Wild Kisses

Wild Kisses

A Wildwood Novel

SKYE JORDAN

This is a work of fiction. Names, characters, organizations, places, events, and incidents are either products of the author's imagination or are used fictitiously.

Published by Montlake Romance, Seattle

www.apub.com

ISBN-13: 978-1503940765
ISBN-10: 1503940764

Cover design by Eileen Carey

Printed in the United States of America

For Marina and Rocco.
Thank you for all your positivity and support.
For being a phone call away with the answer to
my every question.
Love you two!

ONE

Trace Hutton struggled to focus on the rough-hewn stone in his hand as he back-buttered the small slab with cement, but all he could think about was Avery playing with icing downstairs. And how he wished he were playing with her.

The warm scent of chocolate and spice floated up from the partially remodeled kitchen, sweet and infinitely tempting, just like the café's owner. In his mind, the cement in his trough turned to icing, the stone transformed into Avery's naked body, and his hands replaced the trowel and controlled the frosting.

"Thinkin' with the wrong head again." He used both hands and a sharp eye to settle the stone atop the last, building the fireplace hearth, stone by stone.

An upbeat song from Lifehouse echoed through the unfinished space, its lyrics filled with hope and talk of fresh starts. That's what this project was about for both him and Avery—the perfect opportunity for each of them to give their lives a boost.

Too bad that boost didn't include a hot hookup between the good girl and the ex-con, because all he'd been able to think about for weeks was licking buttercream frosting or melted chocolate or caramel whipped cream—really, any of the mouthwatering fillings she created—off her equally delicious body.

His watch chimed, dragging Trace from his fantasies and reminding him of his father's medical appointment. Trace glanced over the hearth, only half-finished. Damn, there just wasn't enough time in the day. He still had so much to do to get this place ready for Avery's opening, just a few short weeks away. The invisible vise cranked a little tighter, giving him a fresh perspective on the concept of time crunch.

Trace was able to lay four more stones before his watch chimed again, signaling he had twenty minutes to swing home, pick up his dad, and get him to his doctor down the street. Totally doable if his dad was in a cooperative mood. If not . . .

Trace checked the last stone he placed with his level. Sweat trickled down his bare chest. This Northern California Indian summer was killing him. It was almost November, for God's sake. He cleaned up his supplies, washed off in the upstairs bathroom—yet another "to finish" on his list—and trotted down the stairs to check on the guys he'd hired to install the booths in the café's main seating area.

The scent of home-baked chocolaty goodness drew his gaze toward the baking area on his way past. In addition to the full kitchen in the back, Avery had wanted a central area where she could bake in full sight of customers. So Trace had created a secondary kitchen for her consisting of a large butcher block with a small inset of marble. As soon as her appliances came in, she'd have an oven, fridge, and sink against the back wall, effectively separating the cooking and baking areas.

To keep debris out of the area so Avery could continue working during most of the construction, he'd installed thick plastic sheets from floor to ceiling, with one entrance held shut by Velcro. Through the murky panels, Trace saw Avery swaying and singing along to her preferred music, a mix of pop and country.

He paused to watch her, loving the way she sang and danced a little, then refocused and became intensely still as she put piping tip to cupcake. A furrow of concentration between her brows, she assessed the next cupcake like an artist looking at a blank canvas. She twisted her pastry bag and bent toward the counter.

Trace's devilish streak sizzled across his shoulders. Grinning, he slapped the plastic aside, ripping the Velcro open. "Hey, Snickerdoodle, how are you doing?"

Avery startled. Her hands slipped, and icing squirted onto the stainless steel counter. "*Dammit*, Trace. How many times have I told you—"

As she caught his grin, her frustration turned hot. She aimed her pastry bag at him and squeezed. Icing shot across the space, splattering his abdomen in a cold blast.

Shock tripped Trace back a step with a laugh. Arms lifted out to the sides, he looked down at the gooey mess and laughed harder. That wickedly playful move was not what he'd expected, but the longer he spent around this woman, the more she surprised him.

Avery looked a little surprised, too, her cheeks turning a deeper pink. But she was laughing. "You deserve it. You can be such a little shit."

Trace approached the counter, swiping a finger full of icing off his gut. "Is this royal or cream cheese? Because you know I hate royal."

The way she pressed her lips together in annoyed humor told him it was cream cheese, and with a laugh of triumph he sucked the icing off his finger. But this wasn't just cream cheese frosting. She'd added spices that made him hum with pleasure.

Her hair was up in a messy bun with wisps falling around her face and neck, and she looked absolutely adorable.

She smiled, her light-blue eyes twinkling. "You ass."

"Just part of my charm." He reached for the cupcake she'd messed up. "Guess that's going to have to be donated to the less fortunate."

She smacked his hand hard, the sting singing through his skin.

He pulled back but remained poised to grab the treat, and he leveled a look at her. "You're feisty today. Am I going to have to fight you for that? 'Cause I was quite the wrestler in high school. My moves combined with all the icing around here . . ." He added a teasing warning to his voice. "It could get really messy, really fast."

"Maybe you will." She tilted her head and narrowed her eyes. The look she gave him—as if she were seriously considering—shot a little thrill through his chest. "I should fight you for it on principle alone."

Oh, the images that flashed in his head . . .

If only.

But he just wasn't that lucky, and this project was just too important to both of them to mess it up with flirtation gone wild.

Trace purposely brought the teasing back to a respectable level. "But you won't because you know it's late, you know I've got to be starving, and you know I won't have time to stop for lunch today."

Her gaze darted to the clock on the wall, and her humor faded. "Oh my God, it *is* late."

She wiped her hands on her apron and turned toward the old fridge. Trace took the opportunity to grab the ruined cupcake while her back was turned. This batch was for a bridal shower / wedding-cake-tasting party, so he knew they would be her best. And after working around Avery seven days a week for two months, Trace knew she made twice as many of everything as she actually needed. So he didn't feel bad about stripping the wrapper and stuffing half of the cake into his mouth.

But the giant bite didn't give him the chocolate hit he'd expected. Instead he got a mouthful of decadent spices blended in a thick-textured, melt-in-his-mouth cake. And the cream cheese icing added a luscious zing that made Trace moan.

"*Trace Hutton,*" she scolded, complete with a two-year-old foot-stomp. "Those *are not* for *you.*"

Trace started laughing and covered his mouth so the cupcake didn't end up all over the kitchen. When he'd swallowed, he said, "Did you *seriously* just stomp your foot? Okay, that was *almost* the highlight of my day." He lifted the other half of the cupcake. "*This* is the *absolute* highlight of my day. But they're not chocolate. Why do I smell chocolate?"

"Because I'm making brownies for Finley's Market." She pushed two brown paper bags across the counter. "Sandwiches and apple turnovers."

Trace stuffed the other half of the cupcake into his mouth, groaning at the way the flavors blended and instantly changed his entire outlook on life for the better. "Oh my God. What *is* this?"

"Carrot cake from scratch with crushed pineapple, and ginger-cinnamon cream cheese frosting." When Trace reached for another cupcake, she slapped his hand again. "You're killing my profits, Hutton. *Get out.*" She pointed to one of the bags. "And hide those apple turnovers until George gets some protein in him. You, too. You both have an insatiable sweet tooth that's going to lead to diabetes if you don't change your diets."

"Says the woman single-handedly keeping the sugarcane industry alive."

She picked up a rag, rounded the counter, and started wiping the icing from his body.

Trace dropped his arms to his sides, giving her full access to whatever part of him she wanted to touch. But he had to fist his hands to keep from touching her back. Over the last two months, their friendship had grown closer and more flirtatious. They'd both walked right up to the line that differentiated friends from something more, yet neither had stepped over.

Which was the way he knew it should stay. Even if her eyes on him made him wish for so much more.

"I think I got it all." She tossed the rag onto the counter and returned to her frosting station. "Now go. You're going to be late."

Most women liked his body. Construction work kept him muscular and fit without additional exercise or weights. But if Avery was impressed, she didn't show it.

"Can I bring one of those to my dad?" he asked, wanting her eyes on him again. Wanting to see if he could catch any hint of heat there.

"Pffft." She didn't look up from her renewed focus in decorating. "Like I believe George would ever see it. Oh—"

She stopped in midsqueeze, set her pastry bag down, and bent to look beneath the counter. The soft fabric of her blouse bowed a little—thank God for gravity—and Trace got a peek at her bra and the breasts filling the cups. Yes, he'd sunk to grabbing peeks wherever he could get them.

She was on the smallish side, but her breasts were round and perfectly proportioned to her body. He was sure they would also feel like silk under his tongue and cradle his cock to perfection.

"When I was restocking at Wildly Artisan," she said, "Carolyn, the woman who has the space right next to mine, told me about this website on music therapy for dementia and Alzheimer patients. It made me think of George. I printed the article out for you."

She straightened and offered Trace a couple of pages.

He took them and pretended to glance over the text, but he was momentarily awed—yet again—by her generosity.

Avery sold her sweets in key places across town as promotion in preparation for the grand opening of Wild Harts, a diner and bakery. She rented a spot in her aunt's business, Wildly Artisan, where artists of all kinds sold their creations. Avery couldn't bake fast enough to keep up with the demands from her space there. She also replenished sweets at the local grocery, Finley's Market, daily, and did a decent Internet business. Not to mention her custom-cake orders for special occasions or her dessert-catering gigs.

She was one of the busiest people Trace had ever met, working sunup to sundown, seven days a week, striving to make her dream a success. Yet somewhere in her "free time" she'd researched a tangential topic she thought might help his father.

And what had Trace been doing? Lusting after her body.

This was exactly why he needed to keep his hands off her.

She was *way* too good for him.

"When I dropped lunch off for George last week and you were at the lumber yard," she said, "I stayed and talked with him awhile. He said he used to play piano in a choir?"

Trace felt a little shift deep in his chest. One that only this woman could create. He nodded, trying to realign all his thoughts and feelings into the appropriate places, but nothing wanted to fit where it should. "That's where he and my mom met."

"I figured it might be worth a try."

Trace folded the papers and pushed them into his back pocket. "Thanks. I'll read it tonight."

Now he felt awkward and lecherous, so he reached for another cupcake. And got another hand slap. And laughed as he headed for the door.

Equilibrium restored.

When he took one last glance back on his way out, he found her gaze on his ass instead of the cupcakes she should be frosting.

Forget the adorable foot-stomp. Ditch the delicious cupcake. Her eyes on his body—*that* was *undeniably* the high point of his day.

TWO

Avery Hart had one goal in life: to create pastries that were better than sex.

But not just any sex. Avery aimed to make her sweets as satisfying as the wicked, sheet-fisting, back-arching, throat-closing, religion-altering kind of sex she'd heard about in conversations among fellow army wives at their monthly Sisters' Sanity Night, back when she'd been an army wife.

Her gaze blurred over the smooth, thick ivory ribbons of icing swirling around the beater in her KitchenAid's stainless steel bowl. She forced her mind off her recent divorce and onto her bright future. Free. She was free to do whatever she wanted, the way she wanted, because she wanted. No more pining over a silent phone or an empty e-mail in-box. No more heartbreak over *another* postponed homecoming. No more crushed expectations.

Only she didn't feel free. In the last two days, Trace had progressed to working on the café's cabinetry, and she'd been relegated once again to the tiny kitchen in her aunt's home. She was staying with Phoebe until Trace finished the apartment above the café, but she tried not to bake here unless absolutely necessary. And as if the space weren't cramped enough, Avery's sister Delaney and her boyfriend, Ethan, had decided to spend their evening here, dominating the doll-size kitchen table and discussing Ethan's most recent brew.

Covered in confectioners' sugar and royal icing, and struggling to work around the lack of equipment and space, Avery still felt a lot like the ex-wife who'd been kicked out of her house, pushed away by her "friends," and disowned by the army she'd so loyally loved for so long.

Now back home in Wildwood and facing old friends and acquaintances for the first time in eight years, she felt like the impulsive girl who'd run away at seventeen and ended up failing at love and life. She felt burdened and stressed and worried. And, yes, she also felt incredibly fortunate and infinitely grateful. On her good days, she even managed cautious optimism—quite a feat considering the risks she faced.

But "free"? No. She didn't feel free.

If she did, she would have more self-confidence. The self-confidence to go after what she wanted personally. Then she'd be rolling in Trace Hutton's sugar and slathered in his icing. Maybe then she'd feel free.

Memories of his tease at the café two days before made her smile. Wrestling in icing with Trace? In a heartbeat—if he were ever serious. But he was just a player, flirting. And that was okay. It gave Avery practice.

"Popcorn?" Delaney's question pulled Avery's gaze across the small kitchen to where her sister sat on Ethan Hayes's lap.

"No," he said, contemplative.

It seemed there was something amiss with Ethan's beer. It was the one he planned to use in his starting lineup for Wildcard Brews, the brewpub he was opening in town with his grandfather and Delaney. Ethan and Delaney had been curled up together on that kitchen chair for half an hour, trying to figure out what didn't taste quite right, while Avery baked stock for the shelves of her space at Wildly Artisan.

Ethan lifted his glass to peer at the amber liquid through the light. "Try some, Avery. Tell us what you think. You've got the best taste buds in the family."

"Only for items containing sugar and butter." *Or Trace.* "Sorry."

"It's really nice." Delaney took another sip. "Especially for this time of year."

Ethan agreed. "But if I don't know how it happened, I can't re-create it. Is it caramel?"

"Close, but no," Delaney said.

Avery lifted her brows and offered, "World's best cinnamon roll?"

Both of them focused on her, their gazes dazed, as if coming out of a trance. Delaney's sharpened first. Her smoky-blue eyes darted to the mixer, then to the trays of cinnamon rolls covering every horizontal surface, waiting for frosting.

Something clicked in her gaze. She pulled in a sharp breath, and a smile broke out over her face. "Butterscotch."

Avery frowned. "There is no butterscotch in these rolls. Maybe you need a taste-bud checkup."

"But there was butterscotch in the scones you made earlier."

Ethan glanced at his beer, his brow tight as he contemplated her revelation. "Butterscotch?" Some sort of wisdom hit, and his face opened with a smile. *"Butterscotch."*

Delaney was already flipping back through Ethan's brewing journal, where he wrote down every detail of his process for every batch. "You must have . . . Here." She pointed to something on the page. "Your second fermentation temperature was low."

He frowned at the note. "Not that low."

"Low enough." She cut a sidelong grin at him. "You can *never* admit you made a mistake."

He gave her a heavy-lidded, how-dare-you-say-that-word-in-my-presence look. "That's because I don't make *mistakes* with my beer. Just ask my mom."

Delaney burst out laughing, head thrown back.

Delight washed over Ethan's face. He set his glass down, took Delaney's head between his hands, and pulled her in for a kiss.

Avery was about to look away, but Ethan's expression trapped her. A look drenched with desire and affection and so much raw want—a want transcending the physical. His gaze held on Delaney's mouth until their lips met and his lids closed. Delaney's grin melted into instant heat, and she wrapped an arm around his neck as she sank into the kiss.

The sight shot a spray of heat through Avery's belly.

I bet Trace kisses like that.

The thought poured fire through Avery's lower body and snapped her out of her trance. "Oh-kay . . ."

She refocused on her bright-red mixer. With a sigh, she pushed the speed control higher, whipping more air into the frosting and drowning out the hums and moans between Delaney and Ethan.

Too bad it didn't unknot Avery's gut or dim the fantasies of Trace in her mind.

She shook her head, silently reprimanding herself. She might not have had a man around in years who had acted like a husband, but her divorce was still only two months old. And Trace worked for her. They were friends. She shouldn't be thinking about him like this.

In fact, he was probably the best friend she'd ever had outside of her aunt and sister. Avery's return home with nothing to show for her turbulent eight years away—no husband, no education, no career—had been the hardest transition of her life. Trace had been a constant source of encouragement and empowerment. Of support and sanity. Of humor and honesty.

And, yes, he'd also been the origination of all her fantasies.

The sight of him, shirtless, with icing sprayed across his abdomen, made a smile curve Avery's mouth. That had been so unlike her. But Trace had a way of making her feel completely accepted, like no matter how she acted or what she said—naive, silly, serious, or awkward—it was all good.

She couldn't imagine him in prison. Couldn't imagine a person as easygoing and as thoughtful as Trace living among the ugliest criminals in the state. It didn't seem right to house someone convicted of a drug charge, but with no violent history, with murderers, rapists, and armed robbers.

The oven timer dinged, and she eagerly switched her focus away from the uncomfortable thoughts. After shutting off the mixer, she grabbed a folded kitchen towel in each hand and pulled more cinnamon rolls from the oven, closing the door with a bump of her hip. She realized too late that she should have thought it through first. The small kitchen's limited counter space left her spinning in circles, searching for a place to put the hot pans.

"I hate to pull you away from your, uh, *moment*," she said to the still-kissing couple, "but, Delaney, could you pop a trivet on that table for me? I don't have any more counter space."

A warm wave of cinnamon and almond wafted through the kitchen, perfuming the air with sticky, sugary goodness. Love in edible form—that's what Avery had dubbed her sweet treats long ago. And even now, she sometimes wondered if the warm, gooey feeling that filled her with every new, delicious batch would ever fade.

She hoped not. It had started her baking during that long, lonely stretch after David's first deployment. It had earned her friends and created purpose in her young life as nothing but a soldier's wife. It had soothed her through their turbulent, vacant marriage. And now, not only was it all she had, it was what continued to drive her.

While Delaney looked through drawers for something to protect Phoebe's table, the heat of the pans leaked through the towels.

The front door opened, and their aunt's voice bubbled through the living room. "Guess who I dragged in from the street?"

Avery didn't care what member of the Wildwood community Phoebe had brought home to sample her latest delicacy straight out of the oven. She deeply appreciated her aunt's enthusiasm, support, and kick start on this venture, but Avery was dead tired and she ached—everywhere. Her legs, her feet, her back, her shoulders, her arms, and God, her hands . . . With as much kneading as she'd done to perfect her baking during the last two months, she'd developed ridiculous strength, along with strains and probably premature arthritis. And even if putting on the good hostess face for Phoebe's guest meant making another sale, all Avery wanted to do now was sink into a steaming-hot bubble bath up to her nose.

Or into bed with Trace.

After she got rid of these hot pans.

"Delaney, I'm going to catch fire in a second."

"Phoebe," Delaney said, opening two drawers at once while Avery sorted out a plan B in her head. The sink, the floor, the patio? "Where are your—"

"Here." The familiar male voice came from behind her and made Avery's stomach jump. By the time she glanced over her shoulder, Trace had stepped past her and opened the oven door. "Put one here."

With burning fingers, Avery didn't have time to process anything other than the pain and dropped the pan. She was already moving the other tray toward the rack when Trace hooked his finger around the edge and pulled it halfway out.

She slid the hot sheet to safety and dropped the towels. "Damn."

Shaking out her hands, she gritted her teeth against both pain and embarrassment. She'd been baking for a decade, professionally for half of that, yet she was still burning herself because she'd failed to plan for something as simple as counter space? And she planned on opening a café and bakery in a few weeks?

"Honey?" Phoebe said. "Are you okay?"

"Avery?" Delaney echoed her aunt's concern at the same time.

Avery glanced up and met Phoebe's blue eyes, still crystal clear at sixty-five. Her indigo sweater made them pop against her creamy skin and silver hair.

"Why didn't anyone ever tell me that shit coming straight from the oven is hot?" Avery said.

Phoebe smiled in relief, a few crinkles appearing at the corners of her eyes. Ethan and Delaney laughed.

"Here," Trace said, crossing behind her to run the water in the sink. "Get your hands under here."

He wasn't smiling when he grabbed Avery's forearm and pulled her around, drawing her to the basin.

"Cupcake, you've got to be careful. These hands are your livelihood." He fanned out each palm, inspecting them as water cooled the burn. A special place warmed inside her every time he used one of the many baking-themed nicknames he'd come up with for her over the last couple of months. "You're lucky. Doesn't look too bad."

Avery didn't respond. She was staring at his profile. At the way his jet-black hair, mussed from the day, still shone like raven's wings. At the prickle of stubble that had formed over his chin and jaw since he'd shown up at the café that morning at six. At the way that shadow framed his lips.

Oh, yeah. Trace Hutton would kiss like every woman's fantasy. The surety of it weakened her knees a little.

He cut a look at her from the corner of his eye and caught her staring. "You okay?"

God, he was so sweet. And she was so tired. So lonely. So needy. Avery closed her eyes and focused on releasing the pent-up stress. Having him close made that easier. Having his hands cradling hers, his thumb rubbing her palm beneath the water as if erasing the burn, made it much, *much* easier.

"Exhausted. You?"

A lopsided grin lifted his lips. "Exhausted."

"Seems to be our constant state of existence lately."

"So it does."

"You weren't working this late, were you?" she asked.

"Not really. I had a special project I wanted to finish."

"Is Zane with your dad?" she asked. Trace's brother helped shoulder responsibility for George as best he could. But Zane's chaotic schedule as a local deputy left most of the burden on Trace. Something Avery had never heard him complain about once.

Trace nodded.

Phoebe had inserted herself into the taste test at the kitchen table, which had transitioned into a discussion over the progress of the brew-pub's construction. With Phoebe's back toward them and Trace's big body between Avery and the others, Avery felt a familiar cocoon of intimacy settle around her and Trace.

Most of the time they worked day in and day out together like buddies. But then there were moments like these. Wonderful, odd, intimate moments Avery couldn't label or define or even understand. She only knew they created a snap, crackle, and pop inside her she was sure could be heard a block away.

"How is it that you happen to be on hand to witness every asinine thing I do?" she asked.

His grin reappeared. Those ridiculously stunning, black-lashed blue eyes did the sparkle-and-dance routine that made Avery's gut ache. "Just lucky, I guess."

Back away from the hottie.

She took one last look down at his hands wrapped around hers and reminded herself that not only was she his employer, and not only was she newly divorced, but she was also in no emotional shape to take on a man in her life right now. Especially not Mr. Six-Foot-Three Rock-Hard Babe Magnet. Trace Hutton was ten times too much man for her, even on her sexiest, most confident day.

"How are they feeling?" he asked.

Amazing. So good she wanted him to never let go. Which was exactly what finally made her pull her hand from his and step back.

"I'll be okay. What about you? That rack was just as hot as the pans."

"My hands are leather at this point." He shut off the sink, picked up a towel to dry his hands, and leaned his hip against the counter. "Sure smells good in here. Did you figure out what was going wrong with your cinnamon rolls?"

"Oh, yes." She clapped her hands around the towel, excited to share her breakthrough with him. "Let me frost one for you. Wait until you taste this. You're going to *die*."

He chuckled and crossed his arms. "I have something for you, too. Though nothing that exciting. I doubt you'll *die*."

She dug out a spatula of fresh icing and spread it over the top of a warm roll.

"What did you do to fix this little demon?" he asked. "He's been costing you way too much sleep. You know you're the only person who can taste all these little changes you fuss over, right?"

She pulled a plate from the cabinet and carefully set her creation in the center. Then with a flourish, she presented it to him with a devilish smile. "For my official taste-tester. You decide."

His eyes did that twinkling thing again, and Avery had to look away. "Go on. Eat. They're better warm."

He lifted the roll. "Whoa," he said, testing the weight. "This guy is chunky. What did you put in here?"

"I'll tell you after you taste."

He lifted it to his mouth and bit down. Avery watched his every move, his every expression, relishing the excuse to get such an intimate look without exposing her overwhelming attraction.

The soft dough gave easily beneath his teeth. The creamy frosting gathered on his full lips. Avery licked her own, imagining what it would be like to suck that frosting away. Then spiral her tongue with his, the frosting melting in the heat of their mouths.

"Oh my *God* . . ." His eyes, wide with a little shock and a little awe, fixed on hers. "What in the hell did you do? This is *amazing*."

Relief eased her shoulders, and her smile grew. "I used a brioche dough," she said, watching him lick the icing from his lips as he unwound a curl of the roll to peek inside. "Let them rise twice as long, which is why they're spiral towers. And I filled them with a marzipan streusel. Then I tripled the vanilla in the icing."

He repositioned the roll and bit again, taking half the gigantic mass. Avery knew the moment all the flavors kicked in and blended. A spark of surprise lit his eyes before all the tension in his face transitioned into euphoria. He groaned. His eyes fell closed. Head tipped back.

The sight shot sparks along every inch of Avery's skin and pounded heat between her legs. A split-second image of him doing the same as Avery took his cock into her mouth flushed her body with fire. The mere idea that she could pleasure a man who had the sexiest women lusting after him was ludicrous, but she let herself enjoy the fantasy anyway.

"Oh God, Avery . . ." he said around a mouthful of dough.

The pleasure dripping from his voice pushed another surge of heat through her veins. And she loved the way he said her name, as if there were no *e*. "Avry" sliding off his tongue in that sexy baritone made all sorts of naughty things flash through her mind.

"You have seriously outdone yourself here."

She did her best to shake off the haze of lust and gave him an *I-told-you-so* smile. "So, you mean, even *you* can tell the difference?"

"This is no ordinary 'different.' This is an *oh-hell-yeah* difference."

Pride and excitement fizzed inside her. Avery's stomach growled, reminding her she hadn't eaten since breakfast. And as Trace continued to devour the roll with moans of pleasure, Avery reached out and took hold of an edge, pulling it from the bun. The melted icing dripped over her fingers.

Trace's hand encompassed her wrist, his blue eyes sharp and bright. "Just what do you think you're doing?"

"I'm hungry." But her attention was on the tingles sliding up her arm from his touch. "Didn't you hear my stomach?"

"You have a whole pan of rolls right there. Get your own." Then he dragged her hand to his mouth.

She pulled back automatically, laughing. But Trace held her wrist deliberately and ate the gooey roll right out of her hand.

When his lips closed over her fingers, when the wet warmth of his mouth registered on her skin, Avery's breath stuttered. Her smile fell away, replaced by shock. Her gaze jumped to his just as his eyes closed, and his expression took on a whole different look of pleasure.

She forced enough air into her lungs to utter a confused, "Trace . . ."

But then, good God, his tongue stroked her fingers, and he hummed softly. He added suction and moaned, the sound almost inaudible. The warm tug on her fingers and the sight of those lips wrapped around them made her brain stall out. Made her nipples peak. Made everything between her legs squeeze and ache.

She didn't know what to do, what to say, how to act. An elemental part of her demanded she pull away. But something even deeper wouldn't let her.

She swayed and grabbed a handful of his T-shirt to stabilize. Then glanced past his shoulder to where Phoebe had taken a seat at the table with Delaney and Ethan.

When she looked back at Trace, ready to break away from . . . whatever this was, Avery found his eyes open and on hers, and the sight shocked her heart. His expression mirrored Ethan's just moments ago when he'd kissed Delaney so passionately—hot and lust-filled.

Oh my God . . .

All her thoughts of putting distance between them tangled. Those blue eyes burned hot on hers as he sucked her thumb clean, then her index finger, then her middle finger. His eyes fell closed again. His tongue swept across her palm and between her fingers—a sensation that made her crave his mouth between her legs, even though she had no idea what that would feel like.

Avery's heart pounded in her neck. Her breath rasped in her throat. "Trace . . ."

Dammit, she didn't know what else to say. Or do. She didn't even know how she should feel. She wanted to beg him not to stop, yet she wasn't naive enough to think sleeping with someone working for her was a good idea. Especially not if it didn't go well, which was more than likely, considering her lack of experience.

As if he could read her mind, regret pinged in his pretty blue eyes. Just a split second of darkness before he lifted his mouth from her hand and lowered his gaze. "I'm sorry," he murmured with a shake of his head. He covered her hand and rubbing it dry. "I shouldn't have . . . I got a little carried away. I'm—"

She pressed her fingers to his lips, then stared at them, surprised to find them there. "Don't apolo—"

"Ask Trace."

Delaney's words tossed ice water on the coals burning between Avery and Trace, and the chill cut straight through the center of her chest. She dropped her hand and curled her fingers into her palm. Falling back a step, Avery turned to the cinnamon rolls waiting to be iced, her mind a mess of conflicting emotions.

"Ask me what?"

Trace's voice moved away, and with her back toward the group, she squeezed her eyes closed against the disappointment.

Delaney and Ethan pulled Trace into a conversation about plumbing requirements for equipment Avery knew nothing about. She washed her hands, regretting the fact that she had to wash off the touch of Trace's mouth.

Trace's mouth.

Sucking on *her* fingers.

Had that even been real?

She shut off the water and shook her hands dry, feeling like an idiotic kid with her first crush. Then busied herself by frosting the rolls, her hands moving automatically after doing it thousands upon thousands of times. She tried to force her mind to engage, to get her even, logical thinking back into place, but all she could focus on was the hum of Trace's voice in the background—a rich timbre that shivered through her while she floated in a strange haze of confusion.

"I'll be right back," Trace said. "I'm going to grab something from the truck."

Phoebe stepped up to the counter beside her. "Sounds like you had a breakthrough with your cinnamon rolls."

Avery pushed her mouth into a smile but couldn't meet her aunt's eyes, sure Phoebe would see in Avery's expression what had happened between her and Trace. "I think so."

"Please tell me this is your last batch tonight."

"It is. I'm exhausted."

"Can I box these for you?"

"That would be so amazing." Avery offered Phoebe a grateful grin. "Thank you."

Her aunt's sharp gaze held on Avery's a second too long. "Are you okay, sweetheart?"

Heat burst at the pit of her stomach and rushed her cheeks. Avery refocused on her rolls. "Sure. It's just been a long day. I appreciate the help."

"Then maybe you'll like this." Trace's voice, suddenly so close again, kicked her heart into a double beat.

She looked up and found him coming toward her with . . . a cutting board? In fact, it was the biggest cutting board she'd ever seen. She checked Trace's expression and found him avoiding her eyes. "What's that?"

"More counter space." He stepped between her and Phoebe and fitted the board over Phoebe's sink, instantly adding six more square feet of countertop to the tight kitchen.

Avery's mouth dropped open, and a space deep in her belly warmed, something that happened on a daily basis around Trace. "Oh, wow."

His gaze met hers with more uncertainty than she'd ever seen. "I know I'm always kicking you out of your kitchen. Thought this might help when you have to work here."

Her smile came straight from that warm place at her core. She spanned the multicolored wood he'd pieced together with both hands, recognizing the precious value of the counter space he'd just handed her. "Oh, Trace, it's beautiful. It's perfect." Damn, the man was so thoughtful. She turned her gaze on him again. "Thank you so much. You didn't have to do this. I know you don't have time—"

"You have even less time," he said. "So I'm glad it will help."

He held her gaze beyond that extra second. Beyond that awkward moment. Beyond that point at which one or both of them should have looked away.

He held it right up until Phoebe said, "Sweetheart, you've been on your feet for eighteen hours." Her aunt opened the pantry and pulled out a stack of specialty boxes for her cinnamon rolls. "Why don't you go take a long, hot shower and turn in?"

Now all Avery could think about was taking a long hot shower with Trace. In split-second flashes, she saw his chiseled body drenched in clear rivulets, his perfect, droplet-covered lips sucking at hers the way they'd just sucked at her fingers . . .

"And on that note, I'll let you all get on with your evening," he said.

Evidently, the idea had the opposite effect on Trace. He turned and set that sexy swagger toward the door.

"Trace, wait." She grabbed a bag from the fridge and another from the counter. "Sandwiches, salads, and a few cinnamon rolls. Figured you and George could use something in the fridge."

She was rewarded with a soft, lopsided smile. "You're a lifesaver. Thanks."

Another extended moment of eye contact made Avery's chest squeeze. Warmth and longing seeped through her body. God, she wished they were alone so they could just continue talking. So this awkwardness wasn't so overwhelming. So they could have taken that whole erotic finger sucking to the next level.

As if he could read her thoughts, Trace broke their gaze. "See you tomorrow."

He turned for the door, and by the time he'd offered a round of good-byes and exited the house, all the heat inside Avery had drained.

"Sweetheart." Phoebe's hand slid down Avery's back. "Are you sure you're okay?"

No. She was a mess. An emotional mess.

Avery nodded. "Yes. Fine."

Yep, perfectly fine.

Great.

Living the dream.

"But, you're right. I could use some good sleep. Are you sure you don't mind frosting and boxing these?"

"Absolutely not."

Avery leaned in and kissed Phoebe's cheek. "Thank you." She pulled back and blew a kiss to Delaney and Ethan. "Good night, lovebirds."

Avery continued to pep-talk herself right into the shower. "I'm fine. Everything is *fine*. Life is good."

It was true. Her heart may not believe it, but facts were facts, and she couldn't deny she had what millions of people wanted—a chance to follow her passion.

She'd just never imagined following that passion without a man she loved beside her. For Avery, love had always trumped money or status or fame or success. Love had always been worth sacrifice and hard work. And here she was with everything *but* the one thing that had always mattered most. Which only made her even more grateful for the way Delaney and Phoebe had rallied around her with unconditional support.

As she ducked her head beneath the hot stream of water and closed her eyes, Avery didn't see lighted glass pastry cases lining the lobby of Wild Harts. She saw Trace and all the mixed expressions she'd read on his face tonight.

"He's not in your stratosphere." Reminding herself out loud helped a little. "And you don't want the mess of a man anyway."

Now, *that* rang true. After David, she didn't even know if she believed in love anymore. At least not true love. If such a thing existed, she doubted her jaded heart was capable of trusting enough to experience it.

No. She absolutely did *not* want the mess of a man in her life.

He would forever be a fuck-up.

Trace cranked the handle on his ancient truck to lower the window and let the October air blow across his overheated body.

The road was all but deserted at 10:00 p.m., giving him plenty of time to replay that asinine move he'd made with Avery.

The renovation of her café was the most important job he'd had since he'd gotten out of prison and reestablished his contractor's license. He couldn't blow it by messing around with his employer, no matter how badly he wanted her. He'd spent the last eight years painstakingly hauling his life out of the gutter with an impeccable work record, a perfect credit record, and a pristine criminal record. He rarely drank, never used drugs, and chose his buddies carefully. In fact, Trace's only "fun" fell into the hot, young chicks category. But his desire for other women had tanked since he'd set eyes on Avery.

"Stupid sonofabitch."

His cell rang. He pulled it from his belt on the third ring, didn't recognize the number, and by the time he'd decided to pick up, the call had gone to voice mail. Better anyway—he wasn't in the mood to talk to anyone.

He rested his elbow on the open window ledge and rubbed a hand down his face, letting it rest on his mouth. His memory flooded with the feel of her long, slim fingers between his lips. Of the raw, open look of lust on her pretty face.

Trace closed his eyes for a brief second and moaned. Hot blood pooled between his legs, tightening his cock. "Stupid fucking sonofabitch."

He slowed in front of the sheriff's substation and turned into the parking lot. He stopped next to a cruiser in the first row, shut off his truck, and stared at the double doors he'd entered far too often in his younger years.

The thought brought reality into full focus. Avery was a beautiful woman, just flowering into life now that she'd shed a neglectful, selfish husband. She deserved fun and freedom. She deserved the experience of dating that she'd missed when she was young. She deserved happiness.

And Trace was nothing but a stain.

He shoved the door open and stopped short when a woman with big brown eyes looked up from the computer at the front desk.

Fuck me.

The moment the thought crossed his mind, he wished he could wipe it clean, because that was exactly what the woman had done.

"Well, hey there, Trace."

Discomfort balled at the center of his chest. Trace pushed his hands into his pockets. "Cindy. Didn't know you worked here."

"You would have if you'd returned my calls."

Great. Fucking great. This just topped off his night.

Trace wasn't going to pull any punches here. When it came to women, he played straight and clean—at least he had until it came to Avery. "We talked about that."

Cindy sighed and offered a halfhearted smile. "A girl can dream."

"Can you let Zane know I'm—"

"Hey." Zane stood in the doorway to the foyer. He always looked so stern in his uniform. So unlike the little brother Trace used to wrestle into the dirt as kids. Zane darted a look between Cindy and Trace, then said, "Come on back."

As they walked down the hall, Zane shot Trace a look over his shoulder and muttered, "Is there a woman in town you *haven't* slept with?"

"Shut up. Where's Dad?"

"Asleep in one of the cells."

Trace fisted the collar of Zane's uniform shirt and yanked him back. Zane immediately swiveled and knocked Trace's hand away with a *what-the-fuck?* look. At Trace's height and weight with a hell of a lot more fight training behind him, Zane was no longer the kid Trace could dominate.

"You put him in a *cell*?"

"I didn't *lock* him in a cell. It's the only place he could lie down." Zane took a breath, still scowling. "Don't fuckin' grab a cop like that, idiot."

"You're not a cop. You're my little brother."

"Who's a cop?"

They continued around the corner to where the office opened to a large area filled with desks pushed together in pairs. Two other deputies sat across the room with their feet up, chatting, Austin Hayes being one of them. Perfect. This night just kept spiraling. "When you've been a cop longer than you've been my little brother," Trace told Zane, ignoring Austin rising to his feet, "you can put 'cop' first." Then he headed toward the cages in the back of the station.

"You're welcome for taking care of him while you finished up work," Zane called after him.

"*You're* welcome for taking care of him for the last five years while you built a career," Trace shot back.

"What are you going to do about the doors? We're lucky Mrs. Coolidge was home when he wandered out."

"I'm installing special locks and a video monitoring system tonight, because, yeah, I've got so much extra time and energy after working for the last sixteen goddamned hours."

As soon as Trace stepped into the row of cells, the familiar chill, the familiar smell, the familiar echoes closed around him and formed a rock in his gut. The sound of his brother's boots on the cement behind him made all his muscles tighten up and his teeth clench.

Trace found his dad asleep in the second cell on the left. He stepped halfway in, his skin jumping with nerves, his mind sparking with flashbacks. "Hey, Dad, wake up. Let's head home, get you into a bed."

Not a bed much better than this cot, but better than any kind of bed inside a cell. Trace had rented a house a little over a mile away from the construction site for himself and his dad for the short term. It had come furnished, but in truth the place was a dump, which was all Trace could afford even with Zane and their grandmother Pearl chipping in to care for George during Trace's work hours. But because of Zane's hours and Pearl's age, Trace still ended up responsible for his dad 80 percent of the time.

"Dad," Trace said again.

George didn't move. His eyelids didn't flutter.

Trace sighed, edged deeper into the cell, and tugged on his dad's sleeve. "Wake up, Dad. Let's get home."

His father slowly rolled to his back and focused on Trace. "Where's your uniform? Are you off duty?"

"It's me, Dad. Trace. Zane's right there." He gestured toward his brother. "It's time to go home."

George pushed up to a sitting position slowly, painfully. By the scowl on his father's face, Trace knew he was in for a struggle. "Where the hell am I?"

"At Zane's station."

Trace relented to reality and sat on the edge of the bunk. His father's dementia had taught Trace a lot of things, but the one he used most often was patience. George's mood varied from day to day. Situation to situation. Hour to hour. Sometimes moment to moment. Nothing moved quickly or easily in George's world.

"Zane," one of the guys called from the office. "Phone call."

Zane left to take the call, and the sight of him walking away while Trace was still inside a cell rocketed ice through the middle of his chest. Anxiety crawled along his skin.

"Come on, Dad—we've really gotta go."

His father rubbed his hands over the top of his mostly bald head and turned his scowl on Trace. "You in jail again, boy?"

A rich laugh sounded at the doorway to the office and scraped its way down Trace's spine. *Austin.* Trace should have known the asshole couldn't resist an opportunity to dig.

"Your daddy's got your number," Austin said, his boots making a slow *clomp*, *clomp*, *clomp* down the aisle. "He knows where you belong. And we all know there's no such thing as a reformed drug addict. Once a druggie, always a druggie."

Trace's jaw clenched. The fight reflex that had been seeded in prison flared, but the control he'd developed since he'd been released prevailed. He stood and shook his father's arm. "It's late, Dad. Come on."

"You ought to save yourself a lot of time and work and take your dad back to Santa Rosa," Austin said at Trace's back, his voice low and threatening. "You can make that old bar as pretty as you want, call it a café or a bakery or a fuckin' museum, but it'll always be the ratty Bad Seed to everyone around here. Avery is never going to make a go of a business in that building, and you're stealing money from her by working on it."

Trace turned on Austin. "Just because you've got a fucked-up way of looking at things doesn't mean others do. The people in this town love Avery, and they'd support her even if she opened a stand on the street corner."

A deep, brewing anger lived in Austin's dark eyes. He may be Ethan's brother by blood, but the two men were nothing alike. Ethan was all light to Austin's dark.

"She'd be better off on a street corner," Austin said, "because I'm watching you, and the first time I get even a whiff of stink coming from your direction, I'm gonna be all over it. If I have to shut down that bar and Avery's business with it, I will."

Trace didn't blame the Hayeses for their contempt for the old bar Avery's father had left to his daughters when he died. If a member of Trace's family had been killed there, he'd hold a grudge, too. It was Austin's abuse of power and attempted manipulation that pissed Trace off.

Austin was nothing but a bully with a badge, and everything inside Trace fought to lash out. He was caught in a battle between emotion and common sense when Austin's radio crackled then hummed with the dispatcher's voice, issuing a call.

Austin pressed the mic on his shoulder and responded to the dispatcher, then smiled at Trace. "I'll be seeing you."

Trace's nerves were still rattling even after Austin left the building. He took a deep breath and turned back to his father—only to find him asleep again.

"Jesus, Dad, come on."

When George came around again, his gaze sharpened on Trace. "Did you get it?" he asked, voice lowered to a tone so familiar Trace would have recognized it over the phone. "The stuff. The good stuff. None of that generic crap."

"Yeah, got it." Lying had always been easy for Trace, probably because his father had coached him so young. But now the lies spilled out as easily as water from a faucet, because reality and truth meant nothing to people with dementia. More often than not, reality and truth caused arguments and anxiety. So in this case, he told his father he had the drugs George was asking for, because Trace knew that by the time they got home, his father would forget he'd asked. "I've got to go pick it up before he sells it to someone else. Let's go."

A fatigued grin turned his father's mouth. "That's my boy."

Trace took his father's elbow and walked him from the jail with a familiar darkness spreading inside him like spilled ink.

On the way home, he picked up his voice mail.

"Hey, Trace, this is your old buddy JT, from Folsom."

The raspy voice turned Trace's stomach to ice.

"I'm free as a bird can be with a ball and chain around its leg. You know how those POs can be. Old nags. Gotta find me a job, and I remember us talking about your contracting work. I ain't got much experience, but I been lifting and running, so I got a strong back, and I'm willin' to do anything you need. No job, no pay too small. Promise I won't give you no trouble. Give me a call. Let's catch up. Later, buddy."

Trace disconnected and immediately erased the message. Suddenly cold, he dropped his phone into the console and turned up the heat.

"Was that Chip?" his dad asked, half-asleep.

Trace cut a look at his father. He hadn't heard George mention the main drug dealer they'd bought from in a long time. "Who?"

"You know, Chip. The guy who's dating Joe's daughter, the oldest one. Can't remember her name."

"Delaney?"

"Yeah, that's her. Her daddy says she's a wild little thing, that one. Chip's always got the best stuff."

Trace ran a hand over his damp forehead. God, he was glad his dad hadn't said that in front of Austin. Talk about dredging up ugly memories. Mention of the man who'd killed Austin's brother could have sent the bully into meltdown mode. And that wouldn't be pretty.

"Yeah." Trace hadn't been this shaken since one of his nightmares of being thrown back into prison. "Go back to sleep, I've got it handled."

Ten seconds later, his father started snoring.

Trace took a deep breath and let it out slowly. He'd definitely done the right thing with Avery tonight. What happened between them was nothing. It had to be nothing. Because he was his father's son. A man wholly unworthy of a woman like Avery Hart.

THREE

Avery threaded her fingers on the linen tablecloth and bit the inside of her cheek to keep herself from butting into the animated conversation between mother and daughter across the table. Avery could suggest and guide, but she believed the final decision on a wedding cake belonged to the client.

She glanced around at the other three dozen family and friends who'd come for the bridal shower. Each guest had already cast a vote for which flavor combination they preferred for Tiffany's ginormous cake. But judging by the continued mother-daughter tug-of-war, it appeared that exercise had been more of a game than a true poll, because Nancy had her mind set on a very specific, very elegant creation with no visible intention of compromise. In that way, mother and daughter were very much alike.

The Mulligan estate in the hills of Wildwood included a five-thousand-square-foot, Spanish-style house on fifty gorgeous acres of vineyards. Now, nearing 8:00 p.m., the land lay in the cool Northern California darkness. From where the gathering took place under a veranda on the patio, with gas heaters cutting the chill and thousands of tiny white lights creating an intimate kind of joyous atmosphere, Avery let her gaze drift over the aqua pool glowing in the dark.

"Uncle Bill is allergic to nuts." Tiffany Mulligan, the bride-to-be and a friend of Avery's since grade school, frowned at her mother. Tiff hadn't changed much over the years. She was still a pretty, freckled blonde. And Avery had been thrilled to discover Tiffany's big heart had only grown with age. "I don't want him swelling into a balloon at my wedding."

"He's been allergic his whole life." Nancy batted away her daughter's concern like a fly. "He's used to avoiding foods that aren't good for him."

"He's walking me down the aisle, for God's sake. He shouldn't have to avoid my wedding cake."

"And I won't have the remaining five hundred forty-nine guests settling for an average cake they could get at any wedding because one person is allergic to nuts. Avery's carrot cake is exquisite. Like nothing I've ever tasted. No one will be forgetting that cake as soon as they leave the reception."

Avery smiled and offered a soft, "Thank you."

The Mulligans could have easily hired a ritzy cake designer from Napa or Marin or San Francisco, but Tiffany had insisted on using Avery, which, every time she thought about it, still created a warm spot beneath her ribs.

She tried to keep her mind on this beautiful moment for Tiffany and Sean, both down-to-earth, damn good people. But her mind couldn't keep from comparing this gallant wedding affair with her own hasty elopement before David had entered basic training. Or her own desolate marriage and how jaded she'd become toward the union as a whole.

So she turned her mind to Wild Harts. Only that brought up an immediate burn of stress. God, she had so many things to finalize—menus, protocols, staff, bookkeeping. And that didn't even touch on the fact that her new, commercial-grade equipment hadn't arrived yet—$20,000 worth of appliances, the installation of which was holding Trace back from finalizing the kitchen construction.

And dammit, there he was again—Trace—in her head. His tongue stroking her fingers. His lips sucking the cinnamon-and-cream-cheese frosting off her skin.

The memory of their sudden and intimate moment three days before wound through her like a spiral of heat. Heat that turned into an uncomfortable burn when she thought back over how he'd been acting since—preoccupied, evasive, distant. Like he wanted to be anywhere but around her. After years of experiencing the same syndrome in her marriage, Avery recognized what was happening with Trace perfectly.

Man, do I know how to pick 'em or what?

"Avery." Tiffany's plea brought her thoughts back. "Tell my mother she can't feed nuts to a man with a nut allergy."

Fatigue made Avery a little snarky. "Depends." She grinned at Nancy. "How well do you like him?"

Tiffany's jaw dropped. *"Avery."*

Nancy started laughing.

"I have to admit," Avery went on with mock seriousness, "it would really put a damper on the wedding to lose someone to a nut allergy. I mean, for years to come, there would be a bevy of nut jokes—"

"Avery!" Tiffany said, half-shocked, half laughing.

Avery shook her head and shooed the idea away as if they'd all been considering it in the first place. "Really all around better if we just skip it."

And Nancy was still laughing.

"I have a solution that should please you both," Avery told them. "Nancy, your brother probably isn't the only person attending the wedding with a food allergy. Nuts, gluten, wheat, dairy, and eggs have become real problems in recent years."

Nancy's happiness turned to frustration, and she threw her hands up in surrender. "Oh, for God's sake. I'm so damn sick of having to be so politically correct. I know, Tiff, let's just forget the cake altogether. What shall we serve? Rice crackers and Cheez Whiz?"

Tiffany covered her face with both hands and groaned.

"I think you'll like my idea better," Avery assured her with a hand on her friend's arm. "I'll make the cake of your dreams, Tiff—a tiered carrot from scratch, with ginger-cream-cheese filling and fondant icing, decorated with exquisite, handmade, crystalline sugar flowers in your wedding colors"—*cha-ching*, *cha-ching*, *cha-ching*, the pair had chosen some of the most expensive specialties available—"and I'll also make a dozen single-serving cakes for guests with allergies. They'll look like mini-versions of your cake and taste so good, the guests won't know they're any different. Instead of feeling shortchanged because of their allergies, they'll appreciate your concern over their individual issues. I'll reserve one of those for your uncle."

Tiffany clapped her hands beneath her chin. "That's *perfect*." She turned to her mother. "Isn't that perfect, Mom?"

"Phoebe told me if anyone could make this work, it would be you, Avery." Nancy glanced at Tiffany. "Go ahead and fill out the order form. We've still got presents to open."

With both Mulligans returned to their buoyant, pre-shower bliss, Avery stood, lifted a wine bottle from the bar nearby, and strolled toward the table where Phoebe sat with several other women, including Willow Holmes, the amazing, mature-beyond-her-years, eighteen-year-old Avery had hired as the manager of the café once it opened, and Willow's mother, MaryAnn.

Avery felt so lucky to be getting Willow. The girl had been working in their family restaurant since she was six years old—a steakhouse just outside town—and had all kinds of experience Avery didn't. Avery could create recipes and bake and build clientele, and, yeah, she could do the basics at a restaurant, but running a café and a bakery while also taking on specialty orders was a whole different animal.

In that way, Willow's year off between high school and college, and her desire to become a pastry chef, was an absolute godsend to Avery. Definitely a win-win for both of them.

As long as the overprotective MaryAnn stayed out of it.

Avery reached over Phoebe's shoulder to refill empty wineglasses, and her aunt grinned up at her. "You managed to keep that little explosion between Tiffany and Nancy under wraps."

Avery smiled, proud of herself. God, how long had it been since she'd truly been proud of herself? Years?

"They just needed to work out the bugs." She smiled at Willow. "Getting excited to start?"

"Yes," she said, her face alight with excitement. "Totally. I've been researching business practices to see how cafés run things differently than restaurants, and I've got some great ideas."

"I can't wait to hear them."

"And I've been trying out some new recipes at home—"

"And I swear *I've* gained twenty pounds," her scarecrow-thin mother teased, raising laughter around the table. "Just remember, Willow's taking the job so she can *stop* working seven days a week at our restaurant. So you can't work her the way you work, Avery, sixteen hours a day, seven days a week."

Don't work Willow too hard. Don't take advantage of Willow's experience. Don't keep Willow at the hostess station. Don't, don't, don't. Every time Avery saw MaryAnn, she got some kind of warning.

"You don't have to worry about that," Avery assured MaryAnn. "Willow and I have her schedule all worked out." She smiled at Willow. "We should get together about a week before opening day. Sound good?"

"Perfect," Willow said, her excitement palpable.

Tiffany tapped Avery's arm and handed her the order form with a huge smile of relief. "Here it is."

Avery stepped away from the table and glanced over the form. This cake was going to amount to a mint. And it would cost Avery at least three sixteen-hour days of work, a mountain of stress, and very, very little sleep. Luckily, the wedding was a few months off, which meant she could have the café up and running smoothly before she tackled this job.

A little flutter of accomplishment winged up her chest, making her smile.

She could do this. She continued to have doubts daily. Hell, hourly. But right now, yeah, she could do this. And the sparkle of independence at the end of the tunnel gave her something to hold on to during these long workdays.

She grinned at Tiffany. "This is going to be one unforgettably spectacular cake."

Tiffany wrapped her arms around Avery. "Thank you so much. This could have turned into such a fiasco without your levelheaded guidance."

She hugged Tiffany back. "Thanks for taking a chance on me, Tiff. I won't let you down."

Tiffany leaned back. "I have absolutely no worries whatsoever. You have my two hundred percent confidence."

Avery laughed and fanned her face. "If you make me cry, I'll kill you." When Tiffany only hugged her again, Avery pulled away. "Let me get you a total for this so you can get on with your night."

As she turned toward the house, Nancy strolled up beside them, a glass of wine in her hand. "I have to hand it to you, Avery. When Tiffany said she wanted to use you as her wedding cake designer, I told her it was bad timing, that it wasn't a good idea. But you've proved me wrong. You've outdone yourself, and I'm so completely impressed at how you're handling your own situation and not letting it impair your work."

This wasn't a new sentiment. Since Avery had returned home, she'd gotten these backhanded compliments a lot. Everyone seemed stunned at how well she was functioning through the divorce, insinuating she should be falling apart, when she had always been the strong one. She was the one who had fought for their marriage long after David had given up.

But she did what she always did—she took the high road.

"David and I may have been married on paper for several years, but the divorce wasn't a surprise."

"Not the divorce, honey," Nancy said, her voice sincere. "I meant David's engagement."

En—what?

Avery's stomach dropped and her throat closed, leaving her speechless.

"And so soon after the divorce," Nancy went on. "You know what that means. He had someone in the wings. Probably someone he worked with. Most likely someone he was deployed with. Both my sons are military. I know how it works."

"Mom, stop it," Tiffany said, her expression aghast.

Nancy waved her away. "Regardless, I've been divorced long enough to know that no matter how your marriage ended or how long ago it happened, news that your ex is getting remarried is always a blow. I just want you to know that, having been there, I applaud your ability to move on and stay positive."

Tiffany took her mother's arm and lifted the wine from her hand. "I'm sorry, Avery. I think Mom's one over her limit."

"No." Avery had to force the word out, her chest now coiled into a hard knot. "It's all right."

Tiffany leveled an apologetic—possibly even piteous—look at Avery and mouthed, "I'm sorry." As she led her mother away, she said, "I'll call you."

Avery nodded, but she remained rooted in that spot while the guests rose from their tables to gather in a seating area that surrounded a fire pit, where gifts had been stacked on and around a chair.

In one way she felt numb. In another, she swore she was on fire. A million thoughts spiraled in her brain, thousands of emotions clashed in her chest. But an overwhelming sense of betrayal clouded everything.

There had been a million things about her divorce and her marriage Avery hadn't understood when they were happening. Things she still didn't understand now. But after all the fights, all the counseling, and all the tears, she'd come to believe that David was simply more committed to his life as a soldier. And that a soldier's life would never be congruous to a wife and family. Avery had believed his reason for wanting the divorce: because his heart belonged to the US Army.

But it was now obvious his heart had belonged to someone else as well—and it hadn't been Avery.

She took a slow, deep breath. The air stuttered into her lungs, and tears stung. Her brain was already busy stuffing the hurt into dark corners to protect her heart. The pain didn't stem from losing someone she still loved or still wanted. This was pain born from the deepest kind of betrayal. She'd dedicated her entire adult life to making David happy, to supporting his dreams and goals, to seeing him succeed—even while sacrificing her own—because they'd made a promise.

Until death did they part.

Which was when she had an epiphany. One she should have had a hell of a long time ago: promises meant shit.

Her parents promised they'd always love each other—lie. Her mother promised she would always take care of Avery and her sisters—lie. Her oldest sister, Delaney, promised she would keep the family together after their mother left—lie. The boy Avery had loved promised escape and everlasting happiness—lie. The man that boy had become had promised their divorce was because of who he'd become in the army, not another woman—lie.

Lies. All lies. Every important turning point in her life had been based on one lie or another.

With her head spinning in confusion, her heart swimming in hurt, Avery turned toward the kitchen and pushed through the swinging door. Staff the Mulligans had hired for the night busily filled pitchers with drinks, arranged trays with more of Avery's desserts, and whisked in and out of the kitchen with wine and coffee. Thankfully, they let Avery have the quiet moment she needed to pull herself together.

She pressed her hands to one of the granite counters, closed her eyes, and took a deep breath to ease the stabbing pain in her chest.

"Congratulations, honey." Phoebe's voice startled her, and Avery jumped, turning toward the door where her aunt had followed her in. She looked so young and fresh in a pretty violet dress that pulled out a purple hue in her blue eyes. Her silver hair was down, styled in loose curls to her chin. "Sorry, sweetie. Didn't mean to scare you."

"I was just thinking about this cake," Avery lied, forcing her gaze to the paper in her hand. "It's going to need structural support."

"Maybe Trace can help you out."

Trace. Avery barely resisted rolling her eyes. Another disappointment. Another rejection. At least he hadn't broken a promise. Yet.

"This is a great foot in the door to the wedding business," Phoebe said, squeezing Avery's shoulder. "Nancy's already raving about you."

Avery nodded, trying to pull herself out of the murky hole she'd fallen into. "Weddings bring in a lot of money."

"And they lead to other events. The Hadleys want to talk to you about catering their daughter's baby shower in July."

"Great." Avery had to admit, Phoebe was a marketing dynamo. Luckily, Avery was also quite good at pretending nothing was wrong. She should be; she'd been pretending for years. Pretending as long as others had been lying. Did that make her a liar, too? "These special events will really help float the café for the first year."

Phoebe patted her hand. "Come out when you're done here, and I'll introduce you to the Hadleys."

"Phoebe?" Avery said as her aunt pivoted to leave. When Phoebe turned with an expectant smile, Avery said, "How about if I set up a private meeting with them, upstairs at the café so they can see how pretty the event space is coming along. Maybe they'll choose to have the shower there. I'll create a selection of my best pastries and serve sparkling wine. Can you just get a few good dates for the meeting? I'm exhausted and starving, and if I don't sit down and eat something without sugar in it, I think I'm going to faint."

Phoebe laughed. "Of course, honey."

On Phoebe's way out, a figure beyond the swinging door caught Avery's eye. She did a double take just as Trace put his big hand against the wood to hold the door for Phoebe, but his gaze held on Avery.

Her stomach jumped, flipped, and fell. God, he took her breath away, even when she saw him again after being gone only a short time. They'd both been on the job site together all day, and she'd seen him a dozen times in passing, but he was showered and dressed in clean jeans and a gray, long-sleeved Henley with LINKIN PARK emblazoned on the front. His hair pitch-black, his eyes electric blue, his body hard as rock.

He definitely released butterflies in her belly and drew her attention away from the lingering sting of betrayal.

"Hi there, Trace," Phoebe said. "Here to pick up Pearl?"

Pearl was the grandmother who'd raised Trace off and on while his mother had been dying of cancer and his father had been hopped up on painkillers.

"I am." His gaze held on Avery's face, then slowly skimmed downward, taking in the dress and heels she'd borrowed from Delaney for the night.

When she'd been standing next to her sister in front of the mirror at the house Delaney shared with Ethan, Avery had felt mildly uncomfortable. The dress was too bright, too short, too sexy. Delaney had turned red trying to convince Avery she'd never looked better, but it was Ethan's shock at Avery's transformation that had convinced her to wear it—because Avery saw this as a transformative point in her life. She couldn't go back, didn't even want to go back. Which only left forward. And she knew from too much experience that if you kept doing the same thing you've always done, you kept getting the same results you've always gotten. This year, Avery wanted different results.

But now, feeling Trace's eyes on the exposed skin of her shoulders, the deep *V* in the halter neckline, the swell of her breasts beneath the chiffon . . . every inch of her body tingled with heat.

"Whoa. You look"—he shook his head, his gaze still scanning hungrily—*"stunning."*

He said the last almost breathlessly, and the sight of the big, strong, always-in-control Trace Hutton so wildly affected by the simple sight of her opened floodgates on her desire. Fire flashed through her body, from the top of her head to the base of her feet, pooling in key areas that made her restless. Made her crave.

"That dress is perfect on her, isn't it?" Phoebe asked. She continued to Avery, "You've never looked more beautiful."

"She's certainly perfect," Trace murmured, his eyes hot and dazed and making sparks fly in every cell of her body. With his attention holding on her four-inch sparkling heels, complete with glittering straps that wrapped multiple times around her ankles, he asked absently, "How'd the tasting go?"

"The tasting was a fabulous success," Phoebe said, beaming. "Avery's got a big new contract to prove it, and another half-dozen people interested in booking events."

Phoebe stepped out of the kitchen, and the door swung closed behind her. And even though staff dotted the kitchen, a familiar and intimate cocoon settled around Avery and Trace again, making her stomach coil.

Trace met her gaze again, his expression something intense and serious and borderline predatory. "Well, congratulations, Cream Puff."

God, that voice, as smooth as the $300 bottles of wine pouring throughout the Mulligan mansion tonight. Low and deep and so sexy, it shuddered through her, creating a fiery friction. And that stupidly adorable pet name just added another layer of intimacy to the moment.

But even as turned on as she was, Avery was also annoyed that he would act like this now, after all but ignoring her at the job site for the last few days. Days during which she'd realized just how ridiculous it was to fantasize about him in the first place. He may as well be living on an alternate plane of reality when it came to their sexual compatibility. He wasn't right for her. He was too confident, too experienced, too smokin' hot. He belonged exactly where he, evidently, already lived—surrounded by light, fun, young, hot chicks he was rumored to hook up with when it suited him.

Avery had spent enough years living her life based on the terms of a man who lived the way it suited him.

Maybe someday she'd be one of those light, fun, young, hot chicks who could pick up a guy on a whim. Someone who could live freely, for the moment, for pleasure. Maybe once she got her shit together. She definitely didn't believe in forever, or even love, anymore.

Now lust, that was a completely different story. At twenty-five, she was feeling her sexual prime coming around, and Trace Hutton had awakened a whole new part of Avery she could only describe as raw lust. The fact that he hadn't seemed to notice her as anything other than an employer or friend hadn't bothered her all that much until he'd gone and opened that what-if door by sucking on her fingers. Now she couldn't seem to think about anything else. That or how an affair between them would surely be a Pandora's box. Which only frustrated her all over again. But at least she'd let go of her anger toward David.

She acknowledged Trace's congratulatory remark with a light, "Thanks." She'd gotten so good at pulling up that nothing-ruffles-me attitude on a moment's notice over the years. "How'd the inspection go today?"

He hesitated, giving her a blank stare for an extended second that revealed his mind was somewhere else. Then the casual, easygoing Trace she knew was back. "Oh, uh, good. Yeah. Inspector signed off. No problems. I'm going to start on some finish work upstairs tomorrow since the appliances won't be here for a bit."

He stepped closer and leaned his hip against the counter. Shifting too close, he tilted his head, those eyes sharp and searching her face. "Hey," he said, voice soft, brows pulled into a concerned frown. "What's wrong?"

A moment of gut-piercing fear that he could see inside her, that she gave off some clue as to what she was thinking, hit her like ice water. But she gave him a *what-do-you-mean?* shake of her head and a smile. "I just got a contract that will replace all my shabby hand equipment. Everything's great."

"Then why do you look like the motor on your KitchenAid finally gave out?"

Her stomach fluttered.

Deny. Deny. Deny.

She laughed him off. "This is a big job. I'm just working out logistics in my head."

She turned toward him and met his gaze head on, shoulders back. If living in the army for eight years had taught her anything, it was how to be tough when she wanted to lean on someone. And, man, what she would give to lean on Trace right now. But she couldn't. She couldn't lean on anyone. Everyone lied. And lies hurt.

"I'd better get home. I still have a lot of work to do before I can hit the pillow. And tomorrow's another early day."

She started to step past him, but with a simple tilt of his wrist, Trace wrapped his big, warm hand gently around her bicep and stopped her at his side. Avery's breath caught. His warmth embraced her. His scent, clean with a hint of very masculine spice, filled her head. Something deep in her body whipped up that craving again. A craving unique to Trace.

He bent his head so close she felt the soft wisps of his black hair brush her temple. Her heartbeat quickened. She couldn't think straight.

"Avery," he said, voice soft but imploring. "I screwed up the other night. I'm really sorry, and I really want things to go back to the way they were with us."

Surprise leaped in her chest, and Avery turned to gauge his expression. His closeness hit her first. Just an inch away. So close, she could see how many colors of blue filled his irises, the curve of his long, spiky lashes, every hair making up his day-old beard.

All she had to do was shift her weight, and her lips would cover his.

Oh . . . the thought . . . The decadent thought had her swaying. But Avery couldn't take any more rejection, and she knew he was only telling her he wanted them to be friends again.

"If things are different," she said, "it's because you made them different. You're the one who's been keeping your distance."

"So it wouldn't happen again." His gaze cut away, definitely guilty. "I promised it wouldn't—"

"Maybe I didn't want that promise." She couldn't quite believe those words had come out of her mouth. But Avery pushed on. Of all the promises made to her and broken, why couldn't this be one of those? "Maybe I liked it. Maybe I wanted it to happen again."

His gaze jumped back to hers, surprised, pained.

And she had her answer—it would never happen again.

She stepped away and pulled from his grasp. "But I understand it's the right thing, so don't worry. Everything between us is fine. I'll see you tomorrow."

Avery walked out, confused, lost, and hurting in ways she didn't understand, wondering whether Trace understood what was happening between them any better than she did. She offered hasty good-byes to several of the guests as everyone made their way to their cars, gave Tiffany a hug, and climbed into the Jeep Delaney had loaned her for the foreseeable future.

Sick with the turmoil in her life, Avery headed to her favorite place in the world. The one place where following simple steps would, time and again, produce successful results. A place where those successful results created warmth and happiness and love.

Her kitchen.

As she drove down the long, lighted driveway of the Mulligans' multi-million-dollar home, she shook her head and murmured, "If only life could be as simple."

FOUR

"Maybe I liked it. Maybe I wanted it to happen again."

Trace couldn't get Avery's words out of his head. Nor could he wipe the image of her in that sexy little deep-pink dress as she'd walked away from him. The way the softly flared skirt followed the curve of her ass, the way it ended high on those toned thighs. The way the open back showed all that creamy, smooth skin beneath straps creating an X between her shoulder blades, joined there with a little bow.

"Maybe I didn't want that promise."

A flash of Avery's gorgeous face flushed with want filled Trace's mind from that night he'd had her slim fingers in his mouth, and his groin swelled with the kind of heat and pressure that demanded attention. The kind of attention he hadn't had in over two months—since he'd set eyes on Avery Hart.

"Trace, honey." His grandmother's voice broke into his delicious memory, and he let thoughts of Avery fade as he glanced toward Pearl in the passenger's seat of his truck. "It's green."

"Hmm?"

"The light, honey. It's green."

Trace's mind snapped into the present, and he stepped on the gas. "Sorry," he muttered. "Was thinkin'."

"Did you hear anything I said about your father?"

Trace searched his mind and glanced at his grandmother. "No, Gram, sorry. I hope Zane doesn't have to pull a double. I've really got to get some extra time in on the café, and I don't want to be worried about Dad when I'm using a nail gun and table saw."

"No, Zane's with him tonight," she said, exasperated. "I was telling you about the music therapy Avery told us about. Have you noticed a change in your dad?"

"Uh . . ." He thought back over the last few days. "I don't know. I see him at night, and you know how fast he goes downhill after five or six o'clock. I've been focused on the project, on following up with his doctors and Medicare."

"Between the café and your daddy, you're burning the candle at both ends. You can't keep this up."

"I'm all right, Gram. Have *you* noticed a difference with Dad?"

"Actually, yes. An amazing change, in fact. I wasn't sure at first, but each small change builds on the one from the day before. I've only had him listening to the music mix Avery made for us for three days, and he's already happier when I get there in the morning."

"Avery made you a music mix?" That was news to him. She hadn't mentioned anything about it. The sweetness of her unselfish act when she had so much to do, so much stress weighing on her, touched him.

"I saw her at Finley's Market, stocking those amazing blondies of hers, and we got to talking about the article. I told her what he used to love listening to, and she put a small selection of music together so we could try it out. I can't believe the difference. The first day, the changes were small. He was more alert, like on one of his better days. But today, when his irritation kicked in around noon, I turned on the music, and, you're not going to believe this, but he calmed right down and started singing along."

"Singing?" Trace looked at his grandmother in disbelief. His father used to sing all the time when Trace had been a kid, but he hadn't heard one note from him since his mother got sick. "Are you sure you were in the right house?"

Gram laughed. "I know. I could barely believe it." She pressed a hand to her heart. "Lord, it was so wonderful to hear that lovely voice of his again. And his mood stays up for at least two hours. It's truly miraculous."

A tiny spark of hope burned in the back of Trace's mind. Anything that helped his dad feel better was a blessing. Because when Dad was happy, life was easier and happier for all of them. "I'll say."

"I'm going to talk to Avery about adding songs or making another mix. Try it out with him tomorrow night. It might make your life easier."

"I will."

"But you need a long-term plan, Trace. You and your brother have demanding careers, and you should both be working on building families by now, not juggling your father like a hot potato."

His lips twitched into a grin as he turned onto one of the many quaint residential streets in Wildwood, but the emotion behind it was dry and dark. A family was the furthest thing from Trace's mind. Once upon a time, before his life had gone to shit, yeah, he'd wanted it all—the wife, the kids, the business. Now he just wanted to drag himself out of this hole, stop making ends meet with grunt work for other contractors, and get his own business back on its feet.

"You'll have better luck getting great grandkids out of Zane."

"Hardly."

Trace chuckled.

"I'm serious, Trace. Are you seeing anybody?"

His mind turned to Avery. "Nope."

"What about Avery? You two get along so well, and she's the prettiest, sweetest little thing. Phoebe says she's dated some, but she isn't seeing anyone seriously. And she can cook."

Trace groaned, turning into the driveway of his grandmother's cottage. He didn't need anyone pushing him toward Avery. Working with her so closely since she'd returned home, he knew exactly who she'd been dating and how often, and he kept hoping one of those guys would stick so he could cut her out of his thoughts.

"She's also almost a decade younger," he said.

"Eight years," Gram countered. "And at your age, that doesn't matter."

"She's also freshly divorced with her freedom at her fingertips. She deserves someone far better than me."

He reached for the keys to shut down the engine and got a stinging slap on the forearm from his grandmother.

He smirked at her. "That is no way to treat the grandson who drove you home."

"It's the way to treat a grandson acting like an idiot."

"If that were the case, you'd have to be slapping me constantly."

"That can be arranged."

He laughed and opened the door.

"Don't get out," she said, her voice filled with frustration. "I can still climb from a truck."

"Not from my truck you can't. Stay put."

"That's no way to talk to your grandmother. And Avery may be freshly divorced, but from the way Phoebe tells it, she hasn't lived like a married woman in years."

He *so* didn't need to hear that.

"Gram, drop it." He shut his door and rounded the front to open hers, already imitating her voice with, "Don't you close the door on me when I'm talkin' to you, Trace Benjamin. I oughta whoop your hide."

She smacked his arm again. "Smart-ass."

"You're going to start leaving marks." He wrapped his arm around her shoulders and walked her toward the porch. "Imagine me trying to explain that."

"You don't have to walk me in. You make me feel ancient."

"Wouldn't matter if you were twenty-seven or seventy-seven, I'd still walk you in."

At Gram's door, Trace took her keys and unlocked the house, then stepped aside as Pearl entered and turned on the living room light.

"I've been thinking," she began.

"Oh, man," he said with dramatic dread. "Thought I told you to stop doing that."

Trace wandered into the kitchen, where he checked the stove burners and the ovens, things Pearl sometimes left on absentmindedly.

"Why don't you move George in with me?" She set her purse down on a side table. "I'm not doing anything I couldn't put aside while you finish the café. Steady work ought to start pouring in once everyone in town sees what you've done with that place, which will give you the money to put him in a facility—at least during the day."

"This move has been hard enough on him. I don't want to move him again." At the back door, he turned the dead bolt and closed the blinds, then returned to the living room. "He's just beginning to settle into a routine and seems to be doing pretty well on his own between the time you leave and either Zane or me get him in the evening. I get by to check on him in the afternoon."

At the wide picture windows, he drew the drapes, then checked the space heater at his feet, another device Pearl often forgot to turn off.

"Well, then, what if we trade houses?" Gram suggested. "I'll move into your house, and you move in here. Then you don't have to move him."

Trace grinned, hugged Pearl, then kissed her forehead and pulled back to look at her. "I really appreciate the offer, Gram, but Dad and I live in a dump, and I wouldn't let you live there if you paid me. Besides, you already raised him once, and you're doing a lot as it is. Let Zane and me pick up some slack now."

"You've already given up too much of your life for him—"

"Ah-ah," he cut her off. "We're not talking about that, remember? Lock the door after me." He turned and opened the door to the night, but the thought of where he was headed and what he still needed to do tonight made him feel heavy. Hopefully he'd get lost in his work and Avery would slip from his mind for a while, giving him some relief.

"How's the café coming?" Gram asked.

He turned and met his grandmother's gaze. "It's getting there. Still have the roof and the appliances, lots of finish work."

"Are you going to have it done for Avery's grand opening? It's getting close."

"Hell yes. I won't miss that deadline." If he did, he may as well kiss future work and all the recommendations he'd cultivated from this job good-bye. To say nothing of disappointing Avery, which would kill him.

"Did you hear that Shiloh is pregnant?"

Trace shook his head. "I don't even know who that is."

"A friend of Delaney's."

"For a girl who left town under a cloud of suspicion and returned kicking and screaming, she sure has developed a lot of friends around this place."

"Sort of like her aunt."

"Sure thing." Phoebe Hart not only knew everyone in town, she knew everyone's entire family tree.

"Well, Shiloh and her husband are trying to get financing for a room addition on their little house on Picket Street before the baby comes. Delaney recommended you for the job."

Trace lifted a brow. "And you know this how?"

"Phoebe."

He grinned. "Of course."

"She also told me that Finley's Market is planning to expand. You might want to stop in and talk to Caleb."

Caleb Finley and his wife had inherited the business in the last year, and the changes they'd made had increased business tenfold. The market had been bursting at the seams for months. Caleb also happened to be best friends with Delaney's boyfriend, Ethan. A great string of connections for recommendations around town. A lousy string of connections to screw up by letting his attraction to Avery get out of control.

"Yeah, I will. Thanks for the heads-up."

She squeezed his arm. "I'm always thinking about you. Have you gotten any new bites?"

"Just a roof for Gabe Snyder." Not something he was thrilled about, but a job he'd take because he needed it.

"Hang in there, Trace. Good things are coming."

"We'll see. One step at a time." Future success in Wildwood, or anywhere else for that matter, depended entirely on how well he followed through on Wild Harts. Which was a reminder to get his ass in gear. He kissed Pearl's forehead and stepped onto the porch.

She moved into the doorway. "Any more trouble from Austin?"

An immediate squeeze tightened Trace's chest.

"He's not a problem," he told his grandmother, hoping he sounded confident. Realistically, Trace knew Austin would be trouble until Trace left town. "Zane's got him under control."

His grandmother's watery blue eyes narrowed. "No one truly has any of the Hayeses well controlled."

Trace forced the raw fear associated with prison away and grinned for his grandmother. "Not true. Delaney's got Ethan hog-tied and lovin' every minute of it."

"An exception to the rule." Pearl's smile put a fresh glint in her eyes. "Don't ever underestimate the love of a good woman, son. It can move mountains."

Trace wouldn't know anything about that. "Go on. Get inside, and let me hear that door lock behind you."

"Get some sleep, Trace." Pearl closed the door and tripped the dead bolt. "Happy?"

Happy? No. Trace didn't know how to be happy. Couldn't remember the last time he'd been truly happy. Of course the question brought Avery to mind because, hell, why not, everything else did. And when he thought of Avery, Trace could almost imagine happiness—with his body buried deep inside hers, their limbs tangled, mouths fused, those clear blue eyes of hers heavy-lidded and sparkling with lust, and those perfectly plump, pink lips forming his name as she rose to orgasm.

Yeah, he was pretty damn sure that was the one thing that could make him happy.

But that would never happen.

So, no. He wasn't happy.

"Yep," he said, patting the door with a flat hand. "Love you, Gram."

"Love you, too."

The drive from Gram's to Wild Harts took fifteen minutes but only because he meandered. He really didn't want to work tonight, but he was behind again, thanks to his father's bizarre tirade that afternoon, something that was becoming entirely too common. He wasn't seeing the calm in George that Gram had described.

Trace's mind drifted to the bathroom mirror he'd come home to earlier that evening. The one his father had broken but didn't know how. Then to the time and money it would cost to fix it—neither of which Trace had.

With his elbow on the open window frame, he scraped a hand through his hair. He really didn't know what he was going to do if his father didn't adjust to this move soon. No one in the family could afford an in-home caretaker, to say nothing of the cost of putting him into a facility. Hopefully they'd hear from Medicare soon.

For now, all Trace could do was take things day by day. With his father. With this renovation. With Avery. And tonight his father was safely sedated into a tranquil sleep, and locked inside their small cottage, freeing Trace up to get some extra work done on the café. As far as Avery went . . .

He rubbed his forehead. "Fuck if I know."

His wild attraction to her was so wrong on so many levels. He'd admit to preferring hookups with younger women, but Avery was way too young—and not just in chronological age. Not only was she eight years his junior, but even more troubling, she was decades younger in sexual experience. From the information he'd gathered between Avery herself, Avery's family, and now Gram, Trace knew she'd run off with David at seventeen and stayed faithful even while David had been deployed for the majority of their marriage. A marriage that, by all accounts, had headed downhill after the first year, becoming far more of a long-term emotional jail and far less of an actual marriage.

If that was true, Trace estimated Avery was about as sexually experienced now as he'd been at fifteen. And he was beginning to believe there was something seriously twisted in his head, because the more he thought about it, the more her inexperience and abstinence turned him the fuck on.

All that beautiful skin to touch and tease in ways she'd never been touched and teased before. All the wild variations of sex to explore that she'd never explored, some she probably didn't even know existed. Owning all that gorgeous, uncharted territory for his very own. Watching her experience pleasure she'd never known—at his hands, his mouth, his cock. Introducing her to the amazing world of sex awaiting her now that she was single and in her prime . . .

"Fuck that's hot. *Why* is that *so hot*?" He shifted in his seat and adjusted the bulge of his cock against his jeans with a groan of frustration. "And *why* am I such a *goddamned idiot*?"

She'd probably had plenty of sex with her husband. They'd probably gone at each other like animals as soon as he returned from a tour and never left the bed until he deployed again. And why was Trace so ready to believe the stories of her faithfulness during their eight years of marriage? He'd been with enough women to know few remained faithful when they weren't getting what they wanted at home—sexual or otherwise. He didn't do married or committed women, but he'd discovered long ago that women lied like demons when they wanted what they wanted.

Then again, he didn't exactly hang out with a normal cross section of the female population. He, admittedly, liked his women young, easy, energetic, knowledgeable, and ready to move on in the morning. Preferably sooner. In short: slutty. Which only made this semi-virginal fantasy playing in his head even more bizarre.

A headache throbbed at the center of his brain by the time he turned onto the drive of the bar-turned-café. With fatigue stinging his eyes, Trace didn't notice the Jeep parked near the kitchen door on the far side of the building until he'd pulled to a stop and shut off his engine.

With his hand still on the keys in the ignition, his mind pinged from one thought to another, in no order, making no sense. "What the hell is she doing here now?"

She should be at Phoebe's with her nose to a sketch pad, planning out Tiffany's wedding cake. Or researching recipes for her opening lineup at the café.

"Dammit." He'd come to get his mind off her, and now . . . "God, I hope she changed out of that dress."

He sat back and stared at the café, illuminated in the exterior lighting and situated on a private corner of the property's five acres. His eyes took in the smoky-green siding of the two-story, turn-of-the-century building, the crisp white trim around windows and doors, and the gingerbread at the roofline, but his mind was somewhere else entirely.

"Maybe I liked it. Maybe I wanted it to happen again." If she'd developed a crush on him, he hadn't noticed. She had probably been drunk. One glass of champagne was all it took with her.

But whatever was happening, he had to deal with it. He had to get it out from between them. He needed this job. He needed her recommendation. But even more, he missed her easy friendship. He wanted things to go back to the way they were before his restraint had slipped and he'd sucked icing off her fingers.

A shiver of lust traveled down his spine, and his mind veered toward other places on her sweet little body he'd like to lick . . . and suck . . . and bite . . .

"*Stop*, dumbass."

Trace stood from the truck, took a deep breath of the cool fall night air, and let the driver's door close quietly. Lights from the kitchen area glowed through the double front glass doors.

After Delaney had realized their father's ramshackle bar was the perfect location for Avery's bakery and café, she'd abandoned her plan to restore and sell the building as a bar. Instead, she'd used her experience as a historical renovation specialist to redesign the interior to accommodate Avery's every need, setting her sister up to grow Wild Harts into any size café or bakery Avery wanted.

Looking through the doors now, past the dining counter and the open plastic drapes, into an open baking area beyond, Trace didn't see Avery. What he did see was one colossal mess. Baking supplies littered the stainless steel countertops, mutilated fruit lay abandoned on the cutting block, bowls and measuring cups and utensils lay haphazardly on every surface or resting in dirty bowls.

"What the hell?"

Something was very wrong. Avery was an absolute perfectionist when it came to her profession. An utter clean freak in her kitchen—even if her kitchen was still only half-finished. Not only did Avery *never* cook like that, but she would never, ever, not in a million years, leave her kitchen like that.

His stomach knotted with apprehension. He jerked the door open, stepped in, and scanned the space, calling a worried, "Avery?"

"Go away." The irritated return bark came from the other side of the eat-in counter.

Relief rolled through him first, instantly followed by confusion. Trace strode to the counter, squeezed between two barstools, and planted his palms on the shiny surface to lean over.

He found Avery sitting on the floor.

Sitting on the floor.

She'd thrown her hair up into a messy bun, and her back rested against the center island, facing the wall to Trace's right. She was still wearing that sex kitten dress that sent Trace's mind in a million inappropriate directions, and those sparkling heels that turned her legs into a curvy, toned, mouthwatering display of perfection. She had the leg closest to Trace bent at the knee, her sparkling heel planted firmly on the floor, causing her skirt to slide all the way to her hip. Her other leg was bent underneath the first and lying against the floor, half cross-legged.

One arm curved protectively around a pie pan with a baseball-size hole missing from the center of the pie; the other hand held a fork mounded with some kind of creamy, whipped-cream goodness. And a bottle of open red wine sat at her hip.

Trace couldn't comprehend what he was seeing. "What in the *hell* are you doing?"

Avery's heart was still racing from Trace's sudden appearance. The disbelief in his voice only raked fingers across a chalkboard. To add to her irritation, shame ramped up her body temperature. Of all the people to catch her in this unholy state, sitting on the cement floor of her unfinished café in Delaney's expensive dress eating a hole in the middle of a pie, Trace Hutton was the absolute worst.

Just perfect.

"Are you blind?" she bit out, embracing her complete loser status. "I'm eating pie. One I made from scratch for no one but me. So go away."

She dropped the fork into the pan with a clank. She grabbed the bottle of wine and took a big swig, so she would be drinking when she heard Trace walk out. But he didn't go anywhere. Avery set the wine down on the cement with a clank, hoping if she ignored him, he'd get the message.

Ah, but no. His footsteps came around the counter, and she took another drink of wine. She didn't want it, but she knew she needed it. At the island, standing beside her, he checked out the disaster she'd left, which only made her cringe.

"Well," he said, his tone matter-of-fact. "This is definitely an Avery I haven't seen yet."

Guilt snuck in as she envisioned the remnants of fruit, sugar, flour, butter, and vanilla she'd left strewn all over the brand-new butcher block he'd installed just two days ago. "I was going to clean it up. If you hadn't come, you would never have even known."

"It's your kitchen, Jelly Bean. I'm just building it. I don't care what kind of mess you make."

"Jelly Bean? What kind of nickname is Jelly Bean?"

"They're sweet. Forgive me for not finding one more closely related to baking. I'm tired, and I'm running out of originality. What kind of pie is that?"

Sweet. Yeah. That's how he saw her. Not like the sexy playthings he was used to.

She licked her fork and sighed. "Mango-pineapple-coconut cream dream."

He turned, hands in the front pockets of his jeans. His gaze darted to the pie but swung back to Avery, openly scanning her legs. "Damn"—he half laughed the word—"that's one hell of a good look on you, girl."

He turned his focus toward his feet, clearing his throat. Then he sighed heavily, pressed his back against the cabinet, and slid to a seat on his ass beside her. Knees up, he wrapped his arms around them and kept his attention straight ahead.

"Gram told me about the music you made for my dad. That was really sweet of you."

There was that *sweet* again. And she didn't want to talk about his father or the music or anything *sweet*. "*Why* are you here?"

His gaze darted to her face, then back to the cabinets in front of them. "I was going to work on your kitchen. But seeing as it's currently in use . . ."

"I guess you're off the hook."

A moment of silence passed. An odd, highly charged silence she didn't understand.

"Why are *you* here?" he finally asked. "My grandma would tell you what she just told me—you're burning the candle at both ends."

"Pearl isn't trying to start a business with every last penny she has in the world. That generally motivates a person to burn a hundred candles at both ends."

After a moment, he turned to face her. "Whatever's going on inside you is bigger than the business."

"Ya think?"

He huffed a laugh and shook his head. "Baby, you give a whole new meaning to the slogan 'Army Strong,' you know that?"

That hit her hard—another one of those backhanded compliments she'd been getting since she returned to town. She might be proud of all she'd endured and how she'd matured, but tonight she didn't want to be reminded that she'd done it all for nothing.

"Don't," she warned him. "Just don't."

"Avery," he said, voice serious and soft. "What's wrong? Did something happen tonight?"

Frustration skyrocketed. She didn't need his smoldering temptation around when she was feeling weak. He was hard enough to resist sober and levelheaded.

"We already talked about this. I'm dealing with it the way I always deal with everything. Which means it'll be fine, just like I told you it would be fine, because I *always* make *everything* fine. I'm the *goddess* of *fine*."

"You're a whole lot of goddess, sugar—that's for sure. And while you definitely look fine," he said, taking a sweeping glance of her legs before looking away again, "you *don't* look fine, if you know what I mean."

"No. I don't know what you mean, because you're sending all kinds of mixed messages." And he was prying at a door she didn't want open. Her eyes teared up against her will. "*Please,* Trace, just go."

"Hey, now," he said, his voice softer as he leaned his leg toward hers until they bumped. "The goddess of fine would never cry."

"You're right, she'd eat." She stuffed one more mouthful of pie between her lips, dropped the fork into the pie pan, and pushed it away, leaving a stupid mess of custard and cream on her mouth.

Trace chuckled, reached over, and wiped cream off her mouth. But as soon as he touched her lips, his finger slowed and deliberately moved from one side to the other, his bright-blue gaze hot as it followed the movement. Then he sucked the custard off his finger with his eyes on her mouth, and the entire atmosphere in the room shifted on a dime.

Avery's stomach pitched and swirled.

"I saw Huck Stevens at the gas station today," Trace said. "He asked about you."

What? If that's where his head was at, she was reading him completely wrong.

"He says you keep turning him down for a second date."

"That would be because I'm not interested in a second date."

"He's a really stand-up guy. Makes good money, smart, great family, and the girls seem to like him."

"Which means he won't have trouble finding female company."

"Why won't that be your company?"

She angled toward him, annoyed as hell that he was trying to pawn her off on another guy. "What the hell do you care?"

His gaze lowered to her mouth. "Just can't figure you out."

What a joke. "You're not trying."

He looked away, focusing on the pie. "Are you really gonna eat that all by yourself? Thought I was your official taste-tester."

This was ridiculous. She was sick of wandering around on eggshells. She just needed to get this over with. Make the move he wouldn't and get rejected; then she could let go of this attraction and focus 100 percent on her business.

"You know, you're right." She rolled to her knees and scooped up another forkful of pie. "I should really get your take on it, shouldn't I?"

Before he could answer, she slid the pie into her mouth, swung one leg across his lap, took his face in both hands, and kissed him.

He made a sound of surprise and grabbed her wrists. Before he could push her away, Avery added pressure. When he still didn't open, she brushed her tongue across his lips with a little mewl of frustration.

That did it. With an answering growl, his fingers tightened on her arms, he tilted his head, and he opened to her.

Avery's breath caught as his tongue stroked in, sharing the sweet, soft cream. He moaned, long and low. The sound rumbled through her mouth, and fire erupted low in her body.

In an instant, she lost track of everything but Trace's mouth. Trace's lips. Trace's tongue. She hadn't been kissed in so long, she'd forgotten what it felt like. Forgotten the heat of a man's mouth. But even if she'd remembered, she wouldn't have recognized this kind of kiss. A desperate, unrestrained, uninhibited, expressive kiss that sparked every single cell in her body back to life.

Wild.

She'd known Trace would kiss like this—absolutely *wild.*

She slid her hands through his hair, let her arms fall over his shoulders, and sank into him with a moan purring in her throat.

The pie was long gone, but Trace kept kissing her, and she kept letting him. His arms doubled around her and pulled her up against his body. His strength took her breath. The passionate way he kissed her and kissed her and kissed her washed away every thought. One hand cupped the back of her neck in a firm, controlling hold that made her feel safe and so completely desired. His other arm moved low and curved around her hips, positioning her sex in direct and perfect contact with his erection.

His *erection.*

The reality shouldn't have been so shocking, but after living in such a screwed-up marriage for so long, Avery had begun to believe she was incapable of exciting a man. And she'd sure as hell never known the thrill of a man guiding her hips into a rich, slow grind that rocketed her straight into intense pleasure.

She was downright euphoric when she turned her head to break the kiss and draw air, whispering, "Oh my God."

Trace froze. His hips stopped their erotic rock; his lips rested listlessly against her temple. And a whole different kind of tension filled him.

"Fuck." His curse was barely a whisper, but it filled Avery with a frantic type of dread.

She closed her eyes and twisted her hands in his T-shirt. "Don't you dare."

"Avery—"

"I swear to God, Trace, if you pull back . . ." The mere thought ground her already-shattered heart into dust. She didn't have an ultimatum handy, but she knew everything between them would change. It had to. She couldn't keep living every day wanting someone so badly only to know she couldn't have him. She'd wasted enough of life that way.

He exhaled heavily, rubbed his forehead against her hair, fisted the hand at her hip. "We can't. You know we can't."

"No. I don't." She laid her hands against his shoulders and pushed back. Would have looked him in the eye, but his were cast down. "Give me one good reason. *One.* Other than the fact that I'm not as hot as your usual hookups."

His eyes lifted and locked on hers with anger flashing. "That's the stupidest thing you've ever said. And you know why. I'm too old for you. Too screwed up for you. Shit, I *work* for you."

"What you are is an idiot, and I said a *good* reason." Hurt joined her anger. "I may not have the experience of your usual flings, but I learn fast. It may not be the best sex of your life, but if you tell me what you like, what you want, I'll make sure you're not disappointed. And you don't have to worry about me holding on. I've been permanently cured of wanting any kind of commitment."

"Jesus Christ." He rubbed his forehead, his voice soft, his expression pained, his gaze sympathetic. "Slow down, honey. I think you might have had a little too much of that expensive wine—"

Anger seared a path down her breastbone. She picked up the bottle and shoved it into his hand. "Have I?"

He tilted the bottle, and through the light-gray glass, no one could mistake it was still more than three-quarters full.

"If you don't want me, then just be man enough to say you don't like what you've tasted. That you prefer something different. But don't use bullshit excuses, and don't put it on me."

Holding the tattered threads of her dignity together, she pushed against his shoulders and tried to stand, which she immediately realized would be more than a little awkward in these heels. But before she could even get one foot underneath her, Trace gripped her waist and hauled her back to his lap. Then slid his hand around the nape of her neck and held his gaze on hers.

"I never said I didn't want you." His voice was gravelly, serious, and edged with something emotional—pain, anger, something . . . "I want no one *but* you. I haven't been able to think of anyone *but* you. I've been trying to avoid exactly this for two goddamned months because I have a job to do here. One that means a whole new life for you. One that means a whole new start for me. And I'm trying like hell not to fuck that up for either of us."

Stunned by his admission, her heart dropped to her stomach. All her anger drained, leaving behind hurt, confusion, and shame. She dropped her focus to his chest with a shake of her head. "I'm sorry. You're right. I haven't been thinking about anyone but me. I'm such a—"

He pulled her in and kissed her quiet. "You're *always* thinking about everyone else." He kissed her again, tasting her in a way that reached between her legs and pulled. "You're perfect." He turned his head and kissed her the other way. "You're beautiful and sweet and so fucking strong you amaze me." Both hands slid into her hair, and his fingers fisted. The sting radiated along her scalp and made her gasp. Trace drank the sound and did things to her mouth with his tongue that made her writhe against him, then broke the kiss suddenly. "Your ex-husband was the biggest fucking idiot on the face of the planet."

That made her laugh. A breathless, dizzy laugh that filled her with warmth from the toes up.

And he kissed her again, this time pulling away to say, "This is a really, really, *really* bad idea."

"Maybe." She scraped her upper lip between her teeth, hoping to quell the butterflies in her stomach. "But none of the ideas I thought were good ever panned out very well, so . . ." She shrugged, scanned his face again until she met his gaze, then forced herself to hold it. Forced herself to own this decision. "Guess I'm really, really, *really* ready to try a bad one."

"Jesus Christ." He dropped his forehead against hers and closed his eyes. "You're fucking fearless."

She huffed a laugh, picked up his hand, and pressed it over her crazily beating heart. "I'm not fearless. I'm just less afraid of being with you than I am of hating myself because I passed up the chance."

She couldn't read all the emotions that rushed across his face or filled his eyes. Only knew they seemed to spill into her body and tangle with her own to make her heart trip and her pulse speed.

"This could backfire big-time," he said. "You know that."

She shook her head and stroked his face with both hands, then ran her thumbs over his stubbled cheeks. "We won't let that happen."

He slid his arms around her and stroked his hands up her back, warm and rough against her bare skin. Then he pulled her in and kissed her again, his mouth gentler now, the kiss filled with the kind of emotion that had been missing in her marriage for so long she wondered whether it had ever been there.

Avery sank in, wrapped her arms around his neck, and soaked it up like a sponge. So needy after going without for so long.

Trace's hands caressed her back, raising gooseflesh and tightening her nipples, before sliding down again, his fingers tugging on the bow holding her dress together. Avery tensed as Trace leaned back and let the sheath fall away until the fabric rested at her hips and she was all but naked on his lap. His gaze seemed to scour her forever while his hands fisted and released in the fabric pooled at her hips.

Avery found it increasingly hard to breathe as negative thoughts pinged through her mind. Her breasts were too small. Her body too boyish. She was too ordinary. The other women he slept with were hot and sexy and curvy—she'd heard the rumors. Seen them, with their long legs and big boobs, come by the site now and then, looking for him.

But then he breathed, "Holy hell." His hands moved back up her body, warm and strong and sure, making her belly flinch, her breasts tighten. "You're fucking gorgeous."

And as if he couldn't wait another second, he pressed his face between her breasts, his mouth open and hot on her skin.

FIVE

Everything seemed to speed and spin around Avery, yet details stood out in relief. The thick, silky feel of his hair between her fingers as she held him close. The spicy, clean scent of his skin as she pressed a kiss to his jaw. The heat of his body warming her everywhere.

He closed his mouth over the side of one breast and worked his way around to the other side before pulling her nipple into his mouth and sucking with a deep moan of pleasure in his throat. Her breath caught, her back arched, and Avery was instantly lost in a swirl of lust that had been repressed for far too long.

His hands gripped her hips and pulled her into him, starting that mind-blurring grind again, rocking her sex against his while his lips moved to the other breast. And when his mouth closed over her nipple, Avery dropped her head back as if it were too heavy to hold up. Another surprised sound of pleasure rolled out of her. Trace growled, digging his hands into the flesh at her hips to intensify their rhythm, his lips tugging hard on her nipple.

"Ah . . ." Avery realized an orgasm was right there too late to stop it. She fisted his hair, uttered a confused, "Trace . . . ?"

He lifted his mouth from her breast long enough to kiss her mouth and murmur, "Gonna come for me, baby?"

"I . . . God . . ." The sensations just layered and deepened, and her body slipped from her control. So quickly. So easily. "Trace . . ."

"That's it," he murmured, biting her neck. "Easy, sugar. Relax. Let it come."

But when his mouth slipped back to her breast and bit gently, there was no relaxing and nothing easy about the orgasm that shocked her body into a tight bow, bending her backward over his arms and pulling a scream from her throat.

Avery shuddered and fisted her hands in his T-shirt to hold on. Her hair fell from the bun, spilling everywhere. Even though she struggled to rein it in, her mind slipped right out from under her. Her body rippled with sensations she'd never experienced—not with David, not at her own hands.

And when her mind slowly returned, and Avery found Trace's heavy-lidded, sparkling-blue eyes watching her, embarrassment flooded her in a heat wave.

She closed her eyes and lowered her head with a confused, "Jesus."

His hand cupped her face and lifted her head. "Look at me, Avery."

She opened her eyes but could barely meet his gaze.

"Don't second-guess your body. It's telling you what you need, however and whenever you need it. There is no right or wrong in sex, and that was the hottest, most gorgeous thing I've seen in a long damn time."

Her chest released and emotions flooded in, wetting her eyes. She wrapped her arms tight around his neck and kissed him hard and deep. Tears spilled from the corners of her eyes and before she could wipe them away, Trace licked them. He then stood, lifting her with him, and set her on her feet.

Steadying her, he let the dress fall to the floor, leaving her in nothing but pink lace panties and heels. His gaze devoured her, while his hands stroked her arms, then threaded their fingers.

Avery's mind drifted to all the light in the kitchen, to the darkness outside. "Should we turn off the lights?"

"No one could see us unless they were standing on the porch," he murmured, distracted. Then added a soft, "You take my breath away."

Another wave of emotion pushed through her. God, it had been so long since she'd felt wanted. And to be wanted by a man like Trace, when he could have any woman, when he'd seen her at her worst . . .

Avery had the sudden and urgent need to live up to her own promises. She stepped into him, wrapped her arms around his waist, and offered her mouth, open and eager. He enveloped her, crushed handfuls of her hair in his hands, and kissed her as if he could never get enough.

With a groan, he lifted her off her feet. Avery held his shoulders tight as he spun and dropped her ass on the butcher block. She gasped at the cold hitting her backside, steadied herself with her hands, and found them sliding in mango juice.

Trace didn't seem to notice or care. He hooked his fingers in her panties and dragged them over her hips and down her thighs, then let them drop to the floor. His hands slid back up her thighs, his fingers tense and sinking into her flesh. His fiery gaze scoured her legs, then settled on her sex.

Avery's nerves started to rise again. She wanted to ask him what he wanted, what she could do for him, but was embarrassed because she should already know.

So she did what came naturally and fisted the soft cotton tee in her hands, pulling it toward his head. Trace lifted his arms and let the shirt come off effortlessly, exposing all that tan skin, all those roped and ribbed muscles, and the dusting of dark hair across his chest that tapered into a line down the middle of his abdomen. And even though she'd seen his upper body dozens of times when he'd been working around the café, somehow he seemed so much bigger now, so much stronger, so much *hotter*. Far more . . . *real*. Probably because she'd become the queen of denial and suppression, and hadn't given him adequate room in her conscious mind.

The pressure of his hands on her thighs dragged her thoughts back as her legs slid open easily, lubed by the juice covering the wood. And when he got a clear, pornographic view of her pussy, he groaned. The sound made her sex clench, and he smiled. He rubbed one hand through the juice, then stroked the cool, sloppy liquid over her skin until he reached her opening and sank one finger deep.

Avery pulled in a sharp breath and gripped the edge of the butcher block until her fingers stung.

I can't believe I'm doing this.

I can't believe I'm . . .

"Jesus Christ . . ." She barely heard her own words over the buzz building in her ears. That felt *so good.*

Trace watched his own hand as he single-mindedly fingered her so slowly she wriggled toward him.

"Hmm, you like that." His lips twitched into a grin, his tongue licked his bottom lip, followed by his teeth, but those eyes stayed on her pussy. On his fingers stroking and sinking deep and stroking again. On the way his touch made her shudder and tense and pant.

And when the pleasure pushed outside her boundaries of control, her hands clenched a little more, back arched a little more, thighs tightened a little more, and the sounds escaping from her throat grew higher, louder, longer, and far more needy. But he kept one big, wet hand on her thigh, holding her open. "No, no. Let me see. Let me watch."

Then he pulled his hand back, met her eyes deliberately, and held them as he took his fingers into his mouth and sucked. Shock burned straight down Avery's chest and zapped her sex like a current.

Trace's eyes fell closed on a long groan. "Mmmm, fuck that's good."

Fire leaped through her body. Her chest was so tight, she could barely breathe. He was even further beyond her sexual expertise than she'd realized. Until this moment, she hadn't recognized just how naive she was. Hadn't understood just how much she didn't know. Hadn't comprehended that even the dirtiest conversation she'd listened to among other army wives hadn't prepared her for this.

For *Trace.*

His hand slid between her legs again, rubbing in the juice before sliding two fingers inside her. Avery gasped, tensed, and writhed into delicious pressure. "God, Trace . . ."

"I *love* hearing that." He released a heavy breath and leaned in, pushing her thighs wider and lowering his head to stroke his tongue across her mouth. "I love hearing my name on these lips."

She opened to him, but he just hovered there, out of reach, his gaze drilling into hers as he moved inside her, driving her a little closer . . . a little closer . . . a little closer to the promise of ecstasy. To the promise of sweet oblivion for several long, delirious seconds.

She was getting so much more than she'd expected. So much more than she knew what to do with.

Yet she still heard herself say, "More, Trace . . ." Her voice came out shaky and weak, and she reminded herself of an addict searching for a hit. "I want more."

He pressed his forehead to hers. "Oh, you're gonna get more. Plenty of time, Cupcake. We've got all night."

The wicked promise lighting his eyes shot twin streaks of excitement and alarm across her nerves. Holding tight to the wood with one hand, she reached out and tugged his belt through the buckle. "I can't do this all night."

He chuckled. "Well, now I'm going to have to prove you wrong." He pushed deep, creating heat and pressure and wild, mind-numbing pleasure that halted Avery's hand. Her mouth fell open, and a surprised cry rose from her lips. "And you know how stubborn I can be."

He covered her open mouth with his and stroked her tongue the way he was stroking his fingers inside her until she was struggling to lift into his hand. "Ah, God, Trace . . ."

"Tell me to make you come."

The pressure centered deep in her body. A wild kind of need that would have had her begging if she didn't feel such a sense of shame about it.

"Trace . . ." She was so close, wanted it so bad.

He put his mouth near her ear and whispered, "Beg me, order me, do it however you want to do it, but I'm not going to let you come until you ask for it."

She squeezed her eyes shut and bit out, "Fuck."

Trace laughed. A hot, nasty laugh as he kissed a trail down her neck. "It's so hot to hear such a dirty word from such a pretty mouth. I can't wait to see the other dirty things that pretty mouth can do tonight."

"Oh, God . . . ," she moaned; her arms burned from lifting her body into his hand, searching for another delicious peak. And his dirty talk was hitting some crazy place inside her, turning her on in a way she'd never believed possible. "Trace . . . please."

"Open your eyes, Avery. Look at me and say it."

She gritted her teeth, frustrated with need, angry he was pushing her to uncomfortable limits. And opened her eyes to his. "Fucking make me come, dammit."

The lust that flared in his eyes burned through Avery, and the smile that glittered across his face could have come straight from the devil. "Well done. Now keep your eyes open and on me."

"Trace—"

Her angry warning was cut off by the thrust of his fingers inside her and the following rub and push and grind of whatever he did. *"Ah . . ."*

Her eyes started to close, but Trace ordered, "Eyes on me. I want to see the orgasm slide through your beautiful face just before it rips through your body."

The climax was so deep, so big, so all consuming, and so slow to come, Avery swore it felt like excruciating moments with her gaze locked with Trace's. She felt as if he saw all the way inside her soul. She felt exposed and vulnerable. She felt controlled and absolutely owned by the time the peak broke.

Her body convulsed and jerked. The sounds that came from her weren't anything she'd ever heard before, not in her greatest pleasure or her deepest despair.

And when the peak broke, all her muscles gave and she fell forward. Trace caught her and held her close.

"So fucking amazing," he murmured in her ear as she shivered down from the peak, sinking into his support, boneless. He kissed her hair. "You're crazy sexy, baby. You have no idea."

With her head against his chest, she heard his heart thrumming hard and fast beneath her ear. "Let me do something for you."

That low, hot laugh tickled her ear again. "Sweetheart, this is as much for me as it is for you."

She didn't understand that at all but couldn't make her mind try to figure it out as he let her rest there, his hands gently stroking her back, her hair, her thighs while she wondered how many showers it would take to get all this juice and sugar off her body.

Then he straightened, chuckling when Avery didn't try to do the same but just lay against him. "I love the feel of this." He used both hands to pull her hair off her face and look into her eyes when he asked, "Will you lie on me after I fuck you? Drape yourself over me? Fall asleep there?"

That whole "after I fuck you" twisted something inside her, and she suddenly found strength she didn't think she had. She tipped her mouth to his and kissed him, so exhausted her mouth was loose and sloppy, and Trace ate it up, licking her, eating her.

When he gave her the chance to breathe, she said, "I'll do anything you want."

He stroked her hair, and a new softness came into his eyes, but he just hummed approval, then leaned over the butcher block, easing her onto her back. He stroked his hands up her arms and back down her body, his eyes following, drinking her in, making her feel more beautiful than she'd ever believed she could.

His hands slipped behind her knees, and he lifted her legs to his shoulders. Another flicker of unease sparked in her gut, and she rolled her head to the side and tried to prop herself up on her elbows, but Trace was already threading her fingers with his and pinning them at her hips.

"What are you doing?"

"Preparing for a meal I've wanted so long, I could swear I already know your taste." With his shoulders wedged between her thighs, his gaze scoured her pussy. "And I'm *really* hungry."

Her body tensed. She'd barely gotten her mind around what was coming next when words spilled out of her mouth. "W-wait."

His gaze jumped to hers.

"I . . . I . . ." *Holy shit. Look what you've gotten yourself into, Avery.* Her face burned with embarrassment. Heart pounded with angst. "I don't know . . ."

"You've never had someone go down on you?"

God, the way he phrased things sounded so dirty, and it still shot sparks through her blood. "Uh . . . no."

He grinned. "You're in for a treat, sugar. Having my fingers inside you will pale in comparison to having my mouth on you."

A shiver trembled through her, and she closed her eyes. "Jesus . . ."

The warm brush of air over her pussy made her body tense and her eyes pop open.

"I'm betting my job"—he paused to blow on her again—"you're going to be writhing against my mouth within thirty seconds."

Her fingers flexed against his, knowing instinctively he was right.

He lowered his head and kissed her inner thigh and squeezed her hands, then met her gaze again. "You say stop, I stop. Deal?"

Avery dropped her head back with a quiet, "Fuck."

"I'll take that as a yes," he said, just before his tongue stroked over her pussy.

The warm, wet, softness was so unique, so different, so bizarre, Avery made a little sound of surprise before he licked her again and again and again. And just like that, Avery was arching against the wood. "Holy *fuck*."

In less than ten seconds she was using his shoulders as leverage to lift her hips to his mouth.

Her fingers strangled his as she half moaned, half cried, "Trace, Jesus."

He growled, opened wide, and covered her completely.

Avery choked out a moan, unable to believe she was rubbing her pussy against his mouth. "Fucking crazy." God, it wasn't enough, and now that she knew the kind of pleasure he could bring, she was greedy for it. "More, please, God, *more*."

He lifted his mouth from her to rasp, "That's fucking music to my ears, baby."

He circled his tongue over her entrance, and sensation washed over her sex, her pelvis, deep into her core. *"Yes."*

He closed his lips and sucked, shooting an electric current through her, and she shuddered. "Don't stop. God, that's so good." She was fighting a frenzy of lust-laden need. "Ah, God, *yes*."

His mouth closed with suction, massaging her gently with a moan of utter bliss.

"*God*, Trace . . ."

The orgasm hit her like a tidal wave, swift, intense, overwhelming. She tumbled and tumbled, the ecstasy dragging her under. And while she was struggling to find the surface, another wave hit, spinning her head over ass again.

She was still shaking when Trace released one of her hands. She threw her forearm across her face, panting, spinning, floating. "Jesus . . . fucking . . . Christ . . ."

Then Trace was pulling her legs around his waist, dragging her up by the arms and lifting her against his body. She wrapped her arms around his neck and held on the best she could. "Where . . . are we . . . going?"

"Shower." He started out of the kitchen, and Avery lifted her head from his shoulder.

"What shower?"

"I finished the shower in the apartment."

She pressed her forehead to his temple to stop the spinning. "When did you do that?"

"Yesterday. I'm going to wash all this sticky off and finally get inside you with water spilling over your gorgeous body."

"Mmm. Love the sound of that." As he started up the stairs, she released his neck and felt for his jeans. Popped the button, forced the zipper down.

Trace stumbled. "Fuck." He leaned against the rail. "Don't do that while I'm trying to get up the stairs, baby."

"Oh, I'm sorry—does that make it hard to walk?" She lifted her head and grinned at him while stroking a hand inside his boxers and getting a handful of long, thick heat. "Oh," she laughed the word. "Guess you were saving the best for last?"

He covered her mouth with a groan and a heavy sweep of his tongue before pulling back with a breathless, "Stop it. Let me get you upstairs."

Now she was having some fun. "Is it hard to think while I'm touching you?" She wiggled out of his arms and pushed more clothes out of the way while Trace settled a death grip on the railing. "How hard do you think it will be to think if I were sucking you?"

A growl rolled out of Trace's throat. He grabbed her around the waist with his free arm and looked directly into her eyes with a clear and predatory sparkle of dominance. "The first time I come, it's going to be inside you."

The ferocity of his tone and the underlying innuendo of ownership in his words ripped away the veil of playfulness. He could tell himself whatever he wanted, but Avery had spent every day around the man for two months, and somewhere between sitting on the kitchen floor and now, this had shifted out of the casual arena. She didn't fool herself—or scare herself—into thinking that meant whatever this was would last beyond tonight, but it exposed his layers. Layers that only made him more attractive.

To balance his intensity, she kept it light, twisting to loosen his grasp with a teasing, "Maybe you're not in control anymore, Hutton." She licked her lip and scraped it between her teeth the same way he had. "Because *I'm* hungry now."

When she finally pulled his cock from his jeans and lowered to take him in her mouth, Trace stepped down a stair, wrapped his arm around her waist, and turned her away from him, then trapped her between the banister and his body. His swift movement and sheer strength whipped a thrill through her chest.

With his mouth at her ear, he rasped, "I'm not going to make it to the shower if you put your mouth on me here. And I told you"—he slowed his words, speaking deliberately—"the first time I come, it's going to be *deep inside you*."

Okay, maybe she had tipped back one glass of wine too many, because somehow, she found this little power trip both sexy and amusing.

She leaned her head back against his shoulder, bit his jaw, and used a jaunty little voice filled with attitude to ask, "Does someone have control issues?"

A low growl sounded in the back of his throat and transitioned into, "Fuck it." He released the banister and reached behind him. "Forget the shower."

"What? Wait, I want the shower—"

"You'll get your goddamned shower." The unique crackle of a foil pouch sounded just before his hips moved away, and he rolled on a condom. Then he gripped her waist and pulled her back against him. His cock rode the curve of her ass, long and thick and hard. "You'll just get it after I get you."

He covered her hands and pressed them to the rail, then pulled her hips toward him and used his knee to push one thigh up a stair.

Nerves tangled with excitement. She glanced over her shoulder but didn't get any words out before his cock stroked along her opening. Her breath froze in her lungs, and her fingers tightened around the rail. She dropped her head back against his shoulder. "Oh, *yes.*"

Trace stroked both hands down her hips, over her ass cheeks, then one slipped between her legs, stroking her, opening her, and guiding the head of his cock inside her.

The pressure was instant and both alarming and thrilling. He growled near her ear, and the sound in the dark as he penetrated her was the wickedest thrill she'd ever known. Her body sang with sensation, with excitement, with lust. Avery lifted her ass and opened her thighs wider.

"Mmmm, that's my girl; make room for me."

That rough voice rippled through her gut, like a stone in a pond. And as he inched his way inside her, insanely patient as he met resistance, his kisses and whispers tightened her chest with something more than sweetness. In the dark, trapped against the stair railing with this mouthwatering man working his cock inside her from behind, this moment overwhelmed Avery with a sense of possession. Of ownership. Of precious, gentle, but demanding domination.

And as much as her mind rejected the idea, her body responded to the carnality. To Trace's self-confidence. To his physical and emotional power. Even to his control. He was only halfway inside her, and she was shaking with the effort to hold back another orgasm.

He kissed her neck. "Fuck, you feel so good." Bit her shoulder. "So tight. So hot."

She whimpered his name. "Trace . . ."

"Right here, baby."

He wrapped one arm around her waist, slid his hand between her legs, and started those movements that made her push her hips into the pressure.

"Trace, don't." She squeezed her eyes shut. "I'm going to come again."

"Yes," he hissed in approval. "Perfect."

"I want to wait." But he already had her on the edge of climax again, making her wonder where in the hell this body had come from. "I want to come with you."

"You will." His breath was quick and hot on her shoulder. "Right now I need you slick and juicy so I can push deep."

The indirect pressure circling her clit was maddening. Her sex opened and took him deeper.

"That's it," he murmured.

The pressure brought the orgasm closer, and she opened more, took him a little deeper. The excruciating cycle of pleasure continued with his rough voice against her skin.

"Take all of me, baby."

The visuals that flashed in her head with his words pushed her to the peak. The orgasm rushed in on a swift upstroke. Avery cried out as her back arched, pushing Trace deeper. She shuddered through another wave of ecstasy, and when her slick walls released, Trace thrust deep with a grunt of supreme satisfaction joining her moan.

Her breath stuttered in and out of her lungs. Her fingernails bit into the wood banister. And, thankfully, Trace remained perfectly still.

"Sweet Jesus," he rasped between pants against her neck. "Never felt anything . . . so fucking perfect."

His hands roamed her body again, his mouth kissing her shoulders, her neck, her temple. "Tell me when you're ready, baby. Once I start moving inside you, I won't last long. Just too fucking good."

She took a deep breath and blew it out, then rocked her hips away and pushed back into him. The movement brought pleasure beyond description. Pleasure she couldn't quite comprehend. His thickness and length seemed to spark sensations everywhere. The pressure spilled a foreign kind of pleasure through her body and tightened her throat.

Trace bit into her shoulder just enough to pinch. "Do it again."

She tilted forward and added force when she pushed back. The head of his cock hit something inside her that was like a pleasure-release button, and sensation washed through her hips. "Ah . . . God . . ."

"Good?" he asked.

"So good."

With a long, low moan—part relief, part need—he wrapped his arms around her, one at her hips, one at her breasts, and whispered, "Fuck me, Avery."

That dark, feral tone shivered over her, and what started as a slow, careful rhythm quickly escalated into a frenzy of pounding hips, slapping flesh, heavy breathing, and moans of pleasure.

"Trace . . ." Exhausted, she paused, even though her body screamed for the orgasm he promised.

But Trace wasn't having it. He tightened the arm at her hips, picked up the rhythm, and added power. Three perfectly placed thrusts, and Avery shattered. Her body shivered so hard, her hip muscle cramped. The pain blended with the pleasure to intensify the orgasm, while the strength of Trace's last few thrusts slammed Avery against the banister.

The tremble of his strong body against hers, the guttural sounds of pleasure vibrating through his chest and into her back were the most intense, most beautiful, most *real* things Avery had ever experienced.

Trace grabbed the banister with both hands, his body wavering in the wake of his release. His hot breath bathed her back, and his sweaty forehead dripped on her shoulder.

An inexplicable smile spread across her face and filled her chest. So many emotions, past and present, combined to sting her eyes with tears again. Happy tears. Deeply satisfied tears. Life-altering tears.

"Holy fuck, girl," he finally whispered, breathless. "That was *wild*."

Avery laughed, curved an arm around the back of his neck, and pulled his head down for a kiss. The meeting of their mouths was solid and warm and lingering.

When she finally pulled out of the kiss, Trace eased from her body. Then, instead of taking the perfect opportunity to break away and disappear into the bathroom, he wrapped his arms around her and pressed his face to her neck. There he sighed, long and satisfied. Then just held her.

A torrent of emotions eddied inside her. Avery didn't know how to feel or what to think. Considering this was supposedly nothing but a hookup, or whatever people called casual sex nowadays, this affection wasn't how she'd envisioned the end of their tryst. And when all she'd ever known was a man who rolled over and fell asleep before Avery had even come close to finding satisfaction, she wasn't sure what to do with this kind of emotion.

To stem her automatic instinct to grab on and hold as tight as she could, Avery stroked a hand along his arm and tried for a light, "Somehow, even at twenty-five, I feel confident saying that I already know nothing in my future will ever top that."

He chuckled, then pressed his lips to her neck and let the kiss linger, in no hurry to escape her. The gesture was so sweet, and her need to be wanted so strong, she closed her eyes against a hard squeeze in her chest.

Trace finally lifted his head and whispered, "Hold off on that premonition, sugar. We've still got all night."

SIX

Trace floated from sleep to distant sounds he didn't recognize. His body felt heavy, and fatigue held his eyes closed as his mind drifted. The delicious scent of yeast, cinnamon, and vanilla filled his head. Warm, loving smells he would forever associate with morning and Avery and the café.

He didn't hear his dad talking to himself, which meant his father was still asleep. And that meant Trace could relax a little longer. A pinch in his shoulder had him shifting to find comfort. Instead he found confusion. He wasn't in his bed. He wasn't in a bed at all.

Trace forced his eyes open and sat up, propping himself up with his hands behind him. He squinted at the light spilling in the big window to his left, filling the small apartment above Wild Harts café with bright morning light.

"What . . . ?"

His memory returned instantly, and a hit of panic struck his chest. He scanned the small room for Avery but found no sign she'd ever been there except a second pillow beside Trace's. They'd fallen asleep in the early-morning hours on the thin foam pad she'd laid down weeks ago for her late nights baking downstairs.

A flood of emotions rushed in—excitement, apprehension, confusion. Regret. Hope.

"Jesus." He ran a hand through his hair and searched the floor for his phone. Scooping it up he squinted at the time. *7:00 a.m.?* "Holy fuck."

He'd also missed a few calls—one from his brother, one from his grandmother, and one from JT.

First things first: he dialed his grandmother. As he listened to the phone ring, Trace threw off the white sheet covering his legs, rolled to his knees, and groaned at the delicious aches and pains all through his body. He hadn't fucked that hard or that long since he'd been a damn kid, and he was feeling every one of his thirty-three years right now. Of course, the twenty-five-year-old he'd fucked all night was already up and downstairs working.

"Stupid sonofa—"

"Good morning, Trace," Pearl answered, as bright as the sun filling the apartment. "George and I are enjoying coffee on the porch. Listen to this."

Movement sounded over the phone; then music drifted over the line. Trace recognized the old song immediately—"You Send Me." He didn't know who sang it, but he sure recognized his father's voice joining the lyrics, word for word.

"Baby, yoooou send me . . . honest you do . . . honest you do . . . honest you do. Ooooh . . ."

The sound swamped Trace's chest with surprise and relief and a kind of bittersweet joy that tightened his throat. He closed his eyes and pressed a hand to his forehead as his grandmother came back on the line.

"Isn't that *amazing*?" she asked.

Trace nodded, working to pull a breath into tight lungs. "Yes," he managed with a rough laugh. "That's amazing."

"And he asked if you could bring home some of Avery's apple turnovers. He actually said 'Avery's apple turnovers.'"

Trace lifted his brows. His father often didn't recognize his own son when he came home from work. "Man. That's . . . wow." He shook his head. "I don't know if Avery's making turnovers today, but I'll grab some if she is."

After they said good-bye, Trace dropped back, threw his forearm over his eyes, and gave himself a few seconds to replay the last twelve hours.

God, he'd really lost his head last night. Sleeping with Avery . . . It was bound to happen. He'd been fighting it from day one. And, man, talk about unforgettable.

Trace caught his thoughts and turned them around. It couldn't happen again. This had to be just another one-and-done. No harm, no foul. He had to let last night slip into the background of their friendship so they could both refocus on their goals.

Voices downstairs made Trace lift his arm and open his eyes. He recognized Cody's drawl, the guy who was going to help replace the roof. Then Avery's warm laugh.

"Shit."

So much for relaxing a full sixty seconds. He rolled to his knees again and searched for his jeans. He found them folded at the foot of the foam pad. Along with his boxers, socks, and shirt. His work boots stood right beside them in a neat little package. The sight created a weird pinch in his chest that he ignored as he dressed in twenty seconds flat.

He took another ten seconds to run the water in the new bathroom sink, splash the cold liquid on his face, and run his hands through his hair. Then he looked at himself in the mirror. Damn, he sure looked better than he'd expected. He looked . . . refreshed, not haggard like usual from all the stress of his father, finances, and deadlines.

He turned off the water and reached for a towel but found them all on the floor where he and Avery had dropped them after drying each other off last night. Their shower flashed in his head, and lust flooded him like a waterfall. He saw her dark hair soaked and falling around her face as she dropped her head back, crying out in ecstasy while Trace hammered her against the tile.

He closed his eyes and gripped the sink to steady himself against the light-headed rush. That little girl had the least experience of any woman he'd ever slept with, yet had given him the most memorable night of his life.

Her voice pulled him back to reality. Last night was over. Now he had to let it all go, head downstairs, and make sure she'd let it all go, too. Then pray last night hadn't screwed up their friendship or their professional relationship, even knowing that was probably too much to hope for.

Resigned, his stomach heavy, he shook off the night and headed downstairs. Halfway down the staircase, right about where he'd pushed fully into Avery's sweet body for the first time, he heard her voice.

"I'm sure he'll be right down," she said. "We had a little problem with the plumbing in the new bathroom upstairs he was checking out. I'll go see how it's—" She turned up the staircase, saw him, and stopped, an uncertain smile wavering on her lush mouth. "Oh. Hey."

They held each other's gaze a long, hot second. A hot second that turned Trace's mind 180 degrees.

He didn't want to let anything go—not last night, not the bond they'd formed, and sure as shit not the gorgeous creature looking up at him.

Either she had clothes stashed somewhere here or she'd gone back to Phoebe's and changed, because she was dressed in her typically adorable country casual again today. Her sweet little print dress was fitted at her breasts and fell in layers of sheer floral to midthigh. And she'd jumped back into her favorite cowboy boots, which she wore with some type of ruffled sock peeking from the top. The cool morning had her in a cropped sweater that fell open in front and off one shoulder.

The only uncharacteristic thing about her was that she had her hair down. In the kitchen, she always wore it up in a twist or ponytail or clip. But today it hung in loose spirals well past her shoulders.

And Trace's mind went completely rogue and darted toward *What if . . .*

"I, um . . . Cody's here." She gestured, then twisted her hands together, her nervous tell. "I was just saying you'd be right down."

Trace continued down the stairs, letting his gaze wander to the banister, where they'd both held tight and found heaven, before meeting her gaze again. He suddenly had a lot to say to her, but they certainly wouldn't be talking about last night with Cody twenty feet away.

So he followed her lead and said, "Plumbing upstairs is good."

Her smile relaxed and grew. The dimple in her right cheek peeked through. "Great news."

Then she spun toward the kitchen again, and her dress lifted, giving Trace a glimpse of her thighs. Thighs he'd had wrapped around him in a number of unforgettable ways last night.

"You and Cody do your thing. I won't be here long. I know you want to work on the kitchen, so I finished up some of my baking early. I'll take my lunch orders to Phoebe's."

While she gathered up her supplies, Trace shook Cody's hand. "Hey, man. Mind doing a walk-around? Check out the materials? They were delivered last week to the south side of the building. I'll be out in a minute."

"You got it." Cody started toward the door. "Good to see you, Avery."

"You, too," she called with that cute smile. But as soon as Cody stepped out the door and they were alone, she turned serious, rushing to put all her things together. "Sorry, I was planning on getting out of your way earlier, but I always seem to underestimate the time I need."

At the counter he braced his hands against the stainless steel. "Could it be because you woke up late like I did?"

A deep breath exited her lungs, and her lips scrunched sideways. "Might have been a little of that."

"You should have woken me."

Her gaze darted up, and a smile fluttered over her lips. Her eyes softened for a second. "Oh, but you looked so . . ." She shook her head, turning stoic again. "It all worked out fine. Okay, I think I have everything. Oh, your coffee." She offered him a tall cup. "I left a few sandwiches in the fridge for you and Cody and George."

She did this every morning. Made him coffee exactly the way he liked it. Put together food for everyone on whatever makeshift crew happened to be in that day and always made sure George was included. Trace's mind drifted to the way she'd bent over backward—literally and figuratively—to please him in bed, let him sleep late this morning, folded all his clothes just so . . .

Instead of taking the coffee she offered, he grabbed her wrist gently.

Her pretty blue eyes jumped to his.

"Avery," he said softly, stroking his thumb across her skin, "are we going to talk about last night?"

Unease shifted in her eyes. She pulled her hand away, dug her purse from beneath the counter, and slipped the strap over her shoulder. "Last night was . . . beyond amazing." Then she smiled, a friendly, businesslike smile. "And it was last night. Today is today. I promised you no lingering ties, and I keep my promises. No worries there."

Disappointment stabbed at his chest, and all the air leaked from his lungs.

Normally, those words were music to his ears the morning after. But it wasn't happening that way today. Today a sense of panic gathered low in his gut, a sense of something really important slipping away. "Yeah, well, I know that was the plan, but last night—"

Her gaze jumped past him as footsteps sounded on the porch stairs.

His "something really special happened" never had a chance. He wasn't going to be able to have any kind of conversation with her here. Not during the day with so much going on.

But maybe that was for the best. This wasn't a good time to bring up the topic of "more" with Avery. Not after a night of blockbuster sex he wanted to repeat—like now. Not when she looked so damned adorable, all fresh and gorgeous the morning after. That was like shopping for groceries when he was starving.

Still, he turned to tell Cody to give him another few minutes so he could at least set up a time to talk with Avery later, but he found someone else at the door.

"Hi," Avery said to the man stepping in, then added a surprised, "Mark Davis? Is that you?"

"Yeah. Hey, Avery." He was dressed in Dockers and a button-down shirt with the sleeves rolled up on his wrists. He was blond, Ivy League, and young, somewhere around Avery's age.

"Oh my gosh, look at you." She lifted her hand to her hair, tugging one long curl forward, a motion he'd never seen her make before. "Last time I saw you, you couldn't fight your way out of a paper bag."

She came out from behind the counter and planted one hand on the stainless steel, the other messing with that one length of hair. Was that a nervous habit? Or one of those hair-petting things young women did, like preening?

Mark gave Avery that schoolboy-with-a-crush grin. "Finally put on some weight and grew into my big hands and feet."

He was a good-looking guy. The all-American hometown boy. And from what Trace knew of the Davis family, this kid was a lot like Huck Stevens. A guy who'd be really good for Avery. A guy she deserved after the shit she'd gone through with her ex.

"Man, you look great," Mark told her. "I've been out of town, just heard you were back, and had to come say hi."

He walked toward her, and Avery obliged him with a hug. Her hair shifted back and over her shoulder again, and that's when Trace saw it—the hickey she was trying to hide. His mind flashed to the moment he'd left the mark, while he'd been teaching her how to ride him like a true cowgirl. And the memory of what an A-plus student she'd been made his blood rush south.

Trace crossed his arms over the new discomfort in his gut. He leaned back against the counter and forced himself to watch her with this other man. Watch the way she smiled up at him as Mark stroked his hands down her arms. Watch the way she lifted her hand to that one curl again, pulling it forward to hide all hints of her night with Trace. And hated the way that all made him fist his hands. Made his stomach ache like a hot coal burned there.

She stepped away from Mark and gestured toward Trace. "Mark, this is Trace." She held Trace's gaze an extra second when she said, "He's making magic happen around here."

If she'd been any other woman, he'd have chalked up her friendliness to Mark followed by a veiled innuendo to her night with Trace as head games. But he didn't think Avery even knew how to play the games most women did.

Mark approached to shake Trace's hand.

"Good to meet you," Trace offered.

Avery's gaze held on Trace, a nervous spark hinting in her eyes. When she looked back at Mark, she said, "Did I hear you bought the building across the street?"

"I did. Hanging out my own shingle."

"Congratulations. An accountant, right?"

He laughed and nodded. "I see the Wildwood rumor mill is working well."

"You must be planning on renovating to meet the standards of that visual nuisance ordinance the mayor put into effect this year."

Mark rolled his eyes and pushed his hands into his pockets. "Stupid bullshit, but yeah. I have to remodel anyway, the place hasn't been updated in decades."

"Well, like I said, Trace has done amazing things here. You certainly can't have him until he's dotted all the i's and crossed all the t's for me, but if you need an awesome contractor, Trace is your man."

Trace really liked the idea of dotting Avery's i's and crossing Avery's t's.

Mark's attention returned to Trace, and the air between them shifted. He picked up an intangible vibe of competition.

Mark nodded. "Great to know. You from around here?"

"Santa Rosa, mostly."

"Trace is Zane Hutton's brother," Avery said. "You know Zane."

Ah crap. As soon as the words were out of Avery's mouth, Trace knew what would come next, and he tightened his stomach for the inevitable hit of his ugly past.

"Oh, right, Zane . . . ," Mark said, his gaze clicking with associations. "Didn't I hear you had some trouble a few years back?"

Fucker. He was definitely interested in Avery. And he'd probably played sports in high school or college, because he'd gone straight for Trace's knees.

Trace had tangled with men who would eat this kid for a morning snack, but he'd left all that behind when he'd walked beyond Folsom's gates, so he offered a smile and a semi-amiable, "I see the Wildwood rumor mill is working well."

Mark nodded, thoughts churning behind his dark eyes. "Where'd you end up?"

Trace's fingers flexed. He deliberately tamped down the spurt of anger. "Folsom."

"Hard time."

Like you'd know, punk. "Very."

"You still have your contractor's license?"

"Sure do."

"Good for you."

Condescending prick.

The way Avery sidled closer told Trace she sensed the subtle confrontation. "Didn't you buy the barber shop? Mr. Stein's place?"

Mark grinned at her. "Good memory."

"It's where my dad used to get his hair cut." She narrowed her eyes a little. "I don't suppose that old piano is still there? I used to pound on it whenever my dad dragged me along."

"As a matter of fact," he said with a sour look as he rubbed the back of his neck, "it's only one of the relics I'm going to have to get rid of."

Her gaze darted to Trace for a split second, but he caught the spark of excitement before she refocused on Mark. "If you're going to give the piano away, I'd love to take it off your hands."

"Really?" Mark asked, hopeful. "Are you sure? I doubt it's any good, and I don't want to dump my trash on you."

She lifted a shoulder. "I doubt it was played much, and we don't have the temperature swings or the humidity that would cause a lot of damage. I'd be willing to take my chances."

"Sounds like you know what you're talking about."

"Just enough to get into trouble. I played in school as a kid."

"Well, I'd be happy to get it off my hands. It's sitting in a corner gathering dust and taking up space."

"Then it's a deal." Avery was beaming, and Trace knew exactly why she wanted that old piano—for his dad. The emotions that hit him when he'd come down the stairs returned, even more intense than before. "And I bet you're probably going to need some nice cabinets right? Come look at my kitchen." She pulled Mark by the arm. "Trace built all these himself. Everything's custom."

She went on about the wood, the hardware, how he'd had to jump through hoops to give her just the setup she'd wanted. And Trace was still wrangling inner turmoil when Mark glanced his way and offered a sincere, "Really nice work."

Trace nodded. "Thanks."

Mark turned, surveyed the butcher block, and planted a hand on the surface—right where Avery's ass had slid over the wood while Trace had eaten her out and Avery had begged him to make her come.

Trace's cock was uncomfortably hard, and he had to shift on his feet to ease the pressure.

Mark stroked his hand across the surface. "This is great."

Trace was already looking at Avery when her gaze cut toward him. "Yes, Trace . . . does amazing work."

His mouth kicked up in a one-sided smile. "It's all about making my client happy."

Avery looked away, pressing her lips against a smile, her face turning bright pink.

"I may have you give me an estimate for a kitchen remodel at my house," Mark said. "I just bought a place on Park Terrace."

Ritzy area. The kid was doing well for himself. And he was exactly the kind of man Avery should be dating. Trace also realized Mark's offer was exactly why he'd taken the café remodel at such a cut rate—to garner more work and get his own construction business under way again so he could stop all that shitty manual labor he'd been stuck with since he'd gotten out of prison. It was also exactly why he should never have slept with Avery.

He sobered, met Mark's gaze, and said, "I'd be happy to come by." He pulled out his wallet, slid a business card free, and handed it to the other man. "Call anytime."

Mark shook Trace's hand again. "Will do."

"Well, it was good to see you, Mark," Avery said. "I'm sorry to cut this short, but I've got to get out of this kitchen so Trace can get started."

"Sure, no problem."

Avery gathered her bags and Mark gallantly took several for her. On the porch, holding the screen open, Avery let Mark go ahead of her and glanced back at Trace with an excited grin and a thumbs-up. "For your dad?"

"It's sweet, Avery, but I don't have the money for the fixes, and I don't know anything about pianos."

"I'll take care of that if you take care of moving it." She gave him the puppy-dog eyes she used when she wanted something special in the remodel. "Please?"

He smiled and shook his head but agreed. "Anything for you."

With an extra bounce in her step, she jogged down the stairs to where Mark waited at the bottom, and they continued toward her car together. Watching her walk away with another man at her side didn't bring Trace relief the way it would have with any other woman he'd slept with over the past year. Or longer.

At some point during the night, Avery had become more than just another hookup. Might have been her sweet laughter in the dark. Might have been the way she'd draped her beautiful body over him, falling asleep with her head against his chest just the way she'd promised. Might have been one of hundreds of other moments they'd shared over the last two months working together. Might have been an all-of-the-above combination.

The what, how, or when didn't really matter. Because regardless, Trace had to face the fact that Avery could never be just another hookup. She was too damn special.

And he wasn't the only one who noticed. On the way to the Jeep, Trace heard Mark say, "I'd love to take you out to dinner and catch up. What are you doing tonight?"

That cut a slice in Trace's gut. He couldn't hear Avery's answer, but they hugged again before she got into the car.

Cody appeared at the base of the steps, and Trace put any lingering thoughts of *what if* out of his mind, stuffed the residual desire and disappointment into a corner, and did what he'd come here to do. For himself and for Avery.

He slapped Cody on the shoulder. "Are you up for moving a piano later today?"

Avery's gaze blurred over the spreadsheet in front of Delaney. She sat in her sister's office at the building that would eventually be Wildcard Brews. The space was in the very early stages of construction, basically a shell housing Ethan's brewing setup. The familiar sound of male shouts echoed through main space beyond the door, drawing Avery's gaze to the window between the spaces. Beyond, the open space was filled with construction materials and wandering men, the sound of power and hand tools.

"Oh, I'm not going to miss that," Avery murmured. She looked forward to the day a little serenity entered her life. At least the large crews Trace had brought on to do the earlier jobs like framing and drywall were gone. Now she dealt with fewer men, usually just Trace and whoever was helping him on the job that day.

"I don't even hear it anymore," Delaney murmured, her brow furrowed as she turned pages.

After years on job sites, Delaney must have grown immune to the sound of construction the way Avery had grown immune to the sounds of a working kitchen.

Avery returned her focus to the spreadsheet, trying to keep her mind present, but it kept slipping back to Trace. "My life's beginning to feel like one big construction zone."

"Same," Delaney murmured, then sat back and looked at Avery, her brow creased with concern. "Your budget is really tight. I agree that the high-grade appliances were worth the expense, but they really sucked you dry. You need an influx of cash. I'd feel better if you could push up your opening date."

"Push it up?" Avery's brows rose. She laughed and shook her head. "I don't see how."

"Well, then you'll have to stay on target. Your operating expenses are threatening to overrun your income. And you've drained the well. There's no more cash to draw on. God, I don't like this."

Delaney's discomfort heightened Avery's. "That's because you're used to working with multi-million-dollar budgets and cash reserves galore. I'm used to operating on a shoestring. It's tight, but I've worked with less."

Her sister wasn't convinced. "How much longer is it going to take Trace to get that roof on? There's rain in the forecast. I'm worried that's going to slow things down and screw up your grand opening date. You don't have cushion for that."

Avery rubbed eyes stinging from fatigue and sighed. "Cody was at the café when I left this morning. He and Trace were consulting on the roof. The materials are already there. You know Trace—he jumps on things. I bet they start tomorrow if they haven't already. I'll look at the forecast and talk to him about it." Avery glanced at her watch. "God, it's three o'clock already. I've got to get back to Phoebe's and start on website orders."

"We need to go over your cash flow." Delaney covered Avery's hand with hers. "Are you okay? You've been under a lot of stress. Working long hours."

"Yeah, yeah, just a little tired." She reached for her purse and searched for her recent deposit slips, flipping her hair out of the way. "The lunch orders keep growing, which brings in some steady cash, and I think that's going to be great for business when the café opens. Phoebe just paid me for this week's sales, and I got a deposit from Internet sales."

She piled the latest receipts in her hand and was about to put them on the desk, when Delaney reached out and pulled her hair aside.

"What in the hell is that?" Surprise and a sassy sort of humor lit her sister's face as she laughed. "Oh my God. A hickey? Aren't you a little old for a hickey? And who, exactly, gave you that? And even better, *when*? When have you had time to . . . Oh, *that's* why you're tired."

Avery pushed Delaney's hand away and pulled her hair over the mark again. "If I'm a little old for a hickey, you're way the hell too old for them, and I see them on you all the time. The only difference is that I have the manners not to point them out."

"Only because you know who's giving them to me. Who's that from?" Her smoky-blue eyes lit up. "Huck? Oh my God, Phoebe's going to be giddy. She's been dying for you to see him again. Wait till she hears—"

"Don't. Phoebe is the last person I want to know anything about my personal life at the moment."

Delaney dropped her elbow on the desk and propped her chin in her hand, eyes sparkling, teeth glimmering in a naughty grin. "Tell me everything. He's so hot. You're going to be the envy of every girl in town, which is good. It'll take some heat off me for snagging Ethan. So? Is he a good kisser? Did you do more than kiss? Tell."

"It wasn't Huck," Avery admitted, her gut heavy with the realization of how her family would feel about her seeing Trace. "And I'd rather not talk about it."

"Not Huck?" Delaney sat back, frowning. "Then *who*? But first, why not Huck?"

"There's no spark. Look, I've really tried to follow your advice and ease Phoebe's mind by dating, but I'm just not interested in anyone, okay?"

Her brows shot up. "Then how'd you get that?"

"It was a fling. One night. Not with anyone I've dated. That's what I want now—easy, no strings. Even the thought of commitment gives me hives."

"Fling with *who*?" Delaney pushed.

"It was just one night, so it doesn't matter who." Avery started closing up the books.

"Well, was it good?"

Avery smirked. "I know some women love to give every detail of their sexual escapades, but I'm not one of them."

"That's not what I meant. I meant that if it was good, why stick with just one night? You're young, single, beautiful, free. And no one deserves some fun, easy lovin' more than you."

Avery pulled the accounting book into her lap and met her sister's blue gaze. "I don't think that would work for me. It's better for me to stick with just one night."

Actually, in hindsight, *one time* seemed like an even better idea. Because in between the multiple rounds of blockbuster sex with Trace during their one night, a lot of other things had happened. A lot of emotional things that hadn't required any words. Caresses and looks, kisses and laughter and whispers. Even their silences had seemed to carry weight.

"Yep, one time would have been even better." Avery stuffed the books away.

"I don't mean to be rude," Delaney said, "but how would you know? You've only slept with one man your entire life. And you hardly got a chance to even sleep with him. So if it was good with this other guy, there's no reason to limit it to one night or one time or whatever you want to call it. You can keep it simple and keep seeing him without letting things get complicated."

Nope. Too late for that. Her feelings for Trace had been complicated from day one.

"And why won't you tell me who it is?" Delaney added with a little pout.

"Because I don't want to talk about it."

Delaney narrowed her eyes and sat back, crossing her arms. "I know him, don't I?"

"You know everyone." She pulled the strap of her bag over her shoulder. "And, frankly, it's none of your business."

"Ouch." Delaney feigned hurt for all of two seconds before her eyes sparked. "Is it one of Ethan's friends? Is that why you don't want to tell me?"

"No. Delaney, just—"

"Oh, it's someone I wouldn't like, isn't it? Or someone Phoebe wouldn't like. That makes total sense. You always hated rocking the boat. You don't want to upset anyone. Well, now you have to tell me." She grinned. "Come on, Avery, I'm not going to give you shit—too much. And I won't tell Phoebe—right away."

Avery laughed as she stood. "I'm headed to Phoebe's to work. Please don't bring this up. I may not have wanted to rock the boat when I was a kid, but if you tell Phoebe, I'll find a way to sink the damn boat and make it all your fault."

Avery pulled open the office door and walked toward the exterior door through the shell and all the activity with a profound sense of relief.

Bullet dodged.

Until she heard Delaney following her, muttering, "When in the hell would you have time to meet—" Her sister's gasp ripped through Avery like ice. "No. No, no, no."

Delaney's quickening footsteps made dread curl in Avery's gut.

Her sister cut in front of Avery just before she reached the door and put a hand on her shoulder. Her eyes were serious when she said, "Tell me it's not Trace."

Avery huffed an exhausted breath, tilted her head, and pretended fire and ice weren't battling for control in her gut. "Unless you want to be the one up until midnight making my highly requested strawberry balsamic caramels, please get out of the way."

"Just tell me it's not Trace, and I'll let it go."

Avery couldn't lie. She could skirt issues, she could distract, she could avoid, but she couldn't lie. And Delaney knew it. But at this point, Avery didn't even want to lie. She was physically exhausted from the night, emotionally exhausted from struggling over her feelings for Trace, mentally exhausted from trying to run a business that barely even existed while that business was bleeding her dry—financially, emotionally, and physically.

But she was no longer the little girl who would scurry away and try to hide either. And as much as she still loved to please, that desire didn't own her. So she just sighed and held Delaney's gaze silently.

Delaney's pretty face tightened with frustration. She grabbed both Avery's arms and shook her a little. "Avery. *No.* You can't afford to get involved with someone you work with. Especially not *Trace.*"

Turbulence kicked up in her gut. "If you were listening to me, you would have heard me say we're not *involved.* We agreed to one night. Which is over." A fact that still left Avery unsettled. Especially after that look in his eyes this morning. Especially with his words still replaying over in Avery's head. *"Yeah, well, I know that was the plan, but last night—"*

"And I know you've had bad experiences with men and work in the past," Avery went on, "but that doesn't mean everyone does. I'm also a very grown adult who's made her own decisions for the last eight years. Very grown-up decisions. They may not have all been perfect, but I'm extremely capable, so please don't treat me like the little girl you left all those years ago."

This time, the hurt darkening Delaney's eyes was real, and Avery immediately realized she'd used the wrong words.

"Damn, I didn't mean it that way. I meant I may still be your little sister, but I'm not a kid anymore."

"You're right." Delaney nodded, but her teasing humor had evaporated, replaced by true concern. "I just want this business to work for you. You've put everything you have into it. It's your dream, and I don't want anything to jeopardize that. Trace . . ." Delaney closed her eyes and sighed. "He's a good guy. A great guy. I would never have hired him if he weren't. But he's got a lot of scars, and people with scars do unpredictable things. He's also got a lot on his plate trying to manage the café and his dad. He's the key to getting that café built on time and within budget. You're both balancing very precariously on high wires right now. If a gust of wind came from the wrong direction . . ."

Avery's dream could fall to its death. "It's not going to go bad because he and I had a clear understanding before anything happened, because we both want the same thing, and because we're both adults."

Delaney took another breath and studied her sister. Avery waited, knowing Delaney hadn't said everything she needed to say. "You know he's a player."

Avery's stomach tightened. "Of course. Who doesn't?"

"You know he was screwed over by his fiancée, and he's not a guy who's going to trust enough to settle down."

No, she hadn't known anything about a fiancée, but she said, "Hello, same. Trace doesn't have any scars on me."

"Yeah, he does." With sadness in her eyes, Delaney lifted her brows. "Prison?"

"He made a mistake a decade ago—so did I. He's been paying for it ever since—so have I. We may have lived in different kinds of prisons, but I've been there, too. And in my opinion, scars only make people work *not* to screw up their lives again so they can get to where they want to be."

Resignation settled into her sister's eyes. "Okay." She nodded. "You've got your head on straight." Delaney's lips twisted, and she gave Avery a sassy smirk. "So? Does he live up to the rumors?"

Avery's neck and cheeks flushed with heat, and she couldn't hold back the smile that filled her face. "Surpasses every one."

Delaney burst out laughing, and Avery laughed with her. Her sister reached out and stroked her hair. "You deserve some good after what you've been through. Just . . . be careful."

"Let me go get some work done so this business doesn't fall flat on its face."

Avery pulled the door open, eager to escape the awkwardness of telling her big sister she'd had a one-night stand with her contractor. A lot of women Avery's age slept around, but this was all new to her, and she was feeling seventeen again in a lot of ways. Only this seventeen do-over was *way* better the second time around.

"Hey," Delaney said. "Have you heard from Chloe?"

Their youngest sister and the true nomad of the family only touched base when she needed money. "She's not calling me back, probably because she knows the café has bled me dry. You might want to have Phoebe try."

Delaney nodded.

On the way to the Jeep, Avery blew her sister a kiss and climbed into the SUV. But she didn't bother to snap on her seat belt for the quick ride around the block to her next stop: Finley's Market.

She parked in the small lot and pulled the color-coded plastic totes out of the back and stacked them, feeling lighter now that she'd gotten that little secret off her shoulders. And it also felt so good to have a sister who cared so much about her—financially and emotionally—that she was supporting her in every way.

Avery thought of Chloe again. Maybe she'd call and offer Chloe a job at the café. It would be so nice to have all of them together.

With a spark of hope for her day, she crouched to gather the totes.

"Ms. Hart." The voice was male and smooth and attractive, but it didn't give her the warm fuzzies.

She released the handles on the totes and glanced toward the man, squinting against the bright morning sun. A cop strolled toward her in a familiar navy uniform. Her mind jumped to Zane, Trace's brother, but he would never call her Ms. Hart, and his voice was warm and happy. Then the man's head cut into the path of the sunlight and his face came into view, and everything made sense.

"Austin." That was as much of a greeting as this asshole was going to get. He may have been Ethan's brother, but he wasn't even in the same gene pool as far as the Hart family was concerned.

She picked up her totes and started inside. Austin stepped into her path and grinned. "I think you meant Deputy Hayes."

Her instincts clicked on, and her walls went up.

She frowned at him over the top of a tote and pretended to think a moment. "You know, I can still remember the first time I saw you. It was in the first grade. All the other boys were out on the yard playing ball, and you were sitting on the benches all alone picking your nose and eating the snot." When the shock registered, and his grin tightened, she said, "So, no, I didn't mean Deputy Hayes. Somehow with that image in my mind, you will forever be Austin to me. Now you have a great day."

She sidestepped him, making a quick path into the market.

"Avery," he called after her.

"Hey, Rita." She ignored Austin and greeted the middle-aged cashier, hurrying through the swinging door leading behind the counter. "I've got more goodies for you."

Austin's boots sounded on the old hardwood of the historical building a few seconds later, stopping near the counter.

"Avery." His tone had gone from solicitous condescension to you'd-better-obey-me-right-now. "I need to speak with you."

Pretend, pretend, pretend. Avery had gotten so good at pretend, sometimes she pretended herself right out of reality. But here, pretend would come in handy. Here, she had to pretend to be that "Army Strong" that Trace saw in her.

"Sorry, Austin, I'm running behind schedule. No time to chat."

She kept her back to him and settled the totes on the floor, crouching to unpack the various brownies, fudge, truffles, and other goodies she'd already cut and stabbed with pretty, bright toothpicks or wrapped in gold foil for tasting. Pulling out the clear plastic cake plates she kept under the counter, she focused on breathing steadily as she arranged them, making sure her marketing sign with the title of the item and the Wild Harts logo was secure and she had plenty of business cards and brochures to lay out.

"I'm not here to chat, and this is not negotiable." His boots stepped into her peripheral vision on the left. His voice sounded directly overhead, quivering down her neck.

Oh, he was so testing her patience. And her strength. And her nerves. But she lifted her voice as if she didn't notice his attitude and this was all just foolery between friends. "Then you best have your handcuffs out and a charge handy, because," she finished in a singsong, "I'm a busy woman."

She turned right instead of left, dodging his interference, and placed a cake plate on top of the counter holding lotto tickets. She'd have to move it, but she'd worry about that later.

"Hey, Joe, Marv," she greeted some regulars. "Take a truffle home to your wives."

"Austin," Rita said, her voice as soft and pleasant as pudding, "there really isn't enough space back here for a man as big as you. And we're really busy."

He ignored Rita, a lot like Avery was ignoring him. She crouched to pick up another cake plate, and Austin's hand closed around her forearm.

"Avery." His bark came from behind clenched teeth.

Avery couldn't take her eyes off his hand on her arm. Her mind flashed back to her father and the beatings she'd received. Every one had started with a hand on her arm just like this. Her insides chilled and quivered. But her mind continued to work. This was wrong. And she didn't have to take it from anyone. Ever. For any reason. That was only one of a thousand things she'd learned during the last eight years.

Her gaze held on a ring he wore. Some kind of law enforcement ring with a To Protect and Serve slogan wrapping the eagle on the front and the name Hayes carved into the design on the side. She reached for her phone, which was sitting on top of the tote right in front of her. "What time—"

"It *doesn't matter* what time it is." He spoke low, but the rise in Rita's voice as she helped customers told Avery people were noticing. She didn't need people noticing. She couldn't afford negative gossip at this stage of her business's growth. She needed Austin to back off and stay off. "I'm trying to tell you that Hutton is bad news. Delaney got him cheap, and you get what you pay for. He's gonna fuck up. All cons fuck up."

Avery moved her thumb over the phone and opened her camera. She didn't know why her fingers weren't shaking because she felt as if she were vibrating on the inside—with fury. With a sense of futility and weakness so ingrained she wanted to scream with it. Her father, David, the military, and now Austin. She was dead sick and tired of feeling helpless.

"He's a criminal," Austin rasped in her ear. "And he lived with other criminals like a pack animal for years. You're not safe with him. And you shouldn't be putting everything you have in his hands."

She clicked the shutter of her camera.

He shook her by the arm. "Are you listening to me?"

"Whose hands do you think I should put my future in?" She held her phone steady and looked up at him, met his gaze deliberately, and said, "Yours?"

Click.

His dark gaze darted to her phone, then to his hand on her arm. He released it as if she were on fire, leaving a beautiful white print where he'd been squeezing the blood out of her skin. Her focus never had to leave his face to know it would be visually stunning. She'd learned that in childhood.

Click.

She slid her phone into her back pocket and stood, then tilted her head and gave him her best Stepford Wife smile—she'd learned that after she left home. Turning herself into the perfect army wife may not have saved her marriage, but it might prove useful in other aspects of life.

"Actually, the time *does* matter, because I happen to be on my way to Mrs. Holland's house to deliver Sheriff Holland's birthday cake. Is there anything—you know, any photos, any video clips, any . . . anything you'd like me to pass on while I'm there?"

Hands on hips, Austin pressed his mouth into a hard line. Avery never looked away.

"Don't fuck with me, Avery."

She lowered her voice for Austin's ears only. "I may have left here a scared little girl, but I had my own training over the last eight years. If you thought Delaney was a bitch, you ain't seen nothin'. So take your own advice." She leaned back and switched into Stepford Wife mode again. "Would you like a truffle for the road?"

He started to turn.

"Oh, and Austin, just FYI, those cameras Trace installed at the beginning of the renovation before I got to town, they're still there, they're still remote, and their footage still feeds directly to a server."

By his I'll-kill-you-later look, she knew he'd caught the reference to his previous threat toward Delaney that had been saved by those cameras, as well as the reference to the ability to catch any future threats swimming in his head now, should he decide to act on them at the café.

Avery waited until Austin had peeled out of the parking lot to turn to Rita, who met her gaze with worried, shocked eyes and asked, "Are you okay?"

Avery laughed with far more relief than humor. "As in, am I crazy? Yeah, I'm probably a little crazy, but yeah, I'm also okay. Do you mind taking care of these when you have time? The samples are out. All you need to do is slide the goodies into their trays."

"Of course not, honey."

She kissed Rita's cheek. "You're a peach."

Avery wandered from the store, drained and numb. She could pull out the strong and use it when necessary, but the truth was, the last eight years had taken their toll. In her two short months home, Avery had quickly adapted to having family around her. Having Trace around her. They shored her up so she didn't have to be strong all the time, and she really enjoyed the stability that created in this crazy world. The truth was, being strong and alone wasn't all that. It also wore her the hell out.

Avery dropped into the driver's seat of the Jeep, ready to find a little peace of mind for a change. Maybe once she found it, she could even figure out what to do about Trace.

SEVEN

As the sun set, Trace loaded the last of the reclaimed maple from the specialty lumber store onto the rails of his truck and tied them down.

With the load secured, he jumped off the running board, pressed his palms to the edge of the truck bed, and closed his eyes until the burn in his shoulders faded. Everything hurt today. He was definitely getting too old to go at it all night if this was how he felt the next day. But he hadn't met anyone he'd been that passionate about in years, so the problem was most likely less about age and more about disuse.

At least that's what he liked to think.

Regardless, he still had a lot of work to do to make up for the time he'd lost. Zane was taking Dad again tonight, so this was Trace's last chance to get caught up on the café for a while.

He straightened and rounded the truck. As soon as he slid into the driver's side, his stomach growled and rumbled. He glanced at the dash and realized he hadn't eaten in eight hours.

Instead of heading back to Wild Harts, he walked across the street to Finley's Market, ordered a sandwich at the deli counter, then wandered to the cooler for a drink. He pulled a couple of water bottles from the case, and when he closed the door he caught sight of Tiffany Mulligan. She was standing in the wine aisle with a bottle of red in her hand, but she was frowning at her phone.

When Trace was living with his grandmother in Wildwood, he'd gone to school here. He'd been in the same class as Tiffany's older brother and had gotten to know the family. "Hey, Tiffany."

She looked up, her expression still distracted, but her gaze cleared and she smiled. "Hey, Trace. How are you?"

"Good, thanks. Congratulations on your wedding. Avery's real excited about doing your cake."

"I know she's going to do an amazing job." Concern returned to her eyes. She leaned her shoulder against the nearest shelf. "How is she? I could tell by the look on her face that she didn't know about David. I can't imagine how hard this transition must be for her. She certainly didn't need the news that he's getting remarried. Hell, the signatures on the divorce papers are barely dry. My mother, I swear."

Trace fought to hide his own surprise. "You know Avery. She's as tough as they come. When did that come up?"

"At the bridal shower. And I feel horrible. I'm the one who saw it on Facebook earlier in the day because I still follow David. I was shocked, and stupidly told my mother. If I'd thought for a second, I would have kept my mouth shut."

"Facebook, huh?" He had ugly flashbacks of his good-for-nothing fiancée who'd left him for another guy at the mere hint of trouble. "That's pretty shitty."

"Oh, it's terrible. There isn't anyone sweeter, more loyal, or with a bigger heart than Avery. I hope she hasn't seen all the comments on his engagement photos. It just breaks my heart." Her phone buzzed, and she glanced at it with a shake of her head. "The comments just keep coming."

Trace flashed to the sight of Avery sitting on the café floor with a pie and a wine bottle. *"I'm the goddess of fine."*

So last night had been a revenge fuck. Or a rebound fuck. *Whatever. Same difference.*

The realization hammered him in the chest. What an idiot he'd been, thinking something real had happened last night. Thinking there might be something different, something special, some sort of unique connection between them.

Worse, he felt like an absolute sucker for believing that she'd wanted him, knowing who he was and where he'd been. That she'd wanted him, knowing she could have any of a dozen other men who were better than Trace in every way that mattered. Yet she'd chosen him.

"I'm cured of ever wanting commitment again," she'd said. And it was a hell of a lot easier to avoid commitment with a guy you really didn't want for anything but a rebound fuck, wasn't it?

Tiffany's phone pinged again. "Jesus. I'm just going to turn it off. I can't take it."

"Mind if I look at the posts?" he asked.

She pushed the phone into his hands. "Be my guest. Then just turn it off. I have to pick wine for a dinner party. Maybe I'm just having pre-wedding jitters, but as soon as I get home I'm unfriending everyone associated with that bullshit."

Tiffany wandered down the aisle, and Trace took a deep breath and turned his attention to the Facebook posts on her phone. He scrolled to photos of David and his fiancée, a cute, chestnut-haired girl. They'd been professionally done, and the two looked absolutely in love in every photo. Kissing. Embracing. Holding hands. Looking deep into each other's eyes. David carrying his fiancée in his arms.

A mess of emotions whipped through Trace, and he found himself filled with an irrational level of both hurt and betrayal on Avery's behalf. But reading the messages friends had posted only angered him more. Things like "Congratulations on finally finding THE ONE," "You're perfect for each other," "Second time's a charm," "Never seen you so happy," and "Hooah, doin' it right this time."

"Jesus." Trace's stomach burned with so much anger in so many directions, he couldn't read any more. He returned the water to the cooler and grabbed a six-pack of Wildcard's high-octane triple IPA instead. Striding down the wine aisle, he handed the phone back to Tiffany. "You're right. That's bullshit. Thanks for being such a good friend to Avery."

Trace checked out without his sandwich, his appetite gone.

Two hours later, nearing ten o'clock, Trace had gone through four of the six beers and laid maple hardwood in half of the café's event space, upstairs and across the building from the little apartment where he'd spent the night with Avery. He was shirtless and dripping sweat when headlights flashed through the windows.

He paused, rubber mallet in hand, and watched Avery's Jeep come to a stop out front. He knew his anger was irrational. Knew she hadn't promised anything more than she'd given, but he still felt like she'd lied to him.

Trace dropped a piece of maple that had once graced the gym floor of the local high school, and followed on his knees. After setting the grooves, he used another piece of wood to hammer the eight-foot length into place.

The front screen door squeaked open, then slammed shut, and the soft tap of Avery's boots sounded on the hardwood downstairs. Despite his hurt, his anger, his disappointment, Trace's stomach flipped and tightened.

"Goddammit," he muttered and stood to grab another piece of maple.

"Oh, wow," she said. "You got the piano moved already?"

He didn't answer. The fact that it was sitting by the front door should be answer enough.

"Trace?" she called up the stairs.

He closed his eyes, rested the end of the maple on the floor, and leaned into it. "What?"

"Thank you."

Why did she have to be so fucking sweet?

When he didn't answer, she said, "You're working late."

"Yep." He dropped the wood and repeated the placement process.

"I'm just here to pick up sugar. I ran out at Phoebe's."

He lifted his hands out to the side. What the hell did he care? "Great."

Her boots tapped into the kitchen, and Trace breathed a sigh of relief. He'd laid two more boards by the time she yelled up the stairs again.

"I'm gonna head out. Do you need anything?"

Yeah, he needed a lot of things, and she was at the top of the damn list.

But he gave her a clipped, "Nope."

She hesitated. "Okay, I'll see you tomorrow."

Trace saluted the empty room. "Later."

More boot taps, another slam of the screen door, and Trace picked up another piece of maple. But this time, he threw it at the floor, dropped his head, and planted his hands at his hips. *"Fuck."*

He lowered to his knees and put his frustration into the hammer. When the piece was in place, he sat back on his heels and wiped the sweat from his face with a gloved hand.

"Trace?"

Her voice startled him, and he swiveled to find her at the top of the stairs looking just as breathtaking as she had that morning.

"What?" he barked.

She hesitated. "Is your dad okay?"

"What?" he asked confused. "He's fine. Everything's fine. Fucking perfect. What do you want?"

Her expression went from open and worried to baffled and hurt. "I wanted to check on you."

"Gee, thanks, Cream Puff. I'm fine. Go get your baking on."

He pushed himself to his feet even though he was spent and grabbed another piece of maple. When he turned to drop it on the floor, Avery jerked it out of his hand.

He spun on her, grabbing it back. "What the fuck?"

"Are you drunk?" she asked, angry now.

"No, I'm not drunk. What difference does it make to you?"

"You're not working drunk. You could hurt yourself."

He laughed. "You're not the boss of me, baby. Go make your cookies. Leave the heavy lifting to me."

He dropped to his knees, which ached despite the heavy-duty kneepads, and bent to place the maple. Avery's boots stepped right in his way. He gritted his teeth and lifted his gaze slowly, trying to hold his temper, trying to ignore her bare thighs, the sway of her skirt, the outline of her full breasts, the fall of her rich, dark hair.

"Woman, you have pushed enough of my buttons today. *Get off* my fucking floor."

She crossed her arms. "What the hell is wrong with you?"

"I've been working fourteen hours straight on about two hours of sleep after fucking you all night, and now you're standing on my floor, which is keeping me from finally getting some good shut-eye. That's what the hell's wrong with me."

"Bullshit. And I'm going to stay standing on this floor until you tell me why you're acting like this."

He sat back, rubbing sweat off his face with his forearm. "I saw Tiffany Mulligan at the market. She told me what you wouldn't—why you were so bent last night."

Avery frowned, shook her head, and lifted her hands out to the sides. "What does that have to do with *anything*?"

He got to his feet and put less than a foot between them, knowing he had to smell worse than the Niners' locker room and not giving a shit. "It has to do with you and me last night."

"No," she said, adamant. "It doesn't."

"If you wanted a revenge fuck or a rebound fuck or whatever the hell you want to call it, you should have just told me that's what last night was about. You should have been straight up with me."

Fury broke out across her face, and she shoved him back with both hands, then followed. "How *dare* you insult me like that. I don't know what your problem is, but don't take it out on me."

"My problem is you"—he shook a gloved finger in her face—"using me to make yourself feel better about your ex getting remarried."

Her mouth fell open, and anger transitioned into hurt. "*That's* what you think of me? You think I'm so weak I need to fuck another guy to bury hurt? If that were the case, I'd have fucked my way through my entire marriage. But I didn't. I coped. I dealt. I believed. I hoped. And what did I get? Nothing. Absolutely *nothing*."

She paced a couple of steps away, then back. "When I heard he was getting remarried, I realized that unless I changed the way I live my life, I would always be lonely. Unless I went after what I wanted, I'd live without any kind of intimacy the way I have for the last six fucking years."

Trace's head was spinning; his heart was beating hard and fast. His emotions were tangled in a knot so high in his chest he thought they'd strangle him.

"I wanted you," she yelled. "I've wanted you from the moment I met you. That's why I haven't gone on a second date with anyone else. Because I want *you*. I knew sleeping with you was a bad idea. I knew I wasn't experienced enough for you. I was sure I would disappoint you, and I couldn't face another failure, so I forced myself to ignore what I wanted. What I needed. Just like I've always ignored my own wants and needs. All finding out about David did was push me to make a decision I didn't have the guts to make before."

She pushed her hands into her hair and turned in a circle. When she turned back, tears glimmered in her eyes, and all Trace's emotions tugged tight until he couldn't breathe—love, hate, desire, anger, frustration, confusion . . .

"What difference does it make to you anyway?" She threw her arms out to the sides. "You got the fuck you were looking for."

He dropped his hammer and grabbed her arms. "I got way more than the fuck I was looking for, goddammit." He hauled her in and kissed her hard. She made a frustrated sound and fisted her hands against his chest. He jerked her back, yelling, "I got the fuck I can't stop thinking about. I got the fuck I want again and again and again."

When he kissed her this time, her mouth softened, and Trace pushed her lips open with his tongue, then tasted her with the hunger that had been building all damn day. Avery swayed into him, tilted her head, and licked his tongue with a whimper in her throat.

Fire exploded through Trace, and he growled into her mouth. He released her arms, ripped off his gloves, and stroked his hands down her body, then back up beneath the skirt of her dress. He moaned as his hands slid up her warm thighs, gripped her tight ass, and pulled her hips into his erection, grinding against her.

Avery broke the kiss on a whimpered, "Yes," wrapped her arms around his neck, and kissed him as if he were water in the desert. The alcohol in his blood was singing, and he was absolutely sure he'd never wanted any woman more than he wanted Avery right this minute.

He pushed her panties over her hips and groaned at the feel of her hot skin in his hands. "Fuck, need you."

"Yes," she breathed, fisting his hair, locking her arms around his neck.

Trace lifted her off her feet. She kicked off her panties and wrapped her legs around his hips. He didn't remember moving until her back hit the wall, and he sank his hips into hers, moaning at the feel of her soft, soft sex giving to his hard cock.

Her hands fell from his hair to rip at his jeans. She was panting, lips wet, eyes hazed with the same crazy need bubbling through Trace's veins. He struggled for a condom in his wallet, ripped it open with his teeth, and pushed it on while Avery swept her skirt aside.

And when he stroked his fingers between her legs, wet heat swallowed them. "Perfect."

He replaced his hand with his cock, and as he pushed into her, Avery sipped a breath, rocking her hips toward him. With her thighs in his hands, Trace pulled her wide and watched his cock push inside her. And, God, it was beautiful. Her hands gripped his forearms, head dropped back against the wall. He pulled back, and thrust again, and again and again. Until he filled her.

Pressure spread through his cock, his balls, his pelvis. Avery's fingers bit into his skin. He fought to slow down, to make this wild passion between them last. Wished he could do this for hours in fifty different positions. Sliding inside her, feeling the slick, hot walls of her tight pussy give, open, then close around him with that delicious squeeze was absolute ecstasy.

Her head rolled side to side, mouth open. "Need it, need it."

He used his body to pin hers against the wall, released one thigh, and slid his hand under her hair to grip the back of her neck. He pressed his forehead to hers. "I want you looking at me when I give you what you need."

She obeyed, and the raw desire flooding her expression went a long way toward healing whatever wound had ripped open inside him. He hoped he could bring her enough pleasure to do the same for whatever pain he'd caused her.

Holding her gaze, he looked into her eyes as he pulled all the way out and slowly thrust.

"Oh, *God*." Her lids fluttered closed, and her back arched as she lifted into him.

"*Fuck*, baby, that is *so* good."

He thrust again, and her mouth dropped open, and that look crept into her eyes, the one she got just before she came. "You want it?"

"Yes," she whispered.

He quickened his pace but kept the thrusts full and deep and strong, tip to balls, and encouraged her to meet him by using her thighs to pull her into the thrust. Which also helped him control the speed, helped him hold it off until she was writhing and shaking.

"Want it, Avery?" he whispered.

"Yes. Please."

Goddamn, there was something about hearing her so needy that just rushed through his blood, and he hammered into her, slamming her back against the wall. When she broke, her pussy squeezed his cock so hard, Trace gritted his teeth to keep his own orgasm in check.

"Fuck," he whispered. "Fuck, fuck, *fuck* . . ."

He gained a wicked amount of pleasure watching her come apart. Hearing the guttural sounds of pleasure thick in her throat. Feeling her pussy soak his cock.

And when her final shudders quieted, he kissed her, deep and slow, and started the build to a joint climax. She peaked again so quickly, he didn't have to control himself long. His passion rose to a rabid pitch until he couldn't kiss her deep enough, couldn't thrust hard enough, fast enough. Couldn't get enough of her even when he had absolutely all of her.

"Fuck, Avery . . ." He buried his face in her neck. "Need you."

She wrapped her arms around his neck, clutched his head, and lifted her hips to meet him thrust for thrust.

She cried out and arched, her hips bucking against his.

Trace matched her need, right on the blissful edge. "So . . . good . . ."

The orgasm clawed its way up his spine, digging deep into his core before it released in an almost violet explosion. Blinding light burst behind his eyelids. His brain went white. Every muscle in his body flexed, squeezed, or bowed. And Avery's name kept coming from his lips.

When the climax subsided, Trace pressed his weight into her to hold her in place until he got the strength to set her down gently.

Long before that happened, extended moments of silence stretched and lengthened and deepened between them—but not in a good way.

Finally, Avery's fingers floated down his neck and over his shoulders, followed by a whispered, "I think we have a problem."

Trace's heart sank, and an empty ache filled its space. He dropped his forehead to her shoulder. "Yeah. Guess we do."

EIGHT

Avery opened the passenger door of her Jeep and pulled the taped list from her last covered tray of sample pastries.

"Okay." She sighed the word and tucked her hair behind her ear, scanning the tray to make sure she had something special for all the big hitters on Dr. Morrison's office staff. "Mandy caves for anything chocolate, Brenda's mouth waters at the sight of lemon, Richard drops to his knees for cherry, and when Vickie tastes the new twist on my cinnamon rolls, she's going to moan like—"

Like I did when Trace was fucking me.

Avery's mind raced back to the night before. To Trace driving into her so hard the sound of her back hitting the wall over and over still echoed in her head. And the memory of him filling her, so passionately consuming her, made a sinful thrill explode at the center of her body and spread like fire. Her sex clenched, and the ache from their fierce quickie still burned between her legs.

She closed her eyes and drew a shaky breath. The look on Trace's face as he set her down appeared in Avery's mind—unmistakable guilt—immediately followed by his words to her their first night together,

"Don't second-guess your body. It's telling you what you need, however, whenever you need it. There is no right or wrong in sex."

She hadn't been thinking about the contradiction last night, but it had probably been floating in her subconscious, because she was still uneasy about the intensity of what was happening between them. She was relieved he'd agreed to a little distance to get their heads straight.

She closed the car door with a bump of her hip, trying to refocus on her mission, but she was already missing him when she approached the entrance to Dr. Morrison's family practice.

Before she could position the tray to free up one of her hands, the door opened and she moved aside.

Betty Baxter, the school librarian when Avery'd been a kid, stepped out of the office with a hand to her chest. "Avery? I heard you were back in town. Look at you. You always were the prettiest little thing."

"Hi, Mrs. Baxter. You look wonderful."

"Thank you, honey." Her smile instantly turned into a sympathetic frown. "I'm so sorry to hear about you and David. Well, you know, we all do crazy things when we're young. I was hoping it would work out with him being in the service and all, but, well . . ." Her smile returned in an instant, but this time it was a little more forced. "Look, we've got you back now, don't we? Everyone's talking about your café. When's opening day? I'm sure someone's told me, but, oh, this old brain. Remind me, sweetheart."

"Saturday, November 20," Avery said, her tone as forced as Betty's smile but hopefully less transparent. She'd been home long enough for everyone to hear about her divorce but not long enough to have seen everyone and receive all the condolences. And every reminder felt like another failure.

"Oh, perfect. Just in time for holiday pies. You know you're going to have some tough competition, what with Penny Stevenson out in Sundance. Her pies have been on everyone's holiday tables for decades now."

This was one of those days Avery didn't need to hear about the walls ahead she still had to scale. So she kept the smile in place and offered a congenial, "I'm sure there are enough people in this county to keep both Penny and me up to our necks in pies this holiday."

"You have the older Hutton boy working on your café, don't you? The one who was in prison for drugs?"

She could remember that, but not Avery's opening date?

"Trace Hutton," Avery said with extra enthusiasm to combat Betty's wary tone. "Wait until you see the place. He's an amazing contractor and a real joy to have around."

"Well, just keep your eye on him. You never know—"

"Can I offer you a treat before these get inhaled by Dr. Morrison's staff?" Avery peeled back the corner of the plastic wrap, grateful for the never-fail distraction.

"Oh, my." Her gaze jumped from Avery to the tray and back, and her smile returned. Her concern over Trace's past vanished. "Well, maybe just one or two for Henry. He loves his sweets. What have you got here, darlin'?"

"A little bit of everything, really. Lemon meringue bars and lemon angel cakes, cherry tarts and cherry cheesecake, Nutella truffles . . ."

As Betty fussed over her choices, her husband's name struck a familiar chord. "Didn't Henry work on the school's instruments? I think I remember him coming in to tune the piano when I was in high school."

"He did." Betty lifted a lemon bar from the tray. "He's retired now."

"Do you think he'd be up for a little side job? I just got a piano donated from Mr. Stein's old barber shop."

Betty's gaze lifted to Avery's, and she smiled. "Barry Stein bought that new from Henry when he worked for Piano Works in Napa."

"If he could make a visit and take a look, I'd be willing to pay you in free sweets whenever you come into the café."

"Oh, dear." Her smile turned sassy. "I doubt he'll be able to pass up that offer."

Fifteen minutes, a piano-tuning date, and far more than one or two treats later, Avery headed into the office, forcing her mind to this marketing call and away from the stressors of the moment.

Belle Davis looked up from her computer at the front desk with a generic smile. "Good morning, how can I—?" Her gaze flicked from the plate to Avery's smile and back to the pastries, and Belle stood from her chair so fast, it rolled back and hit a filing cabinet. "She's here!" Belle slapped a hand over her mouth, then lifted it enough to say, "Dammit, I should have waited until I got my pick before I said that."

By the time the words were out, a half-dozen members of the front office staff huddled around the window, trying to sneak peeks of the tray.

"What'd you bring us, Avery?" Carrie, one of the file clerks, called from the back. "I can't see through all these tall people."

"There's plenty for everyone." Her chance meeting with Betty was the reason Avery always packed her plates full. There was always someone to cheer up or bribe with a treat along her path.

The side door opened, and one of the medical assistants waved at her. "Get back here, girl. We've been waiting on you all day."

Avery's worries fell away, and as she stood in the break room, chatting with staff as they came and went, she felt . . . whole. Content. Everyone was happy. Everyone was smiling. Everyone was chatty and excited as they perused and collected their goodies.

And while she caught up with some people she hadn't seen in years and met others who'd come to town after she'd moved away, a small piece of her mind recognized the insignificance of her contribution. She realized that even though her moment in their lives here was fleeting and probably meaningless, it still gave her joy. And nowadays, joy came in such tiny doses, she was grabbing what she could get when she could get it.

Which spun her mind right back around to Trace. Last night's uncomfortable ending aside, Trace brought a lot of joy into Avery's life.

Before they'd slept together, he'd brought laughter and friendship and a fresh perspective on their screwed-up world. Their first night together had brought more laughter, a bonding deeper than friendship, and ultimately a sense of joy she couldn't say she'd ever experienced before.

Now . . . now she didn't know. And despite her own suggestion they take some time apart, she wondered what kind of message she'd be sending if she went into the café to see him later today.

Two of the front desk clerks wandered from the break room with small plates of fudge, passing Belle on her way in. She stopped short and lifted her brows at Avery.

Grinning, Avery reached for one of the kitchen drawers, pulled out a Ziploc bag, and held it up. "Cabernet, Merlot, and Syrah dark-chocolate truffles."

Belle clapped her hands, squealed like a little kid, and rushed to Avery. She snapped the bag from her fingers just before wrapping Avery in a bear hug and almost tipping her over.

They laughed together, and when Belle pulled back, she leaned against the counter, opened the seal, stuck her face in, and breathed deep. "Oh my God. What a high." She closed and sealed the bag with a grin that just wouldn't quit. One that reminded Avery a lot of her brother, Mark.

"Wait until Toby gets ahold of these." She reached out and squeezed Avery's hands. "Thank you *so* much. This is going to be such a treat for my honey. He's been working so hard."

Belle's fiancé was a PG&E linesman who worked long, tough hours and took a lot of calls. The way they both worked at making their relationship succeed both mystified and touched Avery. "I'm glad."

"I'll pair it with the new nightie I bought from Victoria's Secret and a bottle of his favorite Bordeaux," Belle said with a coy smile, "and I think I'll even the score for that night away in Napa he got for me a couple of months ago."

"I'd say so," Avery told her with attitude. "They're my best batch ever."

Belle laughed. "Perfect." She reached in her pocket and extracted cash. "What do I owe you?"

"Are you kidding? No way." Avery waved her off and crossed her arms, tucking her hands away when Belle tried to push twenties into them. She nodded to the single table, where her tray was almost empty. "This is more than enough. I couldn't ask for a better testimonial than everyone at this office raving about my sweets. Just get them all to show up on opening day, would you?"

"Deal. Thanks again."

"Anytime."

Belle slipped her truffles and her cash back into the front pockets of her scrubs and wandered to the table, picking at toffee crumbs. "Mark's mentioned you more than once." She turned a silly grin on Avery and raised her brows with a playful, singsong, "We could be sisters-in-law."

Avery choked out a laugh. "Oh, jeez, Belle, you've *got* to be kidding." She shook her head, wincing at the mere mention of marriage. "Believe me—I'm doing Mark a favor."

Belle tipped her head and shrugged. "I know. I told him that's why you were turning him down. He usually gets the girls easily, you know? I think he sees you as a *challenge*."

Avery closed her eyes on a sound of dread.

"Just ignore him and he'll go away." The scrape of a chair along the floor pulled Avery's eyes open to Belle taking a seat. She wrapped an arm over the back and leveled a serious, concerned gaze on Avery. "How are you doing? I haven't seen you since David's engagement announcement hit the Internet."

"I'm okay." She lifted a shoulder, not caring much about David's life at this point. She'd created enough of a mess in her own. "Shitty way to find out, but I doubt there would have been a good way. And considering he almost got blown off the face of the earth on his third tour and never bothered to call and tell me about that, it would have been incredibly odd for him to actually make a phone call to tell me about this."

"I'm so sorry, sweetie. I was shocked. Did you know? I mean, about the affair? Did you see the signs?" She didn't wait for an answer before she shook her head. "That's just not something I ever saw David doing. He was so two hundred percent into you when you left. But I guess people change, right? And I guess you really never know someone, right? I mean, Toby and I spend so much time apart that I feel like I'm getting to know him all over again when he's home."

Avery recognized this chatter; she'd heard it a lot over the last couple of years. First from fellow army wives when initial rumblings of the divorce surfaced. Then again once it became a reality. And it started all over when she'd come home.

Everyone wanted some magical insight into their own relationship by way of her failure. Some kernel of knowledge that would give them a sense of security, assuring them that what happened to Avery wouldn't happen to them.

"I knew things weren't right between us," she said, "but I never saw any signs that he'd checked out completely and had found someone else. And, yes, their engagement was fast, but feelings can sometimes happen between two people quickly when the situation is right."

Her feelings for Trace had been instant and ramped up out of control within weeks of working with him. And look at her now.

"David and I were at odds for a long time. I prefer to think he had a friendship that turned into something more once we were divorced. Whether it's true or not really doesn't matter. David went through a lot overseas. We didn't fit the same as we did when we were kids. It's over, and people here might want to hold on to something they see as a scandal, but it's really nothing more than two people realizing they were poorly matched and moving on. I've already let it go."

That was a ridiculous oversimplification of something even Avery still didn't fully understand. Not to mention a ludicrous understatement, glossing over all the loneliness and pain those long years caused her. But her answer made the worry clear from Belle's eyes, and that made Avery happy.

"How's the renovation going?" she asked. "Are you on target for your opening? Is there anything I can do to help?"

Avery's mind turned to Trace first, and it lingered there when she should have been thinking about her business. "Trace is doing a great job on the café. It's really beautiful. More than I ever expected, you know? I feel lucky that Delaney snagged him for the job. I could never have afforded anyone else. And so far, so good on the opening."

"I'm so relieved. When I heard Trace was doing the work . . ." She grimaced. "I'm not gonna lie—I was worried."

After Betty's slight, this one nudged her protectiveness up another notch. Avery forced her frustration to the background. "Why?"

"He's got such a playboy reputation. There are a couple of girls in the office who can't stop talking about him since he got to town. And God forbid they actually run into him when they're out at lunch or after work." She rolled her eyes. "I guess from what I've heard I expected him to be out partying half the night, fucking someone the other half, and be spotty at work."

Avery's gut squeezed until it ached. It took real effort to work up the lousy grin she put on. She just hoped it looked bored, not pained. "Well, you know this town and their rumors. I can't tell you exactly what Trace is doing with all his nights, but I can tell you the man works twelve to fourteen hours every damn day, seven days a week, and he's taking care of his dad, who's suffering from the early stages of dementia."

"Oh, that's right. I think I heard that."

"And if you want to see quality, come into the café. It speaks for itself. If the man can find enough energy to do anything else after all that, he probably deserves some TLC."

Belle grinned. "I love this new, tough Avery."

She huffed a laugh. "This new, tough Avery will get you some flyers. If you wouldn't mind passing them out, that would be great."

"You bet." She stood and slung her arm around Avery's shoulders. "I'll drop by the café and return your plate. That way I can pick up any leftovers hanging around."

Avery curved one arm around Belle's waist. "Better than turning them into compost."

Belle left Avery at the office's front door, and Avery returned to her car alone. Her mind wasn't on her business or the café. All she kept hearing was Belle's *"I guess you really never know someone, right?"*

After everything Avery had been through, she'd have to agree.

Trace hiked a load of old asphalt roof tiles onto his aching shoulder, stood, and climbed the steep pitch of the roof toward the dump truck parked on the opposite side. When he reached the peak, his gaze searched the drive, then the road for Avery's Jeep, the way he had for the second day in a row now.

Still no sign of her. Though she had found someone to work on the piano. Henry Baxter was down there tapping away at keys, and the sound reminded Trace of his younger years, when his mother was well and his dad was clean and his family was happy.

He'd agreed both he and Avery needed some space, some time to think, to cool off. But he didn't like it. In fact, yesterday had been the first twenty-four hours in two months he hadn't seen her, and he'd been miserable. Today was shaping up to be another wretched day. She had to return eventually, but that didn't mean she'd ever want him to touch her again.

He didn't blame her. He'd been a petty idiot. Then turned into a callous bastard, pounding her against a wall after she'd admitted wanting him.

Who did that? Worse, who got hard just thinking about how hot it had been? How it had been the most passion he'd felt in years?

A serious loser, that's who.

"I'm done over there," Cody said, indicating his corner of the roof. "I'm gonna move to the other side."

He met Cody near the gutter and hefted the tile into the dump truck. "I'll restake your safety bracket."

"Nah, I got it."

Trace nodded and started back to the other side of the roof, his own safety line trailing behind him. He knelt, grabbed his crowbar, wedged it under a tile, and pried it from the roof trusses.

The work helped him exhaust his frustration over Avery, but it didn't keep him from thinking about her. About them. He should take the decision out of her hands and call an end to their affair. If he could even call it an affair. Screwing twice hardly made it more than a hookup. But he knew better. There was something between them beyond physical sex. They'd already been friends for months. Good friends. They shared similar life hardships. Had similar values, work ethic, goals. They'd liked each other to start with. That was the problem. Or one of the problems. There were so many, he couldn't keep track of them all.

He tossed another old tile into the pile, shoved the crowbar under the next, and put his back into prying the nails loose.

"I hate these brackets," Cody complained. "They're so goddamned hard to move."

Trace didn't reply. He didn't feel like bitching about the work. Yeah, it sucked to be up here doing the menial manual labor he used to do as a teenager. Especially after he'd worked for years to get his contractor's license so he could have other guys doing this shit. But prison had a way of stripping a guy down to the nuts. He had to pay his dues all the fuck over again.

Which included staying away from Avery.

"I wanted you. I've wanted you from the moment I met you. That's why I haven't gone on a second date with anyone else. Because I want you."

He tossed another tile into the pile and wiped sweat from his forehead with his shoulder. God, he wanted her the same way. Wanted what he hadn't wanted since he'd been screwed over by Corina.

He wanted to take Avery to dinner and stay three hours over drinks, talking. He wanted to sleep in with her cuddled close, eat breakfast in bed, make love all afternoon, and fall asleep together again. He wanted inside jokes. He wanted conversations through a look across a room.

Trace drove the crowbar under the next tile, and the old nails screeched loose.

"This fucker . . . ," Cody muttered.

Trace glanced up and found Cody straddling the roofline, putting all his weight into the crowbar to loosen the stake holding the brace into a two-by-four. Alarm rocketed up Trace's spine. Consequences flashed through his mind in split-second screenshots.

"Hey, don't lean into it." He barked the instruction he'd already given Cody three times that day. "I told you to knock it loose."

Cody looked up but continued to lean into the bar, shoving it with all his strength and placing three-quarters of his weight to one side of the roof.

"Cody, stop." Trace dropped his tool and scuttled toward Cody. "This roof is too old—"

The nail snapped, the rotted two-by-four beneath cracked and pulled through the particleboard. And Cody tumbled head over ass down the slope.

"Fuck!" Trace pushed off with both feet, throwing himself over the bracket and the tearing roof.

Cody hit the gutter, reaching the end of the safety rope. The roof beneath Trace lifted, punching him in the chest. He grunted and lost all his air. Pain crushed his ribs, and for long, excruciating moments, he couldn't breathe. His vision blurred and went dark before his throat finally opened and his lungs greedily sucked in oxygen.

"Ah, God . . . ," he groaned.

He turned his head and found Cody with one leg slung over the gutter as he clung to the roof edge.

"You okay?" Trace called.

"Uh . . ." Cody was breathing hard and fast. "Probably not."

Henry rushed outside and looked up, shielding his eyes from the sun. "Should I call the fire department?"

Wouldn't that be just perfect?

"Cody," Trace called. "Do you need a fireman to save your sorry ass, or can you do it yourself?"

"I can do it myself, thanks. Think my ego's bruised enough."

"We've got this, Henry," Trace said. "Thank you."

The old man didn't look convinced, but he went back inside.

Trace banged his forehead to the hot roof. "Fuck, fuck, *fuck*."

If he hadn't been so goddamned obsessed with Avery, he'd have been paying attention, and this wouldn't have happened.

"Let me know when you're secure," he told Cody. "Then we can figure out which one of us losers is in better shape to drive to the ER."

NINE

Avery had avoided Trace and the café as long as she could. She'd over-stocked her space at Phoebe's shop, filled and shipped her Internet orders, taken care of her lunch orders for the day, dropped off samples all over town, stocked Finley's Market, and even held a successful focus-group tasting to help her refine her opening menu.

Now she needed to spend some time on the small jobs at the café to make sure the opening day happened as planned. And, in truth, as she drove toward the café at 10:00 a.m. after forty-eight full hours away from Trace, her stomach flipped and fluttered with anticipation.

When she saw the state of the roof, excitement joined those sensations, and a smile lifted her spirits.

She parked in front of the café and climbed from the Jeep. Shading her eyes from the sun, she looked up. "Trace?"

Another man peered over the edge, and it wasn't Cody. This man was older than Trace, with sandy hair and a couple of days' worth of beard growth. He offered a bright-white grin and a charismatic, "Hey there, beautiful. You must be Avery."

"JT." Trace's bark startled her. She stepped back and turned to Trace as he came out of the café. He was glaring up at the other man, hands on his hips. "What did we talk about?"

"Oh, right." JT sobered, offered a polite, "Hello, ma'am, I'm JT. Good to meet you. Gotta get back to work now." And he disappeared.

Delaney's warnings about Avery's schedule floated through her head.

"Did you need to hire another guy?" she asked, returning her gaze to Trace. He didn't look quite right—a little pale and a little pained with heavy shadows under his eyes. Her concern changed directions and mounted. "Where's Cody? Are you okay? You don't look so great."

"Let's go inside." He glanced up. "Just let me check on him. I'll be right in."

He walked around the side of the building, and there was no doubt his lazy, sexy saunter had been replaced with stiff, slow movement. When he disappeared around the corner, Avery went inside and found all the upper kitchen cabinets installed. All the crown molding in place. The tables and chairs for the center of the seating area had been delivered and stacked along one wall.

Her thrill returned. A smile brightened her face, and she pressed a hand to her heart, making slow circles to take in how beautiful the space looked with all the finishing touches.

The screen door closed while she was looking at the pristine white subway tile he'd installed as the backsplash. "Trace, it's gorgeous. Oh my God, I can't believe what a difference—"

His arm slipped around her waist, and he turned her. Wrapping her tight, he pressed his face to her hair and whispered, "I'm sorry. I'm so sorry for what I said and the way I acted."

His unexpected, uncharacteristic apology eased her heart open. With her hands on his shoulders, her cheek against his chest, she breathed him in, and the familiar scent of Trace's musk heated her blood. "I'm sorry, too. I haven't exactly been an open book."

She pulled back and felt around his chest, his abdomen. "What's under your shirt?"

"Let's sit down."

Alarm snuck in again. "Where's Cody?" she asked, sitting on one of the new chairs he brought around for her. "Who's JT?"

He sat, too, leaning forward, elbows on knees, and covered her hands with his. "Cody fell off the roof yesterday."

She bolted to her feet. *"What?"*

"He's okay." Trace pulled on her hands, and she sat again, but her heart hammered, and any twinkle of excitement she'd arrived with had been snuffed out. "He hurt his shoulder, and he can't help with the roof, so I hired JT."

"Were you on the roof with him? Were you hurt?" Panic hit her from every angle. "How bad is his shoulder? Why didn't you call me?" She pulled her hands from his and pressed them to her hot face. "Oh my God, I have to call my insurance. Am I covered for this sort of thing?"

Her mind was jumping from one worry to the next, back to the first, then on to another.

"Avery, listen to me, and I'll answer all your questions." Trace's smooth, calm voice focused her. "I didn't call you because I've caused enough stress for you lately and because I had it handled. Cody's covered by my insurance, not yours. And it's just a sprain. He'll only be out of work for a few weeks."

She pressed a hand to her heart and breathed a little easier. "What about you? What do you have on under your shirt?"

"I bruised a couple of ribs. It's a brace that makes it easier to work. It's no big—"

She pushed to her feet again, a hand to her stomach. "You've been working with bruised ribs?"

"They aren't my first. I'm just a little sore. I'm fine with a few Advil."

"You should have called me."

He sighed. "Okay. Next time I'll call you. Would that make you feel better?"

"Next time? No, that doesn't make me feel better." She crossed her arms. "Who's this JT guy? I don't know him. Is he from here?"

Trace sat back, hands loose in his lap. He looked exhausted and Avery heard Delaney saying, *"He's got a lot on his plate, trying to manage the café and his dad. You're both balancing very precariously on high wires right now. If a gust of wind came from the wrong direction . . ."*

"No," Trace said, "he's just a guy I know."

She worked to hold back her fear and frustration. "I know you're working really hard to get this done for me on time. And I know you're under miserable financial constraints. I wish I could do something about that, but I can't."

Her mind was spinning, searching for solutions. But she saw Cody tumbling off the roof, imagined Trace almost following, and her heart skittered. She pressed a hand to her forehead.

"Does this JT guy know what he's doing? Is it safe for him to be up on the roof alone? I'm not sure how we could fit it into the budget, but if we need another guy with experience to be up there with him, I'll ask Phoebe for more money, because you're *not* getting up there again."

She pressed her fingers to her eyes and paced, suddenly overwhelmed again just when she thought she had her emotions under control. "Maybe Ethan can spare a few days. Maybe Delaney knows someone—"

Trace's arms closed around her from behind. His arms doubled low on her waist and pulled her back against him. And oh, God, he felt so good. His big body pressed all along her back, her thighs.

The feel of someone holding her when she was worried. Supporting her when things got tough. It was so foreign. So good.

"I've got it under control," he whispered at her ear, his voice rich and confident. A voice that shivered over her skin, tightened her chest, and created pressure between her legs—like the sexual version of the Pavlovian dog.

She grasped his arms with her hands, turned her head, and pressed her cheek to his chest. "Something really bad could have happened to you." She sounded like a typical shaky female, but she didn't care. "I couldn't handle it if something happened to you." This coming from the woman who'd lived with the threat of losing her husband for eight years. She was beginning to wonder who in the hell she was. "Please don't cut corners on safety. If you need something to be safe, just do it or get it or buy it. I'll find the money somewhere."

He pressed his face to her neck and sighed. "I've missed you like crazy."

Her heart softened. Emotion spilled over and tears pushed at her eyes. David hadn't told her he'd missed her in years, even when he'd been gone for months on end. Being wanted enough to be missed filled Avery with a sense of completeness she'd always craved but had never been able to fill. And even though other men had expressed interest and wanted to continue dating her, only Trace's desire quelled the longing to be loved.

"I've missed you, too," she admitted. This was so out of control. So not what either of them had planned. So not what either of them had wanted at the outset.

He lowered his head and whispered, "Kiss me, baby."

Without hesitation, she turned her head and lifted her mouth, searching for the reassurance of his. His lips were warm and solid and, Lord, the man made her go soft. She relaxed against him, and he tightened his arms. She opened, stroking his lip with her tongue. Trace's soft moan drifted into her mouth as he met her touch with the slow, gentle glide of his own tongue.

This, more than any words, conveyed his regret. Spoke to how much he'd missed her over their two days apart. Avery tried to rationalize her way through the situation, even as her heart stretched to open again after being cloistered. But she'd learned that rationale and emotion often lived in parallel universes, and trying to get them to mesh when they just wouldn't was a losing battle. Like now.

When she let the resistance go, Avery lost herself in him. And her mind had drifted to thoughts of taking him upstairs for a quick reunion when Trace suddenly, almost violently, pulled away, stealing all his heat and support.

Stunned into confusion, Avery swayed. When she'd found her balance and turned toward him, she found Trace facing the front door. He pushed his hands into his pockets and leaned his butt against a table nearby. Before she could form a question, the squeak of the screen sounded and JT stepped in.

Trace looked as relaxed as if he were on a coffee break, but Avery wasn't quite as masterful at pulling herself together. She rubbed a hand over one hot cheek, then over her beard-roughened mouth and looked at the floor.

"Uh . . . sorry to interrupt," JT said in a hesitant voice that told Avery he'd clearly seen them kissing.

"You're not," Trace said, voice cold. "What do you need?"

"I've got that appointment with my PO today. You know how they tweak out if—"

"Go," Trace cut him off. "And take the rest of the day."

Avery glanced at Trace, trying to read him. She'd never seen him act this curt to anyone, and she'd seen him interact with a lot of people over the last two months. Including people he didn't like. Unease spread through her stomach, killing all the heat he'd created.

"Sure," JT said, but he was looking at Avery. And he was smiling in a way that made her feel dirty. "I get it. I'll be here bright and early tomorrow."

Silence filled the space as they watched JT stride to his old Toyota, try to start it up twice before the motor turned over, then drive away.

With a sick feeling in her stomach, Avery narrowed her eyes on Trace. "His PO? Is he talking about a parole officer?"

Trace's jaw ticked, and he kept his gaze on the floor. "I only need him a few more days to get the roof done. The rain will be here soon. It would take me too long to find someone else. And as much as I want to do it myself, I can't."

Avery crossed her arms and paced to the window, anger doubling and tripling inside her. He'd brought a *prison buddy* into her café? That left a dark, icky feeling inside her—a little girl backed into a corner. A shadow on a dark street. Footsteps on the stairs in an empty house.

And when Trace had spent the last two months going above and beyond to make her comfortable throughout the process, she recognized that no matter how badly he needed this guy, bringing him here was out of character.

She took a breath and braced to dig into a part of his life they'd stayed well away from up until now. "What did he do for you?"

Trace's gaze swung toward her, veiled, cool. He'd disappeared behind some kind of veneer, and Avery heard Delaney again, telling her that people with scars don't always make the best decisions.

"What do you mean?" he asked.

"I mean I don't believe you'd work with him, let alone bring him here just because you need help. You have other resources."

"No, I don't. Not if I want to keep you within your budget."

She clenched her teeth, ready to lose her shit. "*What* did he do for you?"

Shame flashed through his eyes before he looked at the floor again. His jaw muscle jumped, and it took him what felt like forever to answer.

Finally, he cleared his throat. "Got between me and another inmate." His voice was low and so dark a chill rippled down her spine. "I'd be dead if he hadn't."

She pulled in a sharp breath. Her eyes stung. Emotions clashed and burned. Austin's words tried to pry their way into her head, which royally pissed her off and sent her into rebellion mode.

She closed the distance between them. He didn't move, so Avery lifted his chin, forcing him to look her in the eye. The pain and guilt and shame turned his beautiful eyes navy blue and stabbed Avery in the heart.

"You stay off the roof," she said. "He's gone the minute it's done. And you keep him away from me."

Gratitude softened his gaze. "Baby, he can't do it himself either. I promise to get rid of him the second it's done, and I promise to keep him away from you, but I've got to get up on that roof if we're going to stay on schedule and on budget." He lifted his hand and ran it over her hair, then squeezed the back of her neck and pulled her forehead to his. "Trust me on this."

Her heart clenched and all its walls slid into place. She wanted to believe, wanted to trust, but experience and common sense wouldn't let her.

She pushed back, crossed her arms and stared at his chest. "Fine." She couldn't control him. Couldn't change him. Pulling in a deep breath, she forced herself to let it go and just absorb the hurt and fear. "I'm here to paint. I'm going to start upstairs, and I don't need any help."

Avery dropped her arms and turned toward the stairs. He reached out, catching her with a gentle hand on her forearm. She met his eyes, and the look there was raw and real and so honest, it hurt her heart.

"Thank you," was all he said.

She didn't know what he was thanking her for, but it didn't matter. She slid her hand down to his, squeezed, then let go and continued upstairs.

TEN

Avery woke late for the second day in a row and drove to the café with bleary eyes and a headache. But she still loved this time of day. At 5:00 a.m. the sun was just cresting and the world seemed so quiet. This was the only time in her life when peace filled her heart and anything seemed possible.

But the pinch at the center of her head reminded her that everything came with a price. The stress was getting to her. She'd endured so much for so long her body was starting to show the symptoms.

Her mind swung toward Trace, and how much stress he'd endured. This situation was taking its toll on both of them. Hopefully that would be over soon. He and JT should be finished with the roof tomorrow. Once Mr. Smarmy was out of the picture, the tension should fade.

They were getting close. The appliances would be delivered right about the time the roof was finished. Those would take only a day or two to get in; then there would just be some finish work, some paint, some final landscaping, and Trace's job would be done.

And Trace would move on.

Whatever was between them would be over.

She turned onto the café's driveway with a heaviness in her chest. "Work, work, work." She parked, shut off her headlights, and climbed from the car. "Focus, Avery."

She'd dressed in jeans, sneakers, and an old T-shirt again, planning to continue painting this morning. But first she had to fill lunch orders and mail out Internet orders.

Soon Trace's wage could go toward assistants to lighten Avery's load. Then she could focus on looking forward. There would be a lot to think about with the holidays coming up.

But once Trace was gone . . .

Trace was gone.

She stretched her arms overhead and arched her back. Painting left her sore, and lack of sleep didn't give her body time to fully heal.

"Someday . . ." Someday she could have a real life with time away from the café to do other things. Develop more friendships, spend time with family, maybe even pick up a hobby unrelated to baking.

She wandered onto the porch, wondering when that someday would come. She reached forward to push her key into the lock, but the door eased open, already unlocked and unlatched.

A sliver of alarm tingled through her belly. "Oh, criminy . . ."

She must not have pulled the door completely closed behind her last night. It had been late, and she'd been so tired.

Inside, she started toward the kitchen, rubbing her eyes. She set her keys down and flipped on the lights. Beautiful canned lighting flooded her equally gorgeous kitchen with soft, bright illumination that reflected off the white tile and stainless steel counters.

Avery's belly warmed, and she smiled. She couldn't wait for her appliances to get here. She'd spent half of her entire divorce settlement on them. Commercial appliances distinguished the professional from the hobbyist. Those appliances would complete her dream.

She pulled her list from her back pocket, spread it on the counter, and wandered into the pantry to gather supplies for the lunch orders.

When she flipped on the light, she caught sight of movement through the opposite door, leading to the main kitchen and a cleaning area with more storage beyond.

Great. She was so tired she was seeing things. Well, it wasn't the first time.

With bread and mayonnaise cradled in one arm, she stepped into the opening between the rooms and flipped on yet another light.

And found a man sneaking toward the back door.

Shock hit her first. Then a mix of alarm and confusion. Then she recognized him, and anger burst free. "JT?"

He spun and gave her that big, charming smile. "Hey there, Avery."

"What are you doing in here?" A million other questions hit her at once. Where was his truck? Why was he here so early? How did he get in?

"I was just going to grab some water before I started work."

"In the dark?"

He hesitated. His smile faded. And Avery got her first real chill of fear.

She backed off the confrontation but maintained control. "I'm sure Trace will appreciate you coming in early. Go ahead and get started. I'll bring some cold water from the fridge outside for you."

His smile flashed again. "Perfect. Thanks."

He unlocked the back door and slipped out.

With her heart beating double time, Avery darted to the door and locked it. Then she rushed to the front door, shut it, and locked it.

Then pulled her phone from her back pocket and called Trace.

He answered on the third ring with a sleepy, "Avery?"

"JT is here," she said in a half whisper, as if JT could hear her from outside. She hated the fear in her voice. She was competent, intelligent, independent, but she didn't feel like any of those now. "He was *in* the café when I got here—"

"Are you all right?" Trace's voice was suddenly alert and stern. "Are you safe?"

"I locked the doors, but—"

"I'm there. Two minutes."

Click.

"Trace?" She lowered her phone and closed her eyes on a quiet, *"Shit."*

She pressed her back to the wall and took a deep, steadying breath. She'd spent eight years in military life. She knew how to handle and shoot a variety of weapons—well. She knew self-defense—well.

She'd never panicked, virtually living alone for eight years, and she wouldn't do it now.

Avery forced the panic to the background. She carried her bread to the counter and started pulling meat, cheese, lettuce, tomatoes, and more from the fridge. When she turned to put them on the butcher block, Trace's truck flashed past the front door, dirt flying from beneath the tires.

Instead of the sight relieving her, Avery's unease amped up. The idea of a confrontation between him and JT suddenly flooded her mind with every bad scenario.

She grabbed several water bottles from the fridge and rushed outside. She found Trace faced off with JT, hands on hips, shoulders back.

"What the fuck are you doing here?" Trace demanded from JT in a voice Avery had never heard him use before. It was cold and harsh. Threatening. And it stopped Avery's feet from moving forward. "I was very clear about the rules. You don't push them out here like you did inside. That's not the way this works. This is my turf. You follow my rules or you get off this job."

JT held on to that affable disposition with a lazy shrug. "I don't know what you mean. Jeez, why are you making a federal case out of this? A guy can't come in early to show some initiative? I'm just trying to do a good job for you here."

Trace took one giant step and grabbed JT by the shirtfront. The move was so fast, so menacing, Avery sucked a breath and held it. Her stomach went cold, and the hair on her arms prickled to attention.

"I know what you're about," Trace said, voice lowered but no less frightening. "So don't try to sell me your shit. If you want this job, then you stay *out* of that café and *away* from Avery."

Those damn seeds Austin had planted in Avery's head tried to take root again. Her heartbeat pounded in her ears like a ticking time bomb, building urgency inside her like a pressure cooker. She didn't know what to do. Didn't know whether she should walk away and let them settle this however men settled things, or step in before a fight broke out. She thought she knew Trace, but she didn't know this side of him, and she didn't know what he'd do if she interfered.

"You'd better back the fuck off." JT's voice suddenly matched Trace's, his facade gone. And when Avery refocused on the men's faces, she saw a war was about to break out. "Because you don't *begin* to know what I'm about. You might be the boss on this job, but that don't mean you can—"

Avery started forward out of sheer fear. She shuffled her feet on the loose asphalt so they'd hear her coming. Trace released JT, but when Avery approached the look he turned on her was completely foreign. His features were dark and tight, his mouth thin and rigid. And that cold space in her belly deepened.

Unfortunately, that look wasn't new to her. She'd seen it countless times on David's face during their many arguments over the state of their marriage.

She offered the water to JT. "Here's that water." She turned to Trace. "Would you mind looking at the fridge? Things don't seem to be as cold as they should."

Before he could tell her no, she slipped her hand around his forearm and pulled him toward the café.

He walked fifty feet with her before he yanked from her grasp but kept pace beside her. "Why the hell did you do that?"

"Because confronting him like that probably isn't the best idea." All those that-only-happens-to-other-people crazy ideas filled her mind.

"He could decide to take a crowbar to your head when you weren't looking. Or push you off the roof. Hell, how do you know he doesn't have a weapon? He's an ex-con. No one knows what he might do."

Trace's feet ground to a stop. "*I'm* an ex-con." In that instant, Avery realized how all the inferences she'd just made about JT also applied to Trace.

She shook her head. "That's not—"

He put a hand out in a stop gesture, but he didn't look mean and dangerous anymore. He just looked frustrated and, yeah, hurt.

Regret swamped her. "Trace—"

"You just deal with your work, okay? I'll deal with mine."

With that, he turned and walked back toward JT.

Avery felt like shit all day. Not only did her guilt and shame grow over the hours following the incident with JT, but Trace's I've-had-it-with-you dismissal had cut Avery deep.

She sat on a stool at the café's bar, scrolling through menu examples online, with residual hurt throbbing in her gut like a physical wound.

She'd finished all her daily baking, painted until her arms felt like they'd fall off, sorted through employment applications for waitstaff and kitchen staff, and was now trying to find a few menus she liked to run past Delaney for her opinion.

Trace hadn't come in for lunch like he usually did. In fact, he hadn't come in at all. He and JT stayed outside from 5:00 a.m. to 5:00 p.m., when Trace opened the door to poke his head in and tell her, "The rest of the shingles are in. I'm taking JT to Santa Rosa to pick them up instead of waiting for them to be delivered. We won't be back for a few hours."

He hadn't waited for her response before closing the door and walking away.

Avery exhaled and dropped her chin in her hand. Disappointment tugged at her chest. They were either hot or cold now. All that fun, comfortable middle ground they'd shared before the sex had vanished. Now she felt like she'd lost a friend, a lover, and something more. Something indescribable and intangible. Something she hadn't realized filled her heart until it was gone.

Avery chose three different menu finalists and e-mailed them to Delaney.

Her cell rang, and Avery pulled it from her back pocket, checking the time before she answered. Already 7:00 p.m.

She didn't recognize the number but rubbed her eyes and answered, "Hello."

"I'm lookin' for my boys." An older man's voice rumbled over the phone, clearly angry. "Did Zane drag Trace by the bar again? You know if you serve those boys, you're serving minors. You can go to jail for that. Get one of those boys on the phone."

Avery's mouth dropped open. Her mind slipped gears. "Mr. Hutton? This is Avery Hart. Do you remember me? I make those apple turnovers you like." When she got silence, she went on. "Trace went into Santa Rosa to pick up some roof shingles. I haven't seen Zane, but I think he's working."

"What the hell are you talkin' about, girl? If you're in cahoots with those boys, you can bet I'll be telling your parents all about it. I'm having a hard enough time keeping Zane out of trouble as it is, even with his brother running shotgun. Now *send them home*."

He yelled the last and hung up with a click so loud, Avery jerked her phone away from her ear. That was an awesome benefit to old-style phones. You could still *really* hang up on someone.

Avery toggled her pencil between her fingers, wondering whether she should tell someone about the call. Pearl had told Avery the music therapy had improved George's disposition, but if that was true, she couldn't imagine what he'd been like before. On the couple of short visits she'd made to his house to drop off food, Pearl had been there, and George had been straddling zombieland. Trace had mentioned something called a sundown syndrome, but Avery didn't remember what that was.

She dialed the sheriff's substation and asked to speak with Zane, but he was out on patrol. She didn't have Pearl's number, but she could get it from Phoebe. If she could get ahold of Phoebe. That woman was busier than a corporate executive.

Avery decided not to get a handful of people upset over a harmless phone call and went back to work. By the time she'd made final cuts to the starting menu and scheduled interviews for potential employees, dusk had turned to night, and Trace still hadn't returned.

Figuring he might have gone straight home, Avery cleaned up and double-checked all the locks on the doors. She'd just drive by their house and make sure his father was okay on her way to Phoebe's.

She locked the front door behind her, tested it, and jogged down the porch steps to her Jeep.

"You there."

The voice felt like a punch to her gut. Avery let out a startled sound and spun.

A shadowed figure shuffled toward her. "You there. Where do you think you're goin'? It ain't quittin' time. I've been around long enough to know last call is two a.m. We ain't even close, and I need a scotch and soda."

George Hutton's weary face came into the beam of an exterior light. With her hand to her chest, Avery exhaled in relief. "Mr. Hutton, you scared me." She glanced behind him, searching for a car, but found the driveway empty and dark. "How'd you get here?"

"Walked, how do you think?"

His snappy tone alerted Avery to his mood. She was trying to decide how to handle him when he walked into the light. He was wearing pajamas—and nothing on his feet.

Alarm tightened her chest. Avery didn't know what to say or not to say, uneasy about upsetting him further. She pulled out her phone again and pressed the speed dial for Phoebe.

"Get off that phone, girl," he said, passing her to hobble up the steps, leaving behind footprints. In blood.

"Holy shit," she muttered as Phoebe's voice mail answered.

He tried the door. "Pretty thing like you shouldn't be cursin'. Not ladylike." He knocked on the glass as if he expected someone to answer. "Come on—open up, Joe. What's wrong with you? You drunk again?"

Crap.

Avery disconnected and followed him to the front door. She unlocked it and held it open for him. "Looks like you might have cut your foot. I'll take a look at that while we wait for Trace to get back."

"Drink first."

"Sure." She flipped on the lights and closed the door.

He was squinting around the bar-turned-café like he'd just walked into an alien's nightclub.

"Do you remember me, Mr. Hutton? I'm Joe's daughter, Avery."

His gaze turned on her. "The middle girl. Sure." He looked around the café again, confused. "What the hell is he doing in here?"

She didn't think he'd take the news that her father had been dead over three years very well, so she said, "Just a little renovation." She took George's arm and led him to a chair. "Let's get you a seat."

He dropped into it with a huff, then sighed. "Thank you, darlin'."

Avery smiled. "You're welcome. Now, what can I get you? Are you hungry? I've got great sandwich fixings. Black forest ham, honeyed turkey breast—"

"Roast beef sounds good. Roast beef and cheddar."

"Roast beef and cheddar it is."

"Don't forget the scotch and soda."

Avery pursed her lips. "I'm afraid I'm fresh out of scotch." In fact, she didn't have any liquor in the café at all. Then she thought of the two beers left from Trace's six-pack. "Could I interest you in a beer?"

"Out of scotch?" He gave Avery a sour look. "Your daddy's really letting this place go to hell."

Avery fought a grin. "Yeah. I'm sorry."

"Fine, a beer then."

She spun toward the kitchen, pulled out one of Trace's IPAs, pried open the top, and grabbed the first aid kit from the pantry before returning to the table. "Here you go. You sip on this while I look at your feet."

She knelt, gently lifted his foot, and found it chewed up from walking over a mile along a dark country road to get here. Trace was going to be beside himself.

"Hey," he said with surprise in his voice, "this is good. I don't usually like beer, but this ain't bad."

"You remember Ethan Hayes?"

"Harlan's grandson. Sure."

For not knowing current time and place very well, his memory for the past sure was sharp. "Ethan and Harlan brew this beer."

"Heh," he chuckled. "The old man loves sharing his hobby with that boy."

Avery wet cotton balls with hydrogen peroxide and cleaned the bottom of one foot, doing her best the get the embedded gravel out. Since George didn't complain, she kept working.

"Wish I could be half the father to Trace and Zane as Harlan is to that grandson of his."

The sadness in his voice tugged at Avery's heart. "I'm sure you're a great father. I know Trace loves you."

He smiled, his gaze distant. "That boy is my pride and joy. Zane's a good boy down deep, but he's a wild one. Trace . . . man, that kid's got heart. Real heart, you know? That's something you can't teach. A kid's either got it or he doesn't. Trace's got it in spades."

Mr. Hutton drank more beer, and Avery started on the other foot, letting the silence linger. Her thoughts turned to Trace. She agreed with George, Trace did have a lot of heart. And a lot of compassion. And kindness. All of which she loved about him.

"Where is everyone?" Mr. Hutton asked, looking around again. "Can't play poker with two."

She pulled out her phone. "I'll call Trace to see when he'll be back. Maybe he can bring enough friends for a game."

Or tell her what to say to his father to placate him until Trace returned.

"Ha. Trace don't play cards," George said. "Trace don't gamble. Trace don't do nothin' wrong."

Avery listened to Trace's rich voice on his message, and yearning pulled in her chest. She ached to apologize for what she'd said earlier. "Hey, it's me. Your dad showed up at the café. Don't worry—aside from cut-up feet, he's fine. I'm bandaging him up and getting him something to eat; then I'll bring him home and wait there with him." She hesitated. "I'd really like to talk later. I didn't mean to insult you with what I said about JT today. I don't see you that way, I just . . ." She sighed. "Well, maybe we can talk about it later."

Mr. Hutton didn't even seem to know Avery made the call. He was still talking about Trace. "Trace don't smoke. Trace don't drink. Trace don't touch drugs."

Avery frowned up at Mr. Hutton, confused. "You mean Zane?"

"No. Zane's got mischief in his blood. Always in trouble. If his mama and I had Zane first, we'd never have had Trace. But Trace." He shook his head. "The perfect kid. A natural athlete, comes home with straight As, always happy." He grew serious and sad. "Boy could have really made something of himself."

Avery added antibiotic ointment to George's feet and wrapped them with gauze. "He has made something of himself," she said, trying to clarify which son he was talking about. "He's a police officer. I'd say that's pretty great."

"No, that's Zane, and ironic as hell. But he says troublemakers make the best cops because they think like criminals."

She finished bandaging one foot, then started on the other. Trying to untangle the thoughts of a man with dementia had to be its own kind of crazy, right?

"But it was Trace who ended up in prison," she said.

"Because of me." George's eyes fell closed and a pained look etched his face. "All because of me." He shook his head, opened his eyes and yelled, "Joe! Where the hell is everyone?" Avery jumped, and her heart banged against her chest. "I want to win back that hundred bucks you stole from me last week."

Avery finished bandaging up his other foot with rattled nerves, then stood. "All right. I'll make you a sandwich, and we'll take it home with you. But I'm driving you this time."

"I ain't going home, missy," he said, annoyed with her again. "I'm playing a goddamned poker game. And I need a scotch and soda. What's this beer doing here? I hate beer."

Avery bit her lip. "I guess I'll get you your sandwich then."

She turned for the kitchen, tapped into speed dial, and hit Delaney's number.

"Hey there," she answered immediately. "What's up?"

Avery closed her eyes and winced when she whispered, "I need your help."

"Wait, *what*? Hold on, hold on—I'm putting you on speaker. Okay, say that again so Ethan can hear."

"Shut up."

"No, not that part, the other thing. You know that word that starts with *h*."

"God, Delaney—" She cut herself off, knowing her sister wouldn't let up until she got what she wanted. "I need your help. Grab a pen and paper and get ready to move."

Once she had Delaney and Ethan on board, Avery made a quick sandwich for George. When she sat it down in front of him, she said, "Maybe when you're done you'll want to try out my new piano."

George's gaze lifted to hers. "Piano? What piano?"

She pointed to it. "It was donated, and I had someone come work on it the other day. Trace told me you used to play in the choir. Maybe you can tell me if they did a good job tuning it."

Without touching his sandwich, George pushed from the chair and hobbled in that direction. He lifted the key cover with a gentle reverence. Henry had not only tuned it but cleaned it as well. Now the old wood shone, and the keys gleamed.

"This is an oldie, isn't it?" George asked.

"It is."

He ran his fingers lightly over the keys, then narrowed his eyes on Avery. "You sure I play? I don't remember playing."

She nodded. "Trace and Pearl told me. You don't remember singing either, but Pearl says you're singing every morning."

He returned his gaze to the keys.

"Sit," she suggested. "Just play around for a few minutes. See if anything feels right."

George lowered to the bench, placed his hands over the keys, and played some quick scales. His gaze jumped to Avery's, and the grin that cut across his face filled her with happiness.

She patted his shoulder. "You just enjoy yourself. I'm going to get ready for our poker game."

ELEVEN

Trace couldn't get that morning out of his mind. He'd been going over it and over it in his head, trying to figure out how JT had gotten in. Avery might think she'd left the door open, but Trace doubted it. Even exhausted, Avery was a creature of habit. And safety was one of her habits.

The forklift eased roof tiles into Trace's truck, and he tossed a thick nylon rope across the bed.

"Can you grab some more nails?" he asked JT. "And wait for the receipt?"

"Sure thing."

JT turned and whistled his way into the office of the building supply warehouse. Trace finished tying down the roof shingles, his mind back on that morning. He didn't believe she'd left the door unlocked, let alone open. And even though—according to the cons at Folsom—no lock was pick-proof, Trace had installed the highest-quality dead bolts to minimize amateur break-ins.

And JT was an amateur.

Through the office window, Trace saw JT talking to the woman behind the desk and slipped into the cab of the truck. With his gaze on the office, Trace grabbed the jacket JT had left on the seat and dipped his hand into one pocket.

Matches, receipts, gum.

He slid the jacket across the seat to reach the other pocket and felt the unmistakable weight of something heavy. He pushed his hand into the pocket and touched metal. Trace pulled out the object—and found a small black gun in his hand.

Trace's stomach went cold, his chest tight. "Fucking A."

"Hell, how do you know he doesn't have a weapon?"

Trace glanced toward the office again before he set the gun aside and dug deeper into the pocket and found more metal. But this was small. And Trace pulled out a key. A single, shiny key.

Rage slammed against his rib cage, demanding release, but Trace knew he had to keep that emotion locked down if he wanted to stay out here in the real world.

JT exited the office with a box of nails and a piece of paper. With his teeth clenched, Trace tossed the gun into his glove compartment, grabbed JT's jacket, and met him in the middle of the parking lot.

He held up the key. "Explain this."

JT's gaze jumped between the key and Trace's face a few times. "Explain what? My apartment key?" His expression turned sour. "What are you doing? Going through my stuff? That's not cool, man."

He grabbed for his jacket, but Trace pulled it out of reach. "What's *not cool* is me going out on a limb to give you a job and you cutting off the branch."

"I don't know what you're talking about."

"I'm talking about the way this key matches up with my key to *the café*."

JT's belligerence turned angry. "You don't know what you're talking about."

"I know exactly what I'm talking about." Trace shoved the jacket against JT's chest. "You're fired. Get the fuck out of my sight, and don't ever let me see your face again. You got that?"

Trace walked backward until he was out of jumping range, then turned for his truck.

"Dude," JT yelled. "You lifted my gun. Give it back."

Trace stopped and pivoted. "You can have your gun or peace with your PO. Which do you want more?"

JT read Trace's threat to tell his PO about the weapon, and fury broke over his face. "That's fucked, man. That's *fucked*."

Trace walked the rest of the way to the truck with JT yelling obscenities and threats, and drove away with JT's furious gestures in the rearview mirror.

He drove two miles, then stopped on the side of the highway, where weeds and bushes lined the fence. Dragging the gun from the glove box, he pulled the clip, emptied the chamber, and wiped down the metal with the hem of his T-shirt—ironically, all things he'd learned *inside* prison. Then he made damn sure there were no cops in sight and tossed the weapon out the driver's window.

Only when he was on the road again, free from JT and rid of that gun, did he breathe easier. Taking him on had been one of the worst decisions Trace had ever made. And the thought of that weapon so close to Avery, of JT so close to Avery, of what he could have done to Avery when Trace's back was turned . . .

His teeth clenched, and a feral sound vibrated in Trace's throat.

He spent the first fifteen minutes of the drive back just wrangling his fury under control. The next fifteen minutes planning how he'd finish the roof on his own before the rain came. And the last trying to figure out how to apologize to Avery in a way that conveyed his epiphany about how wrong he'd been.

He pulled off the highway with a sick knot in his stomach and dragged his phone from the center console to make a call to Gram to see if she could go check on George. Trace had to track Avery down to deliver the news and the apology he hadn't figured out yet.

At the stoplight, he tapped the "Home" button. Instead of lighting up with the background and the time, a row of two missed calls and two awaiting messages faced him—all from Avery.

A lick of panic stung his gut as his mind raced over reasons she would be trying to get ahold of him this late. An urgent problem at the café, an opportunity to ream him for acting like such an asshole today . . . Hell, she could have been calling to fire him.

He tapped the speaker on his phone, held his breath, and played the messages back.

As soon as Trace heard the words, "Your dad showed up at the café," all his air whooshed out.

"What?" He ground his teeth, holding in his fear and anger until he'd heard everything. The apology in her voice hadn't been anywhere close to what he'd been expecting. But he didn't jump to the conclusion that she'd want to mend fences with him, because, well, this wasn't his first asshole moment with her. When her message finished playing, Trace scraped his fingers into his hair. "Jesus Christ."

He deleted her message and played the next one.

"Me again," she said to voice mail. "Just an update. Your dad doesn't want to go home, so we'll wait for you at the café. See you soon."

"Oh, great," he muttered. His dad was having one of his stubborn moments. "Just fucking perfect."

Trace pushed harder on the gas. This was the last thing Avery needed—an ornery old man, with dementia no less—planting himself in the middle of her café at the end of a very long day. And his father's mind only slipped deeper into confusion when he was stressed. The bar's transition into a café, the replacement of Joe with Avery, the absence of alcohol and cards would rattle him enough to twist his thoughts into a dust devil and push his acceptance of change into the negative zone.

All that would trigger irrational anger and mix memories until he made no sense at all and turned belligerent.

Thinking of that stress on top of all the stress Trace had already caused Avery made him anxious as he pulled into the café's drive.

The first sign of trouble hit him immediately—a half-dozen cars in the lot besides Avery's Jeep. The next sign hit a second later—Zane's patrol car among those vehicles.

"Shit."

Fear joined Trace's stress. Reasons for all these cars to be here bounced around his brain, making it hard to think, to plan. He pulled up behind a couple of cars and turned off the truck's engine but left the lights on and keys in the ignition as he jumped out and took the front steps two at a time.

Inside the café, he halted at the sight that greeted him—a bunch of people sitting around two square tables that had been pushed together near the piano. They all had cards and piles of chips laid out in front of them. The lighting was lower than usual, and the murmur of familiar voices touched Trace's ears. Familiar faces registered in his brain.

What he didn't understand was *what* . . . or *why* . . . or *how* . . .

"Okay, yo," Zane said, turning his head toward Ethan, who sat in the next seat, letting a stack of chips slide through his fingers over and over, "we're surfin' the wall here. Are you grabbing your board or not?"

"Speaking English is a requirement to play at this table, kid," Harlan McClellan groused. "If you can't say something we can all understand, then stop your jabberin'."

Ethan tossed his cards toward Delaney, who held the deck. "I'm out."

That pleased Zane, and he turned his sharklike gaze on Phoebe in the next chair. "Come on, Pheebs," he cajoled. "You know you wanna."

"I know I wanna kick your arrogant heinie," she said as she matched Zane's bet and lifted her chin toward Trace's father, who sat across from her. "Take it away, George. Because if I can't be the one to kick his ass, there's no one I'd like to see kick it more than you."

The laughter around the table climbed. And his father was among those laughing. Trace hadn't seen his father laugh in . . . He searched his memory and realized he couldn't remember the last time he'd seen him laugh. Possibly sometime in Trace's childhood.

"Good call," George said, matching his son's sly grin. "Because no one can kick his ass like I can." He tipped his head and shrugged. "Well, except Trace. Trace has a knack for kicking ass."

Trace's confusion deepened into shock. His father sounded positively lucid as he pulled up the corners of his two cards for a quick glance, then tossed in chips to match the others. "I'm in. You gonna wake up to play this hand, Avery? Or just win it while you sleep?"

Trace's gaze slid to the shadowed chair beside his father, just outside the pool of light overhead. Avery had her arm curled on the table and her head resting there. He shifted to get a better look at her face and found her eyes closed. She opened them long enough to glance at the table and throw chips in the pot.

She closed her eyes again. "I'm a multitasking guru."

Trace planted his hands at his hips and watched as the hand moved forward and his brain pieced together the answers to his what, why, and how. It didn't take long for him to realize that because his father still thought this was Joe's bar, he'd demanded to do what he always did at Joe's bar when he'd come—drink and play poker. When Avery couldn't convince him to go home, she'd either had to provide the environment his father wanted or suffer his wrath.

She'd obviously enlisted help from the piano, where the keys were uncovered, and called in the cavalry, soliciting those closest to her to put together the poker game his father had been asking Trace for since they'd arrived in town. Judging by the beer bottles littering the table, it was obvious Ethan had brought the alcoholic refreshments. By the food sitting on the counter, Avery had provided snacks. And between her family and his, she'd pulled together his father's dream night on the spur of the moment.

When it all came together in Trace's head, he experienced a sudden wash of emotions that almost overwhelmed him. Gratitude, affection, longing . . . and so much more. Too much more. He couldn't process it all in the moment. He'd been so lucky to have Delaney call him at the start of this job, doubly lucky when Avery kept him on after the café had traded hands. Now both he and his father had the support of Avery and her entire extended family. Phoebe, Delaney, Ethan, even Harlan had jumped when Avery had asked, giving up their night to satisfy a crazy old man's frivolous wish.

A round of shouts and laughter brought Trace's thoughts back.

Zane jumped from his chair and planted his hands on the table, leaning toward Delaney. "Come on, baby—bring me a diamond."

"Watch who you're calling baby," Ethan said.

"I'm talking to the cards."

Avery chuckled, eyes still closed, head still resting on her arm. "He has to. If you don't have skill, you've got to have a little crazy."

Delaney laughed. "Amen, sister."

Trace could only guess by the body language and card placement at the table that only Avery and Zane remained in the hand, and a shitload of chips were piled at the center of the table.

"Come on, Delaney," Avery murmured. "Pull a lady for me, if for no other reason than to watch Zane writhe in pain."

"Why you gotta be like that?" Zane said.

"You've met your poker match, kid," their father told Zane, then chuckled like the man Trace had once known. "And it's a damn beautiful sight."

Zane ignored George and told Delaney, "You're killin' me here. Just pull it."

Delaney pulled a card and turned it faceup. Trace couldn't see what it was, but by the way Zane dramatically pumped his fists overhead with a, "Yes," it had obviously been a diamond.

"You are the luckiest little shit," Avery said without an ounce of anger.

"Luck of the Irish," Zane said.

Avery opened her eyes and lifted a grin to Zane. "Irish prick, maybe."

The group busted up with laughter, and playing stopped for a moment. Trace realized he was smiling. Realized his chest felt light.

Ethan noticed Trace and lifted his chin in greeting. "Hey, you're back. Pull up a chair—join the next round."

Avery sat up, her dazed gaze searching for him. And when hers eyes slid to a stop on his, Trace felt a warm, gooey knot pull deep in his chest.

A tentative smile turned her lips, and her hair fell over her shoulder, reminding him of the way she'd looked at him during their first night together. "Hey. How was the trip? Did you get what you needed?"

He'd gotten rid of JT, and that was a serious relief to his mind, heart, and conscience. "I did." And he needed to break this up and let everyone get on with his or her life, including Avery. "Dad, you ready to go?"

"Don't you worry about that," Harlan told Trace, pushing back from the table and standing in a slow, stiff movement. "Your daddy's stayin' at the ranch house with me. Gonna plow with me in the morning. You and Zane deserve a night off. George and me got lots of old times to talk about."

"Hey, wait a minute," Zane complained as the hand broke up. "It's not over."

Avery tossed her cards toward the deck, and Delaney slid them back in the cardboard box. "You win, Zane."

"It's no fun to win like that."

"Too bad."

"Jeez." Zane dropped his cards on the table, his shoulders sagging. "Trace, your timing sucks."

But with Avery walking toward him, blue eyes sparkling, he was thinking just the opposite.

"Hey," he said, "thanks for doing this. I'm sorry I didn't get back to you sooner. I didn't hear the phone and didn't see your call until I picked it up to call and check on Dad—"

"It's fine. It all worked out fine."

"Right," he said. "I forgot you're the goddess of fine." But in Trace's book *fine* meant settling. And Avery didn't need to settle anymore.

As everyone collected their jackets and headed for the door offering their "good nights," including his father, Trace told Harlan, "Call me for anything. Anytime tonight, okay?"

"You kids," Harlan said with a chuckle. "You forget *we* raised *you*, not the other way around." He slapped a hand to Trace's shoulder. "Relax for a change."

But Trace felt like a worried father when his own dad walked down the stairs in his pajamas and someone else's shoes, with bandages peeking out around his ankles.

Phoebe followed with a hug for Avery and a warm squeeze to Trace's forearm.

Zane walked out with Delaney and Ethan and paused on the porch. "Do you girls ever hear from Chloe? I was hoping to see her pop up in town since the two of you were back."

"Last I talked to her," Avery said, brows lifted, "she was teaching yoga in Bali."

Zane's mouth dropped open. *"Bali?"*

"Bali."

"Huh. Rough life."

Avery shrugged. "It may seem glamorous, but in a month, she'll call and probably be somewhere in Africa building houses, or in Belize saving turtles, or in Mississippi waiting tables. She hasn't quite found whatever it is she's looking for. When I talk to her again, I'm going to offer her a job at the café." Avery's beautiful face broke into a grin. "I can't wait to hear how she responds to that."

"Keep me posted," Zane said. He promised Trace he'd call and talk about their dad's logistics in the morning.

Before Ethan and Delaney headed down the steps to their cars, her sister gave both Avery and Trace a pointed look. "Be good now."

Standing together, watching the trail of cars flow toward the country road, Trace both relished the quiet and dreaded leaving. "Zane's nursed a wicked crush on Chloe since sixth grade."

Avery chuckled. "Along with every other male in Wildwood. The wild little Hart blonde. I know a lot of people think Delaney was the craziest, but that's only because they'd never experienced how well Chloe could lie, charm, and con anyone and everyone. Zane was lucky she never took an interest in him. In her short twenty-four years, she's left a trail of broken hearts around the world."

"Think she'll come back to take a job at the café?"

"Hell no," Avery laughed. "But a girl can dream. I miss her. She's always so upbeat and positive no matter what. Always fun, larger than life. The girl everyone wants to be, you know?"

"Hmm." Trace didn't know. He'd known Chloe only in passing, and even though her type was the kind of woman he'd sought out for years, the description didn't appeal to him now. Now only Avery appealed to him. Which brought his mind around to Avery's older sister. "Why did Delaney tell us to be good?"

Avery heaved a sigh, one that sounded exhausted. "She has my aunt's intuition. She knows we slept together and isn't thrilled with the idea."

Trace cut a look at her, shock burning in his gut. "You told her?"

Avery lifted a shoulder. "Only after she'd already guessed."

Right. Fucking around with an ex-con wasn't exactly news to write home about.

"Trace," she said, "I'm so sorry about what I said earlier. I know that doesn't make up for it, but I didn't mean to lump you in with all ex-convicts. I was just—"

"You were right." Instead of touching her the way he wanted to, he kept his hands on the railing and held tight to keep them there. Then looked toward the darkness. "I'm sorry I even brought JT onto the property. He won't be back. I fired him."

She rested her hip against the railing. "What happened?"

"Found the key to the café in his jacket pocket. It was brand-new, still shiny. He must have lifted my key and had one made. He wouldn't have had access to yours."

A soft breath exited her lungs, and a moment of silence stretched between them. Then she finally said, "I'm sorry he disappointed you."

That sparkle of compassion was all it took for Trace's barriers to melt away. But the guilt remained. "And I'm sorry I've disappointed you." He met her gaze again. "I'll get the roof done tomorrow myself, then start on the finish work. I promise you, Avery—I'll have this café ready for your opening day."

She searched his eyes, then nodded and stroked a hand over his arm. "I know you will."

A warm, tight feeling gathered at the center of his body. She had every right to doubt him, yet didn't. Every reason to back away, yet stepped closer.

"Thanks for helping out with my dad. I know he's the last thing you needed to deal with on top of everything else today."

"If I wasn't so stretched thin for time," she said, "I'd offer to have him hang with me while I bake. He's quite the piano player. I could listen to that all day."

"He remembered?" Trace asked, stunned. "He actually played?"

She nodded. "The most poignant 'Ave Maria' I've ever heard."

"Wow." He was speechless.

"And boy did his mood improve. He came in all pissed off, and as soon as he sat down at that piano, it was like flipping a switch. Absolutely amazing."

"You're the one who's absolutely amazing," he said. "I overreacted this morning. I'm . . . overly sensitive . . . to being lumped in with the ex-con pool, which is stupid, because that's what I am. I'm sorry for snapping at you."

"We're both stretched thin. I can see how difficult it would be to take care of your father on your own."

He shrugged. "Yeah, well, I was no easier as a kid."

"That's not what he says."

Trace huffed a sarcastic laugh, but a tingle of unease rose along his spine. "Dementia, remember?"

"That's what I thought at first. When he insisted Zane was the troublemaker of the family, I was sure he had to be mixed up. So when Zane finally showed up tonight, I asked him."

His unease turned to fear and vibrated in his gut. It wasn't logical, he knew. But what he'd done to end up in prison hadn't been logical either. Trace was only beginning to realize how much of what he did in life was rooted in emotion.

Like holding out hope she didn't pull away when he lifted a hand to brush a lock of hair from her cheek and tuck it behind her ear.

When she leaned into his touch instead of backing off, he asked, "And what did he say?"

"He said I should ask you."

Trace's mouth quirked. "He would."

He was rolling words around in his head, unsure how to get out of this conversation without giving an explanation about something he'd rather forget, when she lifted her hand to cover his and took another step closer. This time, she closed the distance completely, pressing her body to his and slipping her arms around his waist.

That was all it took for Trace's body to break through the mental restrictions he'd put in place. A craving unique to Avery and getting stronger by the day bubbled low in his gut. Every inch of his body felt tight and hot and hungry. Hungry for the feel of her, the smell of her, the taste of her. He craved the sensation of fulfillment she left in the wake of giving herself over to him.

"You know," he said, laying his hands on her shoulders, unsure how to push her away without hurting her or pissing her off, yet sure that was exactly what he had to do, "it's been a really long—"

"I don't care what your father meant," she said. "It doesn't matter. We all made mistakes when we were kids, right?"

He didn't understand why she always gave him the benefit of the doubt. Why she trusted him at all after what she'd been through with her ex. "I wasn't a kid when I made my mistakes. I knew better."

"So did I, but I still did it."

"You ran off to get *married*. I . . ." He didn't want to get into that. "Forget it. That's beside the—"

"You what?"

"It doesn't matter." He looked around the café for something to distract her and allow him to pull away. "Come on—I'll help you clean up."

But she wasn't having it. She locked her arms at the small of his back and pulled his hips into hers. The feel of her supple belly cradling his cock forced blood into all the right—or wrong, depending on how he looked at it—places, and he couldn't keep his eyes open.

He was gathering the strength to push away, when she said, "You're right. It doesn't matter. We all end up where we're supposed to be eventually."

Where we are supposed to be?

He opened his eyes to Avery's light-blue gaze looking up at him with heat and affection and need. A need that seemed more emotional than physical. Wrapped in her arms like this, Trace realized *she* was as close to where he was supposed to be as he'd ever felt.

But Avery was a completely different story. At only twenty-five, with a supportive, loving family behind her, a prosperous new business on the horizon, and her newfound freedom at her fingertips, she was at the launching pad of her life, not the final destination.

"Eventually, I suppose we do." He ran the backs of his fingers over her cheek. "But you have a lot more life to experience before you'll know where you're meant to be."

"Maybe for the long term." The spark in her eyes dimmed, her soft smile faded, and she let her gaze drift to his chest. "But right now I have no doubt I'm exactly where I'm supposed to be."

She pushed up on her toes and kissed his throat. Fire streaked along his skin, and his cock jumped and swelled. He stroked a hand over her hair, framed her head, and pulled her mouth off his skin. Time for a little dose of reality.

"And what about tomorrow?" He met her eyes directly. "Your sister will still disapprove, to say nothing of what Phoebe will think if she finds out. And I'll still be a struggling ex-con, almost a decade older than you. It might feel good now, but reality is reality, Avery, and that's not going to look very appealing in the morning."

"I've seen you in the morning," she quipped back, "and I promise you, it's extremely appealing." She grew serious, and her eyes did that smolder thing that made him ravenous. "And tomorrow, I'll still see the man I see right now. The same man I met two months ago on the tour of this hellhole."

She slid her hands up his chest and wound her fingers around his wrists. "I don't see the man you see when you look in the mirror, with all the flaws of the past staring back at you, Trace. I see the competent contractor who works twice as hard as anyone I've ever met, while doing twice the job, and all for next to nothing just for the possibility of getting future work from others. I see the man who constantly has his client's best interests at heart, a man who can admit when he's made a mistake and who can apologize for something that's only half his fault. I see a man twisting himself inside out to take care of his sick father and trying to make ends meet."

Trace was slipping again. His chest ached. His body throbbed. And his eyes kept falling to her mouth the way a drunk's clung to a bottle of whiskey. Avery promised him the same blissful relief, the same heavenly escape. If he could just figure out a way to indulge and not wake up with a hangover that continued to gnaw away at him until his next sip.

"You're amazing." He heard his words, realized he'd spoken the thought, and continued. "After everything you've been through, I don't know how you could see the good in any man, let alone a man like me."

She shook her head. "You can't appreciate the good without experiencing the bad. And even though I only have one man for comparison, I spent all my time with very chatty wives of other soldiers. I knew exactly what I was missing in my marriage—emotionally and physically. Which makes me qualified to tell you, Mr. Hutton, that you are way the hell above average, just as you are."

Trace was speechless. Emotions overpowered logic again, and he couldn't stop himself from pulling her to him for just a taste of heaven. Her lips were as warm and welcoming as they always were. Her mouth open and hot, her tongue aggressive, begging for him to respond the same way.

And just like a drunk, one taste, and Trace fell headfirst into the bottle. He slanted his mouth over hers and tasted her. Licked her. Sucked her. And when she made that hungry kitten sound at the back of her throat, Trace wobbled on the edge of losing his mind and doing what he'd done their first night—throwing her onto the butcher block and fucking her until they were both a sweaty, juicy mess.

He broke the kiss and pressed his cheek to her forehead. Taking deep drags of air, he fought to clear his mind. The logical side tried its best, but its wheels spun in the mud with the same weak argument it always threw at him.

She'll eventually hate you for continuing this dead-end fling. She'll end up feeling used. She is exactly why you stick with casual hookups, because women like Avery don't belong with men like you. There's no way this will end well; you are what you are.

"I'm exhausted." Avery's words pulled him from the impossible dilemma, and Trace saw them for what they were—his escape hatch.

He leaned away and nodded. "Yeah. Really long day." He forced his fingers to uncurl from her hair. "You should get some sleep."

"Mmm-hmm." She may have agreed, but not only didn't she release him, she slid her hands under his T-shirt and stroked his belly and chest. "I'm so glad my bed was delivered earlier tonight."

His gaze refocused on hers. "Bed?"

She nodded, smiling like a little imp. "For the apartment. As soon as those appliances come in—which should be any day now—I'll be living here. Personally and professionally. And as hard as I work during the day, I decided I deserve a good bed for my nights." She scraped her fingers through his hair and dragged her lower lip between her teeth. "Come check it out with me. Make sure it's not too soft, not too hard . . . you know—"

"Just right," he murmured, already following her as she pulled him toward the stairs by his T-shirt.

She beamed over her shoulder. "Exactly."

But at the bottom of the steps, that logic caught up with him, and he grabbed the banister, using the physical anchor to stop himself. Her hand slipped from his shirt, and she stopped on the first stair, turning to face him with a curious frown.

"Really, Avery. Don't you think it's better to back off now rather than wait until we're in even deeper and then have to cut it off cold turkey?"

Say yes. Say, "You're right, Trace. Go home."

But just the thought of those words coming out of her mouth cut him down the middle. He definitely had a bigger problem on his hands than he'd realized. He was fucking crazy about this woman.

Disappointment clouded her expression, but within seconds that sadness shifted to resignation. Her shoulders dropped. Her head tilted as if considering. "If that's really the way you feel . . ."

She ascended the stairs backward. Her arms crossed and her fingers grabbed the hem of her tee, then pulled it off over her head, dropping it on the stairs.

Pink lace cupped her breasts, and Trace's mouth watered as his gaze skimmed all the perfect curves from her shoulders down to her waist.

She backed up another stair and slid her hands down her body in an incredibly intimate way that made him think of touching her, of watching her touch herself. Then her fingers slipped into the waistband of her jeans and popped the button. The zipper's rasp sounded loud in the dark.

"I'm not going to force you into my bed if you're ready to move on." She climbed another two steps. Shimmied her jeans over her hips and pushed them down her thighs.

"Avery . . ." Her name came out half plea, half breath, and it was all he could manage, caught between two impossible choices. He could walk away from the most beautiful, most generous, most amazing woman he'd ever met, one who'd somehow snuck into his heart and filled a space he hadn't realized was vacant. Or he could stay with her, love her the way he wanted, the way she deserved, and hurt like a mother when it was over.

She toed off her shoes and stepped out of her jeans, leaving them in a puddle on the stairs as she took the last step to the landing in the prettiest matching bra and panties Trace had seen in a long time.

He gripped the banister until his fingers stung, and a low groan ebbed from his throat.

"Have I ever mentioned that I love the way you say my name?" she asked, reaching into her hair and pulling the band holding it up. "Without the *e*."

Trace had no idea what she was talking about, because all his blood was feeding the wrong brain. Her hair tumbled down in a ragged mess, and she combed her fingers through it.

"Especially," she added, reaching between her breasts to grasp the clip on her bra, "during sex when you use that deep, throaty, can't-get-enough-of-you voice. God, that's *so* hot. I'm already wet."

Snap.

The clip broke open, and Trace's barriers shattered with it. She let her breasts fall free of the bra and looped the fabric around the banister, leaving her in nothing but sexy, sheer, skimpy panties.

Trace went up in flames.

With her hand on the matching banister at the top of the stairs, her gorgeous body shadowed in the dim light, she said, "Well, then . . . I guess I'll be rolling around in my brand-new bed with brand-new sheets by myself tonight. Sleep tight, Trace."

And she turned and disappeared up the second half of the split-level staircase.

TWELVE

Avery stood in the dark of her barely-more-than-a-studio apartment above the café, her thumbnail gripped between her teeth, the other arm crossed tight over her middle, unable to believe she'd just undressed in front of him after he'd rejected her. And in hindsight, what she'd thought would feel playful and look sexy probably looked more like desperation.

She closed her eyes as another surge of embarrassment pumped through her, then lifted her hands to rub her burning cheeks. And as she stared out at the darkness, listening for Trace's footsteps, she took consolation in the fact that no one knew how mortified she would feel if Trace walked out after that lame attempt at seduction.

He was right about cutting off their involvement now. She knew that. At least logically. Ending their intimate connection now while they could remain friends made a lot of sense. Especially when she knew cold turkey was going to throw her into withdrawal. Yet emotionally and physically, she both wanted and needed him so badly she ached with it. And there was just no reasoning with that kind of desire.

In the back of her mind, she realized her moments with him were dwindling, and she wanted to grab as much of him as she could, while she could.

His boots sounded on the hardwood, and her mind hyperfocused on the present. Within three steps, the thump faded, and she realized he was headed for the door.

Dammit. She squeezed her eyes closed, curled her hand into a fist, and pressed it against her forehead. The knife in her belly twisted, and her stomach burned. The *snick* of the front door's dead bolt sliding home was the final blow. A blow that seemed to shift everything inside her.

A few soft thumps sounded near the porch, and Avery turned away from the window. She didn't want to watch him leave. Logically, she knew this situation wasn't anything like her marriage, knew he had good reason to leave. But having the man she wanted walk away from her still felt the same—like a knife straight to the heart. It didn't matter that he'd be back every day for several more days to install the equipment and complete the finish work. She had to accept that her mini-affair with Trace Hutton was over.

She pulled a T-shirt from a pile in the laundry basket she'd brought over earlier and tugged it over her head. As soon as she pushed her arms into the sleeves, she knew it was one Trace had left behind.

"Guess this is as close as I'm gonna get to having him in my bed tonight."

Or ever again whispered through her head.

Pacing across the room, she rested her back against the wall, wrapped her arms around herself, and stared at her bed with its crisp, new white sheets and white down comforter. The thought of sliding in and sleeping alone . . .

God, sometimes it felt like she'd spent her entire life alone. There might have been short spans of time when she'd felt connected and loved—like she had with David at seventeen, or with Trace when she was in his arms. But she was quickly realizing those short spurts weren't enough to sustain her soul.

The room's night chill spread across her skin, and Avery rubbed her arms. Maybe, after Trace was out of sight, she'd go back to Phoebe's to sleep. Maybe it was too soon to think about living on her own. As much as she'd been looking forward to her own space, her own things, and her privacy, this all just felt too empty. And she'd already spent way too many nights of her life lonely.

The thought of dating other guys fluttered into her mind, and she realized that her desire for no strings would leave her in this position a lot—watching men leave, sleeping alone, living with loneliness.

The sound of soft footsteps on the stairs touched her ears. Her heart jumped and rattled. She turned her head just as he stopped in the open doorway and planted his hand on the frame.

The sight froze the breath in her lungs.

He came back? No one ever came back for her. Not her mother. Not Delaney. Not David.

In the shadows, it was hard to read his expression, but she felt the tension between them like a crackle in the air. He'd taken off his boots and socks and looked ridiculously relaxed and adorable and smokin' hot in those worn jeans with his tousled hair, scruff, and bare feet.

"Does that offer still stand?" His voice was soft but thick and heavy with desire. "'Cause after that insanely hot display, I can't make myself leave even though I know I should."

Her excitement hit a wall, crashed, and burned. He'd come back for exactly what she'd promised him: no-strings sex. And ten minutes ago, that would have been enough. Now . . .

"You're right about us," she said quietly, "turning down the heat now will make your leaving more bearable."

His jaw muscle jumped, but he held her gaze and gave a single, slight nod, not so much agreement as acknowledgment. A sensation of loss clawed at her gut, and she was suddenly overcome with a frantic sort of angst to explain—to him and to herself.

"I may not be cut out for the fling thing after all. I mean, it's what I wanted when we started. It's still what I probably need, considering how I feel about marriage and commitment, and you know, relationships in general, but what just happened, that . . . exchange of me wanting you and you walking away . . ."

She shook her head and gave a little shrug. "It was too . . . familiar in a really ugly way. And, somewhere over the last two months, I guess . . . I don't know." She blew out a breath, frustrated that she couldn't spit out her words in any sort of comprehendible way. "I just know I care too much about you to keep sleeping with you under that arrangement."

He nodded again but still didn't move, and Avery was trying to think of something else to say, some way of explaining her Jekyll-and-Hyde behavior, sure he had to be regretting getting involved with someone so inexperienced, so . . . naive.

"Me, too." His words came out rough.

Confused, she shook her head. "You, too, what?"

"I care too much, too. That's why I didn't leave." He dropped his gaze to the floor, flexed and released his fingers from the door frame. "What if we didn't go cold turkey when the project ends?" He lifted his gaze to hers. "What if we just, you know, let whatever this is run its course? When you decide you want something more, you move on."

Her heart squeezed, and she huffed a sad laugh. "And what if I decide you're everything I want? Then where will we be? In even deeper?" She shook her head. "No, I—"

"I can live with that."

She dropped her arms and narrowed her eyes, frustration rising. "Live with what? What are you talking about?"

He did that silent jaw-jumping, intent-staring thing again.

She lifted her hands, palms up. "Trace—"

"I know I should walk away. I know you deserve better. I just . . . I got to the door, and the thought of going home and fighting through another sleepless night was too much. I'm not ready to let you go. I will if that's what you want, but . . . if I'm making decisions based on what I want, I definitely want more of you."

Her lips parted, but her brain and her heart tumbled into free fall. She couldn't find or form words.

When she didn't respond, Trace's expression took on a spark of hope, and he took his damn sweet time sauntering toward her. "And if you want to keep it a secret to minimize the flak you'll get from your family, that's fine. It doesn't need to be public. We can keep it just between you and me."

He was standing right in front of her now, less than a foot away. And even though he didn't reach for her, his eyes flashed with affection and vulnerability.

"Just tell me no, and I'll be gone." He lifted his hand to her jaw and cradled her face. His gaze searched her eyes, expectant, hopeful. "Say something, Avery."

She couldn't. Her throat had swelled tight, and she had to drag in shaky breaths. Avery fisted her hands in the front of his T-shirt and took a step across the distance separating them, pulling him in.

Their mouths met with a force that made Trace sway, but he immediately wrapped Avery in a fierce hold and opened to her demand with a long, low growl, the sound part passion, part relief.

The kiss took on a life of its own, lips sliding, tongues stroking, filling Avery's chest with pressure. Her mind wiped clear of everything but Trace—the way he held her like he wanted their bodies to fuse, the way they fit, the warmth and strength of him, his taste, his smell.

His shirt was halfway up his chest by the time she realized she was pulling at it. And he broke the kiss for only a second to let the fabric pass over his head. Avery braced herself when he kissed her again, but she still bowed backward over his arm.

She gripped his biceps, slid her hands over his shoulders, wrapped her forearms at his neck. God, she'd never been wanted like this. And now she didn't know how she'd lived without all this passion in her life for so long.

He broke the kiss, leaned away to grab the hem of her T-shirt, then froze. He was breathing hard, his eyes narrowed. "Is this my shirt?"

Avery stroked her hands over his abdomen and up his chest, then leaned in to press a kiss over his heart. "You left it here, and it now has a very purposeful life as my sleep shirt. Possession is nine-tenths of the law, which means it's now officially mine."

His gaze jumped to hers. "I haven't seen this shirt in over a month."

She slid her hands around his waist and let them roam over the warm muscles of his back. "What's your point?"

"You've been sleeping in my shirt for *a month*?"

Alarm tingled in her gut. Was that bad? Did that signal that she had schoolgirlish romantic fantasies and couldn't be taken seriously?

Screw it. She was who she was. "Longer. It smells like you." She pressed another kiss to his chest. "And I have no intension of giving it back, so just write it off now."

He eased her back by the arms and looked down at her, a faint grin easing the tight line of his mouth. "I have no intension of asking for it back. I love the thought of you sleeping in it." He gripped the bottom again. "But not tonight." And he drew it off over her head in one quick pull. "Tonight," he said, dropping the shirt to the floor and stroking both hands over her shoulders, down her sides, and up her belly to cup her breasts, "you're sleeping in nothing but skin. You, me, skin, and sheets. All. Night. Long."

He bent at the knees, wrapped his arms around her waist, then straightened, carrying her with him. Avery laughed and wrapped her legs around his waist. And when he tilted his head toward hers, she wound her arms around his neck, met his kiss, and sank deep.

The moan that rolled through Trace's chest gave her gooseflesh. Thick and low, like an animal's warning growl, it vibrated from his body to hers and trembled in her throat. And when he leaned over the bed to lay her down, Avery reached for the waistband of his jeans. But he eased out of reach, kissing a hot trail down her neck, her chest, pausing to tease her nipples into peaks. His fingers dragged at her panties while his mouth traveled over her stomach and finally, finally covered her sex.

The rush of excitement burned straight up her body, and she moaned and arched. Trace dug in, eating at her like he'd been starved for weeks. And, sweet Jesus, Avery didn't have to know anything about oral sex to know the man used his mouth like a god.

She threaded her fingers through his hair as his tongue did things that brought her to the edge of orgasm in seconds. And when she was about ready to fly, he lifted his head, leaving her throbbing, hot, and a little frantic for release.

He was breathing hard as he ran his tongue over his lips with a hum of pleasure. "God, I love the way you taste." He turned his head and kissed a path along her thigh from her knee toward her sex. "I love the way you moan." Instead of lavishing attention on her pussy again, he turned his head the other way and kissed the opposite leg from her knee to her sex. "I love the way you lift into my mouth, like you crave the feel of my tongue." He blew on her, hot and soft, and Avery felt her sex open, felt wetness slide inside her.

With one hand fisted in the sheets, the other in his hair, she propped herself up on an elbow. "Don't tease me, Trace. I need you."

Trace pushed to his feet, then eased over her, laying his body on hers. She smiled as she sank into the mattress, then laughed as he rolled to his back, taking her with him. She sat up, straddling his hips, and reached for the waistband of his jeans. But her hair fell into her eyes, and when she lifted a hand to push it out of the way, Trace gripped her waist and lifted her until her thighs flanked his shoulders.

"Show me how badly you need me," he said, his tone demanding as he gripped her hips and pulled her pussy straight to his open mouth.

Avery gasped at the sensation rocketing through her sex, and she bowed backward. "Oh my God . . ."

Her fingers curled around his wrists, holding on as he ate at her pussy the same way he ate at her mouth, creating a frenzy of shock waves through her body.

"Trace, Trace, Trace . . ." She had no idea why she kept repeating his name, but it tumbled out of her mouth among moans and mewls of ecstasy. Her orgasm rushed forward, and she couldn't keep her body still. She had to move, had to rock to meet Trace's mouth until they found the most insanely perfect grind. She'd never felt anything so wickedly good in her entire life. "God . . . Trace—"

The orgasm peaked, shuddering through her like an earthquake. She cried out while Trace kept licking and kissing and sucking two more mini-quakes from her.

"Oh my God . . ." She fell forward and rolled to her side, muscles limp, vision blurred.

Trace pushed her to her back and lay half on top of her, half on the bed. He pressed his face between her chin and her shoulder and kissed her there with a rough, "You blow my mind."

Avery was breathing hard, her head filled with shards of light. She was pretty sure *he* was the one who'd blown *her* mind, but she couldn't get the words out. His mouth traveled lazily over her shoulder before he tilted her face toward him and covered her mouth with his.

But this time his kiss was languid and deep, and even though the rigid, denim-clad line of his cock pressed hard against her thigh, he just sank into the kiss as if he weren't dying to be exactly where Avery had just come from.

Still floating, she slid one hand over his shoulder, down his arm, his chest, then wedged it between them so she could stroke him. He was so thick and hard, and the way his needy sound rolled from deep in his chest sparked something elemental inside Avery.

But just as she closed her fingers on the tab to his zipper, Trace closed his hand over hers, threaded their fingers, and pressed their joined hands to the bed alongside her head. "Uh-uh," he murmured, soft and quiet. "Not yet. I just want to be for a while."

She let her other hand sift through his thick hair. "Be?"

He turned his head and rested it against her chest, his ear over her heart. "Be. Just . . . *be*. With you." He made an inpatient sound in his throat and repositioned his thigh so that his cock wasn't rubbing against her leg. "I want to touch you. I want to taste you. I want to inhale you. I want to crawl under your skin and *nest*."

Avery laughed. "You're already there, handsome." She sighed. "Already there."

They fell into silence. Silence while their breathing returned to normal. Silence while they touched each other. Silence while they lay skin to skin. A comfortable silence. A sweet silence.

"Are you getting up at four again tomorrow?" he finally asked, kissing a path between her breasts.

"Unless I'm given incentive to stay in bed."

He rolled to his hands and knees and hovered over her, grinning with that sexy little glint in his eye. "I might have the knowledge and the equipment necessary to provide such incentive."

She slid her free hand down his body and stroked his erection. "I know for a fact you have both."

He kissed her again, but it was still filled with sweetness and affection, not the passion and lust she was accustomed to, and she had to admit, that threw her off a little.

Pulling back, he broke the kiss and searched her eyes with a serious expression. Thoughts were churning in his head; Avery could see them getting batted back and forth in his eyes.

She lifted her free hand to his face. "What?"

"I just . . ." He gave a little shake of his head, then murmured in a voice that seemed more for himself than for Avery, "*How* in the *hell* did he let you go?"

Her stomach floated to her throat, and her chest squeezed. Yeah, she was in deep shit with this man. She really needed to check her emotions.

"We were young." She shrugged. "Stupid. He was fulfilling his family duty to continue the military lines of his father, grandfather, great-grandfather. I was running away from turmoil and loneliness. We weren't exactly thinking straight."

He eased his lower body onto hers, twining their legs. "And then?"

"And then?" she repeated, her mind lost in ways to get him out of his jeans.

"You ran away, he joined the military . . . and then . . . ?"

She laughed. "Sounds like we ran away and joined the circus, which I guess would be an accurate description of our life a lot of the time—jumping through hoops, pretending I was someone I wasn't, feeling like every day was high-wire act, with me waiting for that inevitable day someone showed up at my door to tell me my husband died performing unfathomable acts of folly . . . or, in his case, heroism."

Her stomach clenched at the thought, far more of a conditioned response than a current emotion. She shook off those old fears. They didn't belong to her anymore. They belonged to his fiancée now. And, in all honesty, Avery had a steadfast better-her-than-me attitude about David's marriage. The failure of their own still ate at her. His betrayal still stung. But she didn't want that life back. And she didn't want David back either.

"He was deployed to Syria for his first tour and came back a very different man. We worked at reconnecting, went to counseling, but . . . Like I said, we were young. He didn't understand my life; I didn't understand his. He sucked at talking about it; I sucked at asking the right questions, giving him space, understanding his moods. And when we couldn't bridge the gap, he started taking longer tours, which pushed a deeper wedge between us. He'd come home for a month or two even more distant, more complicated. We'd grow that much further apart. It was a lousy downward spiral."

Trace pulled a pillow under her head, pressed a hand to her chest, and rested his chin there. "Why didn't you leave sooner?"

"Because we were *married*," she said with a what-kind-of-question-is-that laugh. "I didn't get married just to hang around for the good stuff. I was in it until death did we part. I went into it committed five hundred percent." She shrugged. "But you can't force someone to love you enough to stay and fight."

"You stayed and fought for eight years?"

"Eight very long, very painful, very lonely years."

"I'm sorry." His thumb skimmed her cheek, his gaze distant. "I can understand why you're not interested in commitment."

"What about you?" she asked. "Delaney said you were engaged once."

His lips kicked up on one side, but the smile wasn't humorous or even sweetly melancholy. It was jaded. Very jaded. "Yeah, well, my fiancée was about as committed as your husband. The second a whiff of trouble came my way, she bailed."

Avery offered a sympathetic hum. She and Trace were kindred spirits in a lot of hidden ways. "Because of prison?"

"Well before that fully played out. She didn't wait to hear whether or not I received a prison sentence." His lips tightened and his brow pulled, creating a V of wrinkles between his beautiful, bright eyes. "About prison . . ." His gaze lifted to hers. "Is there anything you want to ask me?"

"That's sort of a strange question." Concern pulled at her lingering euphoria, and she pushed a hand through his hair and scratched the back of his neck the way he liked.

"You've never asked, and everyone's curious. Most more in a morbid way than a hey-what-was-that-like way. Sort of like they're looking for that shadow it left on my soul." His gaze held hers pointedly. "Do you wonder?"

"I know we didn't meet that long ago, and our pasts have been very different, but in a lot of ways I know you better now than I ever knew David. I feel like we understand each other. Like we're on the same page. So, no, I don't wonder."

The lines around his mouth and etched into his forehead faded, and he seemed to breathe easier. And the look in his eyes . . . It made it hard to breathe. A soft, deeply affectionate, foundation-altering look she'd once seen in David's eyes so very long ago, back when he'd still loved her.

"You're so"—he shook his head—"so, I don't know, wise or something. So mature for your age. Every twenty-five-year-old woman I know is worried about her nail polish and wants to talk about shopping."

Avery laughed, long and hard. "You make it sound downright revolting. Those are important things to most normal twenty-five-year-old women. I'm not normal. I had to grow up fast when my mom left and my dad got lost in a bottle. Then Delaney took the low road out of town. And getting married sure didn't solve anything. I ended up taking care of everything while David was gone—the bills, the house." She sighed. "I think I skipped from sixteen to thirty."

She threaded both hands into his hair and smiled. "Why are we talking about this crap when I could show you what I learned on the Internet?" She lifted her feet to his hips and tried to push his jeans down. "But you have to get out of these first."

"Internet?" he asked with a laugh. "Were you surfing porn when you should have been making truffles?"

"I wasn't surfing porn." Her tone came out appropriately chastising. "It was *soft* porn. And it was for *educational* purposes."

That made Trace burst out laughing. He wrapped his arms around her and rolled to his back. With his knees bent, clasping Avery's hips between his, he said, "Don't you worry, Cupcake—I'm going to want to experience every single thing you found interesting." He pushed a piece of her hair behind her ear, and the sweet move softened her heart a little more. "But I get so little time with you alone; I want to just soak you in. Besides, I haven't figured out what makes you tick yet."

She stroked his jaw. "Well, when you figure it out, let me know. In the meantime . . ." She wiggled out of his vise and scooted down until she could reach his waistband, where she finished unfastening his pants. "I have some playtime on my mind."

THIRTEEN

Trace closed his hands around hers before she managed to free his cock. He wanted her mouth around him in the worst way. Wanted to watch her watch him for cues as she practiced technique and went all out to please him.

Just the thought spread fire through his body. But first things first.

He sat up, sliding her off the bed and to her feet at the same time. Grabbing her waist, he lifted her against him and started for the bathroom.

She wrapped her legs around his hips, her arms around his neck, and looked at him with a quirky, confused little grin. "What are you doing?"

"Jumping in the shower. I've been working all day." He set her feet on the ground by the tub and kept his arm wrapped around her waist as he reached down to turn on the water. Then he turned back to her, brushed her hair off her face with both hands, and cupped her jaw. "And I love seeing your gorgeous body all wet."

She got that soft look in her eyes, the one that pinched his gut in the sweetest way; then she turned her head and kissed his palm. The same deep, pulling sensation he'd felt at the door that had kept him from leaving twisted inside him now, sweeter, stronger, more intense.

He dragged her mouth to his and kissed her with desire that doubled and tripled with each encounter. And like always, she opened to him, heart and soul. He could feel it. Feel the difference between what was happening with them and what had happened with other women.

Avery's hands stroked down his sides and around to his ass. After a quick squeeze, she pulled his wallet from the pocket, set it on the sink behind him, and returned to their kiss as she slipped her hands to the front and worked his pants open.

She had a unique way of making his mind blur. He could completely let go with her in a way he couldn't with other women. With Avery, he could just let things happen. He didn't have to control the situation, didn't have to orchestrate, didn't have to plan his exit strategy before they'd even gotten fully naked.

Because he didn't want to leave her.

And he didn't want her leaving him either.

A warning bell went off somewhere in the back of his mind. One his instincts told him to heed. But Avery pulled out of the kiss, pushed his jeans off his hips and down his legs. And before the denim had even hit the floor, her hands moved on his cock, stroking and tugging and squeezing.

A lightning strike of pleasure bolted through his shaft, his balls. He groaned at the pressure gathering at the base of his spine as he stepped out of his jeans.

Fuck the warning bell.

He turned Avery toward the shower, holding her arms to steady her as she stepped over the tub edge. Then he followed her in where he wrapped her tight from behind, pulling her close and burying his face against her neck.

Heaven.

All her warm, soft flesh up against him made him groan. Made his hands roam as the hot water bathed their bodies, caressing her flat belly, her trim waist, up her ribs, pausing to cup and squeeze her breasts.

"You're so beautiful," he murmured against her neck, kissing her there, then letting his hands slide down her body again. He wanted her so badly, he felt like he wanted to slide under her skin. But he wanted more than their wild and passionate sex. He wanted more of Avery. So he slowed down. Way down.

He purposely explored her body with his fingertips, stroking every curve, every dip, every swell. He cupped her ass and parted her cheeks, snuggling the length of his cock between the soft mounds. The billowy pressure automatically forced his hips forward, and he slid easily along her hot, wet skin.

Avery's moan coincided with his as she arched her back, forcing her ass back to meet his thrust. The delicious pressure spilled through him, and Trace growled, wrapping one arm low on her hips. Avery twisted enough to pull his head down, treating him to a searing, wet, hungry, openmouthed mating of tongues.

He groped for the liquid soap on a ledge, pulling out of the kiss to pour a generous amount in his palm, rub his hands together, and slide them down the front of Avery's body.

But she wasn't interested in getting clean or being pampered. Her blue eyes glinted with a determined and devilish spark as she slowly lowered to her knees. She scooped some body wash from his hand, rubbed it between hers then closed all ten fingers around his cock and slowly stroked base to tip.

Sensation exploded through his hips and up his spine. He clenched his teeth around a curse, planted one hand against the tile to keep his balance. "Fuck, Avery . . ."

Her smile grew. Turned even hotter. And she lowered her gaze to his cock, just inches from her nose where she stroked and squeezed, varying touch, strength, and technique. Just when he thought it could get no better, she let one hand dip to his balls and rubbed. The other continued to work his cock until the fingers of his free hand were in her hair and his body trembled.

"God damn . . ." he growled through clenched teeth. He wanted to tell her to stop while hoping she'd never stop. Then Avery's hands slipped from his body, leaving Trace throbbing, dizzy, and more than a little on the wild side.

She leaned sideways, allowing the water to rinse his body, then grinned up at him. "I think you're plenty clean now." Her gaze lowered to his cock as if assessing. "You make me so hungry."

Before Trace could catch his breath, Avery had his cock in her mouth, and the first stroke of her tongue over his head shot a jolt of exquisite current through his whole body, making him jerk. She slowly slid him deep, and opened her throat to tuck his head into the tight space. The combination of heat, wetness, pressure, not to mention the sight of her on her knees with his cock down her throat, had to be the most delirious thrill ever.

But it wasn't enough.

He combed his fingers through her hair and said, "Suck, baby."

Her lashes fluttered, and her eyes met his. Her mouth closed around his cock with gentle suction, and the tantalizing sensation stole his breath. Made his mouth drop open. Made an animalistic sound grind from his chest. His eyes fell closed, but he forced them open to watch the sexiest sight ever—Avery watching him, watching her, suck his cock.

"Fuck that's so good," he rasped, rocking his hips back and dragging his length from the heat of her mouth.

Avery immediately understood his need. She closed her eyes, gripped his ass with one hand, and pulled him into her, taking his cock all the way to the base, then adding suction as she moved back.

"God*damn*." His voice was as raw as his need. And as Avery went to work with the same single-minded determination she gave everything that mattered to her, Trace cupped her head with both hands, blown away by the way she used her mouth to bring him pleasure. His fingers clenched and released as his excitement mounted, tangling in her hair.

Her low moan of pleasure rumbled over him and made him realize just how close to the end of his control he'd slipped.

"Need more." Trace drew his cock from between her lips, and leaned down to pulled her to her feet a with rough, "Need all of you."

He reached behind her and hit the water controls, then lifted her into his arms. He grabbed his wallet on the way out, struggling to carry her to the bed while she was infusing him with wild, passionate, hungry kisses.

He braced one knee and one hand on the bed, lowering her to the fluffy white comforter, then dug a condom out of his wallet. "You look like an angel."

She pushed herself upright, thighs wide and wrapped around his, and took the condom from his hand. She ripped the package and rolled on the condom, her touch making Trace flinch and his hands fist. Then she looked up at him, her gaze both hot and . . . a little uncertain. "I may look like an angel, but I want you to love me like the devil."

Fire licked through his veins. His cock jumped, as if coming to attention. He wrapped an arm around her waist and pulled her onto his lap, holding her gaze while he positioned the head of his cock against her slick softness. Then he lowered her slowly, reveling in every soft inch of penetration. Of passion. Of possession.

The emotions that passed through her eyes seemed to grab on to his heart and sink in. Lust, awe, pleasure . . . Her expression showed more emotions than he could read. But the one that tied knots in his chest was the one spreading over her beautiful face once he filled her completely—a look of bliss, of fulfillment. Of something Trace could only label as . . . acceptance? As if she, too, felt the overwhelming power between them and was acquiescing to his need to take ownership of her—for as long as that lasted.

His chest filled with a sudden and unexpected mix of emotions that both terrified and excited him. But he couldn't think about those now. Not when his cock was buried in her wet heat. Not when her body belonged to him. Only him.

Trace pressed his forehead to hers, wrapped his arms low on her hips, and started to move with an overwhelming need to infuse her with pleasure. More pleasure than she'd ever known. More pleasure than she'd ever even believed possible. In some small corner of his mind, he was equating pleasure with longevity. As if he could provide enough sexual satisfaction to make up for all the other differences between them. As if giving her the best sex of her life would allow her to overlook the fact that he was an ex-con. As if physical pleasure alone could make her stay.

Trace shoved those irrational thoughts aside and purposely held her gaze as he moved slowly and thrust deep. Her every little gasp, every little chirp of surprised pleasure, thrilled him beyond reason. He let his hands roam, caressing her skin. Let his mouth travel, kissing her lips, her cheek, her neck. He whispered her name but little more. They didn't seem to need words to communicate this bond growing between them. He saw it in her eyes, tasted it in her kiss, felt it in her body. They were in sync. They were speaking on a deeper level than anything he'd ever known. And what he heard, body and soul, reached inside his chest and pulled hard.

As her pleasure rose, she tightened her arms around his neck and rocked her hips into his thrusts. The feel of her body undulating beneath his hands combined with the slam of pleasure with each thrust, was insanity inducing.

Soon his entire world, his entire existence became Avery and the sensual rock of her body, the feel of her pussy stroking and squeezing his cock, her quick breaths and moans of pleasure.

She leaned back, one arm still around his neck, and pressed the other to his thigh for leverage to lift her hips into his with more force.

Her brow furrowed in that borderline-climax, pleasure-pain expression that ticked up the heat in Trace's blood. He was already slick with sweat, but he pumped his hips harder, ridiculously pleased when her mouth dropped open and a sound of ecstasy floated from her chest.

"Yes, yes, yes . . ." she murmured.

"Do I feel good, Avery?"

Her eyes opened and fixed on his face, and she managed, "So good." But her eyes said, *Way more than good,* and her head dropped back on an, "Oh God . . ."

Her climax loomed, urging Trace to push things into high gear. He pumped harder, deeper, faster, losing himself in their perfect rhythm and the rise of his own pleasure.

And when Avery's head dropped back, her mouth open on a cry of release, her pussy tightening and gushing warmth over his cock, Trace let go, too, driving home for an orgasm that twisted every muscle and blew every brain cell. He pressed his face to her neck and breathed her in, surrounded himself in her skin and her scent to cement the moment in his memory as sensations rippled through his body, again and again.

When the orgasm released him, Trace's muscles gave, and he rolled to the bed with Avery. He kept most of his weight on his forearms so he didn't crush her while they caught their breath. But Trace's mind wouldn't start working properly again anytime soon. And he didn't give a goddamn, because he planned on lying in this bed all night with her—no escape plan in sight.

And, God, he was still awed at this explosive chemistry. This was just so . . . "Fucking amazing."

Her quick breaths bathed the skin of his chest, stuttering when she laughed softly. "So it's not just me. This isn't just wildly mind-blowing for me because I'm so inexperienced?"

Trace laughed and lifted his head from her shoulder to look down into her face. She was flushed and glowing, and the smile in her eyes made them sparkle in the moonlight. "No, baby. This is just that fucking amazing because of you and me, together."

She stretched out and relaxed into the bed beneath her, and the smile she gifted Trace was like a lantern in the darkness, offering him all the light he'd ever need.

She reached up and stroked his face, and that familiar softness warmed her eyes again. "I like the sound of that, you and me, together."

Trace's heart turned warm and gooey, and emotions rushed to the surface. Emotions and the fears that tagged along with them. For now, he pushed them away and reveled in the way this woman turned him inside out.

FOURTEEN

Avery floated to consciousness with light pressing against her eyelids. She was warm and comfortable and happy. Trace's muscular legs were still tangled with hers, his front side curved around her backside, his strong arm pinned across her waist, holding her against him.

She forced her eyes open and looked for the clock she'd positioned on the windowsill since she couldn't afford nightstands yet.

"It's only six." Trace's voice startled her. She twisted to look over her shoulder and found him propped up by his elbow, hair tousled, eyes bright, a grin tilting his mouth.

"Hey. You look like you've been up awhile." She relaxed into the pillow again and frowned. "What are you doing?"

"Watching you sleep." His grin grew. "You talk in your sleep—you know that, right?"

"I do not."

He laughed. "Yeah, you do."

She turned a little more and rubbed his erection tucked against her ass. "I'm not sure I like that. What did I say?"

His hand slid back and forth over her stomach, and his hips rocked restlessly against hers, creating a familiar heat between her legs. "I don't know. I was a little distracted."

She wrapped her arm up and around his neck, pulling him down for a good-morning kiss. Their tongues lazily stroked, and Trace sucked at her lips, then growled a moan and pressed his face to her neck. "Warning: if you don't get up now, you won't be getting up for a while."

She pushed her hips back and into his erection and murmured against his temple, "I'm good with that."

His mouth opened against her neck with a groan of pleasure and relief. "Baby, you are such a dream."

The hand at her stomach slid up her body, between her breasts, and cupped her chin as he took the kiss deeper.

A heavy knock at the front door downstairs jerked both of them out of the bliss. They stared at each other for a second, as if each was wondering whether they'd really heard that.

"What?"

The knock came again, louder, followed by the deep, serious voice of someone calling Avery's name. Alarm snaked down her spine, and Avery sat up, looking around the floor for clothes. "Shit."

"Who in the hell is that?" Trace swung his feet off the bed and pulled on his jeans.

"I don't know," she said, frustrated as she followed Trace's lead. "But I'm sick of one fire after another around here. I'd like one full night of relaxation for a damn change."

He yanked his shirt over his head and grinned at her. "Then you'd better stop hanging around me, sugar. I have no intention of letting you relax."

"Your brand of relaxation I'll take any night of the week." She ran her hands through her hair and dragged on the jeans and the T-shirt she'd had on last night before she headed downstairs in bare feet.

"I'm *coming*, for God's—" She hit the bottom of the stairs and looked toward the door. Through the glass all she saw was blue. A mass of navy-blue uniforms. Cops. Four of them, standing on her porch.

Trace almost stumbled over her and caught her around the waist, managing to keep both of them from hitting the floor. "Baby, what—?"

Rap, rap, rap. "Open the door, Avery."

Deputy Tom Potter, a man in his late fifties who'd been a family friend for years, was surrounded by three other deputies Avery didn't know.

Fury and embarrassment flared in a hot streak through her chest, and she started toward the door. "Austin, that piece of—"

"Avery." Trace's direct tone grated on her already raw nerves, and she spun on him. His gaze had hardened into an expression she'd never seen before. "This is bigger than Austin."

Rap, rap, rap. "Avery."

She ignored Tom. While David had become an expert at obeying authority, Avery had discovered in all those years fending for herself, there was a time to obey and there was a time to resist. She'd also discovered that often ignoring, combatting, or avoiding authority got her a lot further than trying to go directly through it. "Trace?"

His eyes moved back to her and he nodded. "Open the door; then step aside. This isn't about you."

"How do you know?"

"Avery, honey," Tom said through the glass. "Don't make me break this brand-new door. Alice'll have me in the doghouse for months."

Tom's reference to his wife and one of Avery's best customers via Wildly Artisan melted her anger like a flame to ice. Avery continued to the door, unlocked it, and opened it a foot. "What's this about, Tom?"

He offered her a folded group of papers. "I'm sorry, Avery. We have a warrant to search the premises."

"For what?"

One of the other deputies pushed the door open, Tom stepped in and urged Avery aside with a gentle hand on her arm. The other three swept in, and one started calling directions.

"Step aside, sweetheart," Tom said. "Let us do our job and we'll get out of here."

"Tom—" Her threat was cut short by the sight of more deputies climbing the stairs and flooding into her shop. Deputies that included Austin. Fury exploded, wiping out any ability to think rationally, and she broke out of Tom's hold, starting for Austin. "You piece of *shit*—"

She lunged for him but never made contact. Trace caught her around the waist with one arm and pulled her back.

"No, no, no," Trace crooned in her ear, wrapping her in his arms and holding her tight.

She glared at Austin, who never flinched, never blinked. He didn't look pleased or annoyed or angry. He looked blank. Like he couldn't care less about her outburst.

"Just let them look," Trace said. "They'll be gone before you know it."

"Let go." She elbowed Trace until he released her; then she turned on Tom, just this side of hysterical. "If they break or ruin one thing, Tom, *one thing*, I swear I will plant my ass on Holland's desk and *handcuff* myself there until the city *pays for it*."

"Now calm down, Avery. All my deputies have strict instructions not to damage anything and to put everything back the way they found it."

Two deputies she didn't recognize approached and addressed Trace. "Mr. Hutton, come over here please."

"What?" Avery swung that direction. "Why?"

Trace put up a hand to Avery. She didn't know if it was meant to reassure her or shut her up, but it did neither. And when she turned back to Tom to demand answers, she saw Zane climb out of a patrol car and jog toward the building.

"Thank God." She pulled out of Tom's grip and went to the door. "Zane," she said before he'd even reached the porch. "Please tell me what the hell is going on."

He put his arm around her shoulders and said, "I don't know, but I'm going to find out."

When they stepped back into the room, Avery froze at the sight of Trace with his hands pressed to the stainless steel countertop. His feet were spread wide, and one cop patted him down while the other stood watch. Her stomach turned icy, and in that flicker of an instant she saw her whole world shift. She imagined Trace being sent back to prison. Imagined herself as one of those women who spent their weekends in cement visitation rooms, talking to their boyfriend through glass over a phone.

"You shouldn't be here," Tom told Zane, drawing Avery back to the present. She turned away from Trace, now standing but still guarded by the two cops. "You're not even supposed to be on duty for another hour."

"You should have at least advised me," Zane said. His blue eyes, lighter and grayer than Trace's, were dark with anger this morning, but he softened his voice when he asked Avery, "What happened with JT?"

Avery crossed her arms over her middle, suddenly cold, dizzy, and nauseous. She felt like she'd missed a whole chunk of the conversation. "What about him?"

Tom glanced at a small notebook in his hand. "He alleges Trace was selling drugs out of this location."

"Bullshit," Avery bit out immediately. "JT's pissed because he got caught breaking into the café yesterday morning. Trace had the good sense to fire him, and JT's just trying to get revenge."

"Did you report that break-in?" Tom asked.

"No," she said, struggling to justify what probably looked to others like a lapse in judgment. "I came in so early, JT didn't get a chance to take anything."

"When's the last time you saw JT?" Tom asked.

Avery's head felt sluggish. "Uh . . . yesterday." She tightened the cross of her arms, unable to get warm. "Before he and Trace went into Santa Rosa to pick up supplies."

Tom pulled a photo from his pocket and showed it to Avery. JT stared back at her, with a split lip and a bruise beneath one eye. "Did he look like this then?"

Her brow tightened. "No. So what?"

Tom tucked the picture away. "So he's saying that he and Mr. Hutton got in a fight over drug proceeds, and that's why Trace fired him."

Avery huffed a disgusted breath and rolled her eyes. "For God's sake, Tom, JT just got out of prison. Trace has been a model citizen for half a dozen years. Who are you going to believe?"

"Mr. Hutton," Tom said, "lift up your shirt."

Avery gave Tom a *where-the-hell-did-that-come-from?* look, then glanced at Trace, who pulled his shirt up, exposing bruises across his abdomen.

"How'd you get those bruises, Mr. Hutton?" Tom asked.

"Jesus Christ," Avery said, her anger bursting into the growing tension in the room. "He got those on the roof."

Tom's gaze cut to Avery. "Did you see him incur the injury, Avery?"

"No, but—"

"Let's go talk outside." Zane cut her off and steered Avery toward the front door.

Avery resisted. "I don't want to leave Trace—"

"He's a big boy," Zane said, pushing her out the door and onto the porch. "I promise he can take care of himself."

Outside, standing among all the police units, Avery's mind started to fragment. News of this stupid raid or search or whatever it was would be all over town by noon. Her mind whirled around the rumors it would stir and the problems it could cause. She worried over the implications it would carry and the impact it would have on business.

Avery reached in her back pocket for her phone, but it wasn't there. She stopped and turned toward the building again. "My phone . . ."

"You can't go back in right now."

"I just want my phone." Her voice broke, and she pressed her fist to her forehead to keep herself together. "I want to call Delaney and Phoebe. Shit." She dropped her hand and looked up at Zane. With a lowered voice she asked, "Does Trace need a lawyer? Should I call someone for him?"

"If they don't find any drugs in your building, Trace won't need a lawyer."

"They aren't going to find—" The ice re-formed in her gut. "Oh, shit. What if . . . what if JT left some there?"

"Why would he do that?"

Avery threw her arms in the air. "Shit, I don't know." She paced in a circle, then returned her gaze to Zane but pointed to the café, livid. "Is this JT or is this Austin? 'Cause I've got shit on Aus—" She sucked a breath and swiveled toward the building. "My phone." She spun back toward Zane. "You need to get my phone. I have a picture on there that Austin doesn't want anyone to see."

Zane squinted toward the building, his expression stern. His phone rang, and, without taking his gaze off the café, he answered, "Yeah."

A high-pitched, quick-speaking female sputtered on the other end of the line. Zane lowered his gaze to the ground. "Slow down, Gram, I can't . . . No, he was fine when Harlan dropped him off . . . Well, how in the hell did he . . . No, I have no idea." Zane put his free hand on his head and turned away, pacing a few steps before he stopped and heaved a sigh. "Christ, we can't afford an emergency-room visit."

Now Avery was caught between Zane's drama and her own. But she could handle only one at a time, which meant she had to solve this mini-crisis within the major crisis before she'd be able to think straight.

She started back toward the café, climbed the stairs, and stepped inside. Her gaze fell on Trace where he sat in one of the dining chairs, leaning forward, elbows on knees, hands clasped, gaze on the floor. His shoulders were hunched. His jaw ticked. And Avery's heart twisted.

"Avery," Tom said, interrupting his conversation with another deputy, "you need to stay outside."

Trace's head came up, and his eyes met hers, but the man she knew didn't live there. The man in those eyes was broken and dark. And it absolutely killed her to see such a good man unjustly dragged so far down.

She turned her gaze on Tom. "No, I don't. Show me in the warrant where it says I have to stay outside."

He heaved a sigh. "I'm sorry, I phrased that wrong. It would be better if you stayed outside."

"I need my phone. It's upstairs."

He gestured that direction. "Go on and get it."

When she turned and glanced at Trace, he was scrubbing his face with both hands; then he threaded them through his hair and clasped them at the back of his neck, never lifting his eyes to hers again.

She jogged up the stairs with a fiery boulder in the pit of her stomach and tears burning her eyes. When she reached the landing and turned toward the apartment, she saw Austin looking through her dresser drawers.

Fear streaked through her chest. She may never use the picture, but she wanted it as insurance, because Delaney had proven holding insurance over Austin's head kept him in line. And because Avery needed every little thread of power she could get right now—real or imagined—to help her feel in control.

As soon as she stepped through the unfinished doorway, Austin straightened. "You can't be in here."

"Yes, I can." She stepped to the head of her bed and scanned the floor for her phone where she'd left it, but it wasn't there. Avery crouched and looked underneath.

"Hey." Austin closed in. "Get out of there."

Her heart pounded in her throat, and she dropped to her knees for a better look, growing a little frantic when she didn't see her phone. She swept her hand along the floor underneath the bed.

Austin gripped her bicep. "I said—"

Metal touched her fingers. Avery's eyes closed, and her breath whooshed out in relief. Austin jerked her arm, pulling her partially to her feet. She wobbled off balance, falling sideways and hitting the wall.

"Hey man," the other cop said, frowning at Austin. "Take it easy."

Avery straightened and pulled her arm from Austin's grip. "That's just his normal, everyday abusive style—isn't it, Austin?"

His lip twitched into a sneer of a smile, and he lifted his chin to the bed and its disarray of sheets. "And this is yours. Fuckin' the bad boys now? I tried to tell you about him." He shook his head with that superior smirk. "Guess you turned out more like Delaney than I thought."

His reference to Delaney's slutty reputation as a youth sleeping with the worst of the worst to get any morsel of attention from their father struck Avery funny considering how fantastic Delaney had turned out.

She huffed a laugh, lifted the phone, and waved it. "And you turned out a lot more like our daddies."

Austin evidently didn't care for the comparison to Avery's dad, an abusive drunk, or Austin's own father, the narcissistic bully who ran Wildwood and who'd threatened Delaney in an attempt to run her out of town.

Austin's expression went from annoyed to pissed in an instant. He came at her, and Avery braced herself, clutching her phone, but the other deputy grabbed Austin by the bulletproof vest and hauled him back a step. "Dude, cool the fuck out." Then to Avery he said, "Ma'am, it would be better if you waited downstairs. We're almost done here."

"Yes, sir." And she trotted down the steps.

At the bottom, Tom asked, "Did you get your phone?"

"Yes, thank you." When Trace kept his hands threaded in his hair without looking up, her heart started to numb around the edges. She could only hurt so long before she started to shut down. She wandered toward the door, doing her best to ignore all the blue uniforms messing with her stuff. Before she exited, she met Tom's gaze and said, "Not that it makes much difference, because Trace wasn't selling drugs here, but he had those bruises the day before he even hired JT."

"You said you didn't see the incident that caused them," Tom said.

"No, but I saw the bruises."

"And when would you have had occasion to see those?"

God, she was *so* sick of being questioned. "We're *sleeping together*," she said loudly, deliberately, so no one would have a question as to what she'd said or meant. "I have occasion."

Trace swore softly, and his hands slid out of his hair to cover his face.

Avery's chest pinched. She'd been able to push away the embarrassment over exposing her sexual habits to stand up for him. But his reaction made it wash back in on a tidal wave, creating a whirlpool of emotions. Anger vibrated in her voice when she asked, "Any other questions, Tom?"

"Not right now."

She walked out of her café, head high, but she avoided meeting anyone's gaze. She wasn't strong enough to battle judgment in the face of Trace's reaction.

At the bottom of the stairs, now confused, hurt, disillusioned, and still scared, she paused near Zane.

"Did you get it?" he asked.

"Yeah. What's wrong at home?"

"My dad. Somewhere between the time I picked him up from Harlan's and put him back to bed so he could sleep until Gram got there to do their regular morning routine, Dad figured out how to get past the locks and went on a walkabout—right into the construction zone three blocks away."

For God's sake. Avery was about to blow a gasket. "Is he okay? What happened?"

"Luckily—I don't know how, but luckily—he came out of it with minor injuries. He's at the ER waiting on X-rays and stitches, and Gram has a really important echocardiogram she needs to get to, so she can't stay with him. After all you've already been through with our family, I hate to ask, but I'm in a real bind."

"What do you need?"

"Would you mind going to the ER and sitting with him? Not only is he the biggest baby on the planet, but stress seems to make his memory worse. He's going to need someone to hold his hand and remind him of what's happening and why. I need to stay here and make sure everything stays kosher for Trace. Get him an attorney if he ends up needing one. But someone needs to be with Dad."

All the tasks on her to-do list went to hell, and a terrifying sense of impending failure tightened her chest. At this stage of her business there were two priorities—quality and follow-through. If either of those faltered, she'd lose current customers and damage the possibility of potential customers. And when she'd spent every penny she had and was counting every dollar she earned, every customer's opinion of her business was vital.

"Of course. Can you have Pearl come relieve me after her appointment? I've got a full day on my plate."

"Absolutely." Zane squeezed her shoulder. "Thank you so much."

She glanced at the café, and a million nerve endings sizzled. "Would you mind getting my keys? They're under the counter on a shelf in the kitchen. And my boots would be nice. If I go in there again, I might claw Austin's eyes out."

Zane broke into a grin, nodded, and headed inside.

Now, standing alone in the parking lot, barefoot, commando, and watching cops swarm her café, powerless to help Trace, her guts churned with stress and fear. And made Avery realize just how much of her heart was wrapped up in there—in both the business and the man.

A man who evidently hadn't wanted to be pinned down as her lover. All his talk about being willing to keep their affair secret the night before to benefit her now looked more like a twisted way of pushing it under the rug for him.

Which begged the question: Why was she settling for someone who didn't want her?

Again.

◆ ◆ ◆

Trace might have been sitting in the café, but he may as well have been back in prison. That's where he was headed. He had no doubts. Between all these prowling cops and JT's accusations, drugs would show up somewhere. Drugs that would put Trace back in prison.

Pearl and Zane would have to juggle responsibility for Dad until Medicare came through. If Medicare came through. And another disruption in his dad's life would only make the dementia worse.

Trace kept focusing on those issues because he couldn't face the repercussions of how this would affect Avery. Of how it would taint everything she'd worked so hard to achieve.

Trace curled his fingers into fists and pressed them against eyes burning with tears. Tears of fury, self-hate, regret . . .

"All right, Mr. Hutton." Deputy Potter's voice crawled down Trace's spine. A numb barrier of protection expanded in his gut, preparing to be sucked into the prison system again. And this time, as a second offender, who knew for how long? He certainly couldn't afford a decent lawyer. "You're free to go. I'm sorry for the inconvenience."

Free to go?

Trace didn't respond. He didn't even *understand.*

"If you've touched something in here," Potter called to no one in particular, "it had better be exactly, and I mean *exactly*, where you found it. The Harts are family friends, and my wife is especially fond of Avery, so unless you want every one of your mamas hearing from Alice, you'd best all double-check your work. Now wrap it up and hit the streets."

Trace floated in a cautious state of disbelief, but within five minutes, the last of the deputies filed out the door, including Austin, and all the cruisers vanished from the parking lot. All but one.

Trace pushed to his feet, went to the stairs, and called a hopeful, "Avery?"

"She's not here."

He turned to his brother's voice, feeling shaky and uncertain. "Where is she? And what the fuck just happened here? You know as well as I do that I should be in handcuffs right now."

"JT obviously thought up that story after the opportunity to plant drugs had passed. And Austin knows there are cameras here. He wouldn't risk planting evidence."

Trace's breath whooshed out, the relief so profound he slumped against the wall, bent at the waist, and pressed his hands to his knees. "Jesus Christ," he muttered. "I thought I was going back."

"I keep telling you criminals are criminals because they're idiots. That's why I ended up a cop."

Trace lifted his head and glared at his brother. "You ended up a cop because I kicked your ever-loving ass until I shook the stupid loose."

That made Zane laugh hard.

"This isn't funny."

"Ah, no, you're right, it's not," Zane said easing from the laughter. "But man, you had me scared as shit, bro. It feels good to laugh."

Trace straightened, but the tension in his gut had wound so tight he was going to lose the bile burning his stomach. "Where's Avery?"

"Dude, you need to get your little head out of your ass and start thinking with your big head for a change. After what you just put Avery through, I doubt she's very interested in talking to you. In fact, you'll be lucky if she doesn't fire you."

Trace closed his eyes and pressed his back against the wall. God, he couldn't feel worse.

"Seriously, Trace, sleeping with her? Of all the women you could screw around with, you have to go and mess with Avery? That's just . . ." Zane's face pressed into a scowl of deep disapproval. "I don't even know. It's like defiling an angel or something."

"Fuck you." He lifted his chin to the door. "Get out."

Zane started that direction. "Oh, and when you finally get your lazy, hedonistic ass dressed, maybe you could head over to the ER when your busy schedule permits."

Zane paused at the door, looked back at Trace, and explained what had happened with their father.

"What the . . ." Trace pushed off the wall with dread tingling down his spine. "*How* in the *hell*?"

"No idea. That must be where I got my B and E skills. He's a little banged up, but he'll be fine. Gram had to go to an appointment, so I'm sure he'd appreciate seeing you. And you'll have to rethink those locks today."

Before Zane closed the door, Trace yelled, "Could you at least tell me where Avery went?"

"She's at the ER, watching after Dad until one of us can get there to relieve her. Think you can take care of that? And while you're there, do the right thing and break it off with Avery. She didn't sign up for this bullshit."

The sound of the door latching reached Trace; then the café fell silent. The ramifications of everything that had happened in the last twelve hours lay heavily on his shoulders. But what kept pushing to the forefront was Avery and the intensity of her inner strength. How she could stand in the middle of a room swarming with male cops and not only blatantly challenge them but challenge them while *defending him.* Then throwing herself under the bus by admitting to sleeping with him? And now she was at the hospital taking care of his father when she had a million other things to do and sure as hell didn't owe Trace a damn thing.

Zane was right. Avery hadn't signed up for this, and she deserved so much more. So much better.

"Do the right thing and break it off with Avery . . ."

Zane's words echoed in his head as he turned for the stairs. "Fuck."

Trace moved into the bedroom and tried like hell not to look at the bed and all its pristine white sheets tangled from their passion the night before. He felt like his heart had migrated to the pit of his stomach and beat there, one painful throb after another.

"Do the right thing and break it off with Avery . . ."

He pushed into socks and boots, hurried back out front, climbed into his truck, and started for the emergency room, all while worrying what his past had cost Avery today and thinking Zane was right. Trace *should* break things off with Avery.

FIFTEEN

Avery sat on the edge of George's gurney in the emergency room with a handful of cards, humming "Silent Night." She was scraping the bottom of the barrel for songs that would keep George calm.

She pulled the ace of diamonds from her hand and laid it on the six of diamonds on the pile. "Your turn," she told George. "You need a six or a diamond."

He put down a ten of spades. "Where'd you say Trace was?"

"Working at my café," Avery said for at least the twentieth time since she'd arrived. She drew a card from the pile for George and slipped it into his hand of cards. "He would have come, but he was caught in the middle of something. I'm sure he'll be here as soon as he can." She put down a ten of spades. "Your turn. You need a ten or a spade."

George heaved a sigh and stared blankly at his hand. "Oh, honey, I'm sorry. I think I'm too tired to play anymore."

Avery closed her fan of cards, then did the same for George's. "You've had a rough morning." She squeezed his hand. "Put your head back and relax. You should be able to go home soon."

She straightened the deck, slipped it into the cardboard box, and set the box on the counter for the nurse who'd brought them in. When she returned her gaze to George, his eyes were still open, and the one on the side where he'd needed stitches along his cheekbone was developing a bruise.

"It isn't like Trace to be late," George said.

Avery lowered the head of the gurney and pulled the blanket higher on George's chest. "Are you warm enough?"

"He's such a good boy. Zane probably drug him off somewhere again."

Avery glanced at the time on her phone, noticed there was no message from Trace, and pulled a chair up alongside George's bed. She curled her fingers over his to check their temperature, but when he closed his fingers around hers, she left her hand in his.

"It isn't like Trace to be late," he said again. "Zane probably drug him off somewhere again," he repeated. "Do you think we oughta call school?"

She squeezed his hand. "No, I'm sure he's fine." To redirect his mind, she said, "Tell me about Trace."

George's gaze met hers, and his mouth quivered into a smile. "Oh, he's such a good boy." His gaze drifted to the ceiling. "And smart. That boy could be anything he wants to be."

"What does he want to be?"

"An architect. Wants to build *big* skyscrapers, like the ones in San Francisco and New York."

Avery smiled. "Big dreams. Why didn't he become an architect?"

Avery swore George aged ten years right in front of her eyes. "My fault," he muttered, almost unintelligible. "All my fault."

She leaned forward and squeezed his hand. "Why, George? Why was it your fault?"

He just shook his head and closed his eyes.

Avery released a sigh, uncurled her fingers from his hand, and sat back. *Whatever.* It didn't matter. She didn't know how long he'd had dementia. Maybe that had interfered with Trace's ability to go to school.

The curtain across the door swayed, drawing Avery's attention to the doctor entering again. She didn't look much older than Avery, which made her wonder what she could have done with her life if she'd made different decisions back when she'd been seventeen.

Water under the bridge. And lesson learned. She didn't need to make the same mistake with another man.

"Did you get ahold of Zane?" Avery asked.

"I did. He's signed off on everything, so as soon as we finish up the paperwork, you'll be free to take Mr. Hutton home."

George mumbled something unintelligible but didn't open his eyes, so Avery told the doctor, "Great. Thank you."

"No problem. The nurse will be in with instructions on wound care and bandaging. It's pretty straightforward. I understand that you may only be with him a few hours today, so if you can just pass on that information to his caretakers, that would be great."

"Absolutely."

"Unfortunately, we aren't going to be able to send him home with any prescription pain medications. He'll have to stick with Tylenol or Advil."

Avery winced. "I sat through those stitches. Isn't his face going to hurt like hell when the numbing wears off?"

The doctor's sympathetic gaze slid toward George's cheek, and she lifted her brows. "Probably, but, unfortunately, his history of addiction prohibits us from prescribing narcotics."

Avery chuckled. "Sorry. I just remember my dad, who taught me the meaning of falling-down drunk. He was always hurting himself and his doctors still gave him prescription meds."

"They're definitely both addictions, but since Mr. Hutton's addiction began with pain meds, he's at an extremely high risk of abusing those again. Couple that with his dementia, and sending him home with pain meds that he could easily become addicted to, yet not remember how many he'd taken, could be deadly. I'll send him home with some stronger doses of Tylenol and Advil. If he's in considerable pain, try using the two together for a synergistic effect. I'll make sure the nurse explains everything and . . ."

Avery's mind slipped out of the conversation, caught somewhere back around "since Mr. Hutton's addiction began with pain meds." She'd heard Trace had stayed with Pearl on and off over the years because of his mother's cancer and his father's trouble with the law. For some reason, she'd thought George had been using street drugs back when Trace had been younger. Or maybe she'd just assumed. But she certainly hadn't known he had an addiction.

"Ms. Hart?" the doctor said.

"Hmm, what? Yes, sorry. Long morning."

"I was just saying that we'll give him something to help him sleep, which should get him through the worst of the pain."

"Thank you so much."

The woman slipped through the curtains, and George stirred. "Pain," he mumbled, as if repeating the doctor. His eyelids fluttered open, his blue eyes hazy. "Need something for pain."

"The doctor's sending us home with—"

"Not that shit," he said, irritated. "Where's Trace? Trace knows where to get the good stuff. We don't need no doctor. Trace'll just find Chip."

Chip.

The name flooded ice through Avery's veins. Chip was the straw that had broken her family apart. Her mother may have deserted them, her father may have been an alcoholic, but she and Delaney and Chloe and Phoebe had been together. They'd had one another to lean on. To depend on.

Until Chip.

Until Chip pushed Austin's brother too hard in a bar fight. Until Austin's brother's death had been blamed on Delaney, even though she'd had no part in the event. Then Delaney, the one dependable constant in their lives, the family glue, had left town, and everything had started to unravel.

But George's reference to Chip didn't make sense. He had to mean a different Chip.

"George," Avery said. "What do you mean, Trace will find Chip? Chip who?"

"That boy your sister's seeing."

Holy shit. He did mean the same Chip.

"The one your daddy hates." George sighed and closed his eyes. "He's always got the best stuff, and Trace always knows where to find him. Don't need no doctor. Just need Trace. It's not like Trace to be late. You think I oughta call school?"

Avery huffed a frustrated breath and rolled her eyes. *Forget it.* Chip and Trace's drug use were in the past.

Now, if only Avery's problems could join them.

Trace was guided back into the ER by a woman he'd dated when they were both about sixteen. She was still very pretty and now very married and very pregnant. And as he walked toward Room Six, where his father was waiting to be released, he realized just how much of his life he'd missed out on over the last decade.

Approaching the door, he heard voices and paused, glancing through the partially open drape. His father lay on the gurney, eyes closed, but he was flailing against Avery as she tended to him.

"George Hutton, stop it right now." The words might have been stern, but her voice was soft, and she gently manipulated his hands out of her way to lay something ever so lightly over the cut on his cheek. "I know it's cold, but it's going to keep the swelling down."

Trace's gut stung as if he'd swallowed a horde of bees, and he took a step back. He thought he'd prepared himself on the drive over, but now that she was within touching distance again, he realized he wasn't ready to face her. He didn't know what to say. "I'm sorry" wasn't going to cut it, and he wouldn't insult her by even trying to smooth over a rift like the one ripped open between them with words repeated so often they meant nothing.

"There you go," she crooned to his dad, one arm arched over his head to hold an ice pack on his cheek, while her free hand held his to keep it still. She sighed and laid her cheek on his forehead, but continued to murmur to him as if he were a child. "There you go. Relax. This will be numb in just a minute. Lucky you, you won't even remember any of it."

That made Trace smile. But with the smile came a rush of unexpected emotions he'd been trying to keep in check—fear, loss, guilt, sadness. Before he knew how, his eyes burned with tears for the second time that day.

He stepped away from the opening, pressed a hand to the wall, and squeezed the sting from his eyes. Then he took a deep breath, straightened, and stepped past the curtain.

Avery had closed her eyes, and Trace was overwhelmed by the sight of her so lovingly caring for a man she barely knew, all because he was Trace's father. He was trying to figure out how one person could have so much good in them when Avery's lashes fluttered, and she opened her eyes to check the ice pack.

And just as her gaze darted to him, he said, "Hey," as softly as he could.

But his father still heard Trace's voice and opened his eyes. "Is that Trace? Is my boy here?"

"I'm right here." He stepped up to the other side of the gurney and put a hand on his father's arm. "Hold still. Avery's trying to help you."

His muddy-blue eyes rolled toward her. "Oh, Avery." He sighed. "Such a sweet girl."

Then, with one hand on Trace's arm and one hand curled into Avery's, George drifted into sleep again.

Avery sighed deeply, a sound of pure relief. Trace new exactly how she felt, because he felt it every time he handed over care of his father to his grandmother or Zane. But when she lifted her gaze to his, her blue eyes, always so open and light, were definitely different.

"I guess they cleared everything up at the café?" she asked, quiet but cool and businesslike.

Trace experienced yet another wave of profound relief and nodded.

She did the same. "I'm glad." She picked up some papers from the counter and set them on the blanket covering George's legs. "He has the cut on his cheek that needed stitches. Otherwise he just has a few superficial cuts and bruises. Doctor says he'll be sore for a while. These are his discharge papers. We were just waiting for someone to help us get him to my car. They should be here any minute."

"Avery—" God, he didn't know what to say.

"You're going to need some time with him, I know. It's fine. I'm going to postpone the café's opening."

"No—"

"It's no big deal. I've been pushing for this opening too hard. It's cost us all too much—"

He reached across the gurney and curled his hand over hers. "Avery."

With her eyes downcast, she pulled in a shaky breath and shook her head but didn't speak and didn't pull her hand away. With her lips pressed tight, blinking quickly, Trace knew she was fighting tears, and the sight clawed at him.

"I want to say something that will make today go away," he said. "I know it was wrong to hire JT. I know I was wrong to let such a piece of shit near you. I know this has cost you rumors that could hurt your business—"

She jerked her hand away, and the look she leveled at him, so hurt, so angry, cut straight through his heart. "I don't give a shit about JT. I don't give a shit about rumors."

The nurse stepped in, took one look at them, and murmured, "Um . . . I'll come back." She exited, closing the drape quietly behind her.

"The only thing I gave a shit about this morning was *you*," she continued, her voice low and harsh. Tears slipped over her lashes, and she broke his gaze to push them away. "I don't ask for much, Trace, but I deserve truth and respect."

He pushed a hand into his hair as his mind spiraled backward. When *hadn't* he given her both?

"I was going to sleep with you anyway," she went on. "We'd already set up the ground rules, for God's sake. But to change them only to turn around and yank the rug out from under my feet?"

"Whoa, whoa, whoa." He rounded the end of the gurney and gripped her waist, holding her tight even when she tried to twist away from him. "No. Tell me what the fuck you're talking about."

She wouldn't look at him. "I'm talking about you being ashamed of sleeping with me." Her bluster faltered, and she was shaking. "Afraid I'd ruin your image?"

He cupped her chin and lifted her eyes to his. "Baby, I would *never* be ashamed of sleeping with you."

She got that stubborn jut to her chin, and tears glazed her eyes. "Then why did you swear and cover your face when I said it earlier?" Her cheeks got red-hot, and her words started spilling out again. "I was trying to help. I wanted them to know—"

Trace stopped her mouth with a kiss. She responded at first, then jerked her head back and pushed at his chest. "Forget it. That's not going to work anymore."

So he kissed her again. Cupping her face he sipped at her lips, licked at her tears. Then he pulled back and pressed his fingers to her mouth so she couldn't start talking again.

"Avery, you're the hometown sweetheart starting a new business with every last penny to your name, and you stood in the middle of a room full of the worst gossips on the planet and admitted you were sleeping with the ex-con playboy who is still struggling years later to scrape his life back together, and who was, at that moment, suspected of a new crime. That's why I swore and covered my face. It wasn't exactly a glowing testimonial to your better judgment."

"Well . . ." She was wearing the cutest little pout, half-belligerent, half-embarrassed. "Screw you," she said with absolutely no heat, "and the horse you rode in on."

For an instant, all Trace's pain and fear fell away, and he laughed, pulling her close. "You are so damn adorable."

Avery relaxed into him, wrapped her arms around his waist, and pressed her face against his chest. And she broke into a combination of tears and relieved laughter. "You scared the living shit out of me, Trace."

"Knock, knock." The nurse peeked around the curtain. "Is it safe to come in now?" She glanced from Avery to Trace and smiled. "Aw, all made up. I knew a little time and talking would fix everything. Usually does." She pushed the drape back and introduced the man at her side. "This is Tanner. He's going to help you get your father to your car."

Avery followed Trace to his house, and together, with George's arms around their shoulders, they walked him inside and put him to bed.

She stood in the hallway, watching how great Trace was with his dad—positioning his pillow so it didn't press on his cheek, covering him to make sure he was warm, waiting until he was sure George was asleep before he backed slowly from the room and closed the door with a featherlight touch.

Her mind was spiraling so fast, thoughts clicking and forming before she could process them, that the words rolled out of her mouth before she'd thought them through. "You'd make a great dad."

He looked at her as if she'd invited him to the pumpkin patch or something equally as out of left field.

"The way you are with him," she clarified, pressing her hands behind her as she leaned against the wall. "I can tell you'd make a great dad."

An awkward sensation heated her face, and she decided space might be the best plan for them right now. "I need to get back to the café. My day has spiraled out of control." She turned and started toward the kitchen. "I should go over his care and medications with you. He's got antibiotics and pain meds."

"No." The tight, obstinate tone drew Avery's gaze. Trace was frowning at the plastic bag she'd brought in from the car. "He shouldn't have been given pain meds."

"The nurse said they were just—"

"Just nothing." He shook the bag's contents onto the kitchen table. Among the bandages were three pill bottles. He picked up one.

"Those are antibiotics," she said.

"These," he held up the other two bottles, "are the pain meds?"

"Yes, but they're not—"

"They're not staying in this house." Without reading the labels, he turned the tops and lifted his hand over the sink.

Avery stepped up and put a hand on his arm. Her mind spun with unfinished thoughts. The nurse's words floated into her head. "Since Mr. Hutton's addiction began with pain meds . . ." Immediately followed by George's words, "He's always got the best stuff, and Trace always knows where to find him."

A tingle started in the pit of her stomach and radiated through her belly. Her mind was split between two possibilities for his actions.

Either Trace was also addicted to the meds and had to get the temptation out of reach or . . .

"Trace, that's a waste. Those would have been good to have around. With you fallin' off roofs, you could probably use them now and then."

"I don't make a habit of falling off roofs." He pulled from her grasp and poured the pills down the drain. "Besides, they make me sick. I'd rather be in pain than puking. And if he gets his hands on this . . ." He turned on the water and flipped on the garbage disposal. Then turned everything off with a satisfied, "That shit's dust."

Avery's mouth still hung open with unfinished words.

And she knew.

Knew without any doubt.

He'd just explained everything with perfect clarity.

Avery started laughing. It wasn't funny. But, oh, it was. Because she understood. She understood so perfectly it brought tears to her eyes. She put a hand over her mouth, trying to control the spill of emotion.

Trace turned to her with surprise and alarm. "Avery? What . . . ? Ah, shit. What the hell did I do now?" He came to her, slid his arms around her, and frowned. "Are you laughing or crying?"

"Both." She shook her head and pointed to the sink. "I just saw myself at twelve pouring my dad's whiskey and vodka and brandy down the drain. Oh my God, I got such a beating for that. Left a scar on my shoulder."

Trace's expression went slack. He eased her back to arm's length as Avery kept talking.

"And I remember answering the door and only being able to crack it because my dad was passed-out drunk behind the door, but I'd tell whoever it was my daddy was out, because it was true—he was *passed* out. I used to lie for him, hide shit for him, steal for him. I was conditioned to do *anything* for him. And I would have, right up until I ran away with David."

She framed Trace's face, and as she stroked her hands down his jaw, the sadness seeped in. "But you didn't get that get-out-of-jail-free card, did you?"

His gaze lowered, and his hands dropped away. He tried to turn.

"You can't hide anymore, Trace." She pulled him back and tilted her head to look into his eyes, but he kept them averted. "Not from me. I may not know exactly how you got caught with the drugs, whether you were buying them for your dad or the cops came and you took them off your dad before he got caught with them. Or maybe he did get caught and the words, 'They're mine' just sprouted wings and flew from your mouth. But the drugs weren't for you, and you weren't the one who deserved to be in prison. Were you?"

He turned away and braced his hands on the counter but said nothing.

Avery followed, slid her arms around his waist, and pressed her body against his. "Baby, you just threw over-the-counter Tylenol and Advil down the drain like it was arsenic without bothering to look at the labels."

He cut a look at her over his shoulder.

She lifted her brows. "The nurse wanted George to have enough to get through the night in case you didn't have any at home."

His eyes slid closed, and he hung his head.

Avery let him be for a minute, resting her cheek against his back, stroking her hands across his abdomen. "I know why you did what you did then, but why don't you tell people how it happened now? Why hold on to the ex-con stigma?"

"You make it sound like something I want." His voice carried more disgust than anger. "All you ever hear from cons—in or out of prison—is 'I'm innocent.' 'I didn't do it.' No one believes them."

"I'll believe you," she said softly. "Tell me what happened."

He turned, gripped her waist, and pulled her between his legs. After a heavy sigh, he said, "My dad hurt his back while he was taking care of my mom during her treatment. That's when he first got the pain meds. It was also when the first hints of his dementia showed up. Between his depression over my mom and forgetting whether or not he'd taken his own meds, he got hooked."

Avery closed her eyes, so easily envisioning the sad situation. "Oh, Trace . . ."

"I didn't know how to take care of my mom or my brother, and I was convinced my dad would get killed in prison. When I was twenty-two, those fears were very real, and I didn't see any help on the horizon. When I was twenty-two, I didn't know what prison was like or how much it would change me. When I was twenty-two, I didn't know how being an ex-con would label me for the rest of my life."

He released her waist and slid both hands down her arms. "Which brings me to the topic of us."

Avery was already shaking her head. She curled her hands into his shirt. "Don't even."

"It's the smart thing, Avery. You know it. Your entire business model is based on word of mouth. And your entire future is based on this business. After today, the gossip will be flying. If you quash it now, you'll minimize the damage—"

"I'm not going to lie. And you said it yourself, the floodgates are already open. There's no getting that water back in the dam. If you want to stop seeing me because you want to stop seeing me, that's one thing. But I'm not going to live my life based on what other people think. I tried that with David and his parents, and no matter what I did, I still never lived up to their expectations. So walk away from me if you don't want me, but you'll have to tell me to my face."

He curled his fingers around her forearms and dropped his head back on a groan of frustration. "You know I want you."

Avery scanned the quick pulse at the base of his neck, scanned the way his muscled chest and arms pushed at the cotton of his long-sleeved tee and grew hungry. "Yeah," she breathed, grinning. "And it thrills the hell out of me."

She slipped her fingers beneath the hem of his shirt and scraped her nails low on his belly. He flinched and laughed, the sound filled with wicked desire.

"While you're thinking," she said stroking her hands over all the taut, warm flesh of his abdomen, "I'm just going to . . . snack."

She bent her head and pressed her open mouth to his belly.

He flinched again. "Avery, I can't think while you're doing that."

"Mmm, that's too bad. 'Cause I sure can. I can think of all the things I want to do to you." She let her hands slide all the way down his abdomen, into his waistband, and flicked the button of his jeans open. "I can think of all the new things you're going to teach me." She dragged his zipper open. "Maybe your brain needs some stimulation."

She pushed her hand into his jeans. Pressed his cotton-covered erection into her hand and let her eyes fall closed on a moan. "Well, lucky you. I had to go commando all morning."

He groaned. "I didn't need to know that."

"I think you did." She pushed his boxers clear of the thick head of his cock with hunger tightening her chest. "Mmm."

Without hesitation, she took his head between her lips and sucked. He was warm and smooth and hard. His familiar musky, salty taste teased her tongue, and his moans of pleasure fulfilled her ingrained desire to please.

Each time she took him in her mouth, she discovered something new. But today it felt like everything she'd learned in the past coalesced—the wet slide of him between her lips; the hard pressure of him against her throat; the rub, push, and pull of him all through her mouth; the supremely male, intensely intimate taste of him on her tongue. All the sensations layering over the sounds and sights of pleasure she brought him was a wild and heady thrill. One she could easily become addicted to.

"Baby . . ." His voice was soft, filled with barely restrained passion, and his hands threaded through her hair. "You have work—"

She opened, drove him deep into her mouth, closed down, and sucked hard.

"Holy *fuck*." He arched, and his hands closed in her hair. His hips bucked, pushing him deeper into her mouth.

A smile curved her lips as she slowly pulled back. Satisfaction radiated through her chest, and pleasure coiled between her legs. Oh, yes, this was dangerously good.

Avery lowered to her knees and got aggressive with his boxers.

"Baby . . ." He was panting now. "My dad . . ."

She stroked his wet length with her hand, licking her lips in anticipation of getting him back in her mouth. "He'll be sleeping for the next twelve hours." She grinned and flicked a hot look up at him. He loved it when she looked at him while she sucked him. "Imagine what I could do to you in twelve hours."

"Hell. You're not playing fair."

"Seems extremely fair to me." And she took him into her mouth again. He tensed, his hands tightened in her hair, stinging her scalp. She slipped her free hand to the base of his cock, then lower, cupping his balls.

"Ah, God, Avery . . ." He gripped the counter with one hand. "Fuck. I didn't teach you that."

She started laughing and had to draw him from her mouth. She was laughing so hard she pressed her forehead to his hip and curled her hand in his jeans. He combed his hands through her hair, and when she finally stopped laughing and looked up at him, the grin on his face and the sparkle in his eyes looked a lot like love to Avery. It might have been a long time since she'd seen that look, but she'd known it a very long time ago.

Her own heart lurched in response, but like a tiger in a cage, lunging for raw meat outside the bars, Avery couldn't quite get to the same place. She could see it. She could want it. But there were barriers to escape and dangerous ground to cover before she could get there. And she didn't feel quite equipped for that journey.

At least not yet.

"Are you saying you don't think I can't be innovative on my own?" She stroked one finger from the tip of his cock to the base, then drew circles on the very tip with her tongue until he moaned and rocked his hips forward. "Because I'm ready to prove you wrong, Mr. Hutton."

He framed her face with both hands and stroked her cheeks with his thumbs. The soft look in his eyes was laced with heat that Avery wanted to turn into an inferno.

"Mr. Hutton." He grinned. "Next thing I know you'll be calling me sir."

She didn't know if she'd go that far, but two weeks ago she certainly hadn't believed she'd be on her knees in Trace Hutton's kitchen either. She lifted her brows and playfully planted kisses down the length of his cock. "Stranger things have happened, am I right?"

Avery didn't wait for his answer. She was tired of talking, and in her opinion, they communicated just fine in bed without a word . . . although his words in bed were nice, too.

She turned off her mind, set aside all her worries, and allowed both her and Trace this time for themselves. But she didn't get a chance to dive in. Trace bent, grabbed her by the waist, and lifted her against him.

Avery automatically wrapped her arms around his neck and her legs around his hips, and murmured, "God, I love the way you do that," before meeting his hungry kiss.

Trace carried her toward the bedroom and had her shirt over her head and her jeans unfastened before he even laid her on the bed. He pulled her pants free of her legs with one hard jerk, then stood there and stared with a hot, pleased-with-himself grin as he let her jeans slide from his fingers and crumple on the floor.

Avery was about to sit up and strip him when he put a hand out. "Don't move. You're almost perfect."

She lifted her brows. "Almost?"

"Take your hair down."

That voice of his and the way he could both ask for something and order it at the same time, all while making you think it was your idea, turned her inside out in a way she'd never dreamed possible.

She reached for her clip while his gaze raked down her body, and he swept his shirt off over his head in a split second. As she shook her hair loose, he pushed his jeans down his legs and came over her on hands and knees.

"You're so fucking beautiful." He lowered to one forearm, combed his hand through her hair, and dropped a sweet kiss to her lips. And the way he pulled back to scour her face while the backs of his fingers traced her cheek made her feel precious and gorgeous and self-conscious all at the same time.

Avery pressed her hands to his shoulders but had to put real effort into rolling him to his back. When he gripped her hips and lifted into her, rubbing his hot cock against her slick sex, she almost forgot why she'd flipped him in the first place.

"Talk about an addiction," he rasped with his hands sliding over her hips, her waist, pausing to cup and squeeze her breasts. "Baby, you are the worst kind."

Addiction. Now she remembered. "I was just thinking that about you"—she pushed up on her knees, scooted down his legs, and settled back down with his cock in lickable range—"on my knees in the kitchen."

She closed her mouth around the head of his cock and sucked while circling with her tongue and moaning with the pleasure of having him back in her mouth.

"Ho-oly fu—" His hips bucked, one hand gripping her head and the other fisted in the comforter.

The rush that his pleasure whipped through her was far more potentially addictive than any substance she'd ever experienced. And that reaction was one she'd never gotten before either. So she combined the sucking, licking, humming trio again, thrilled when she had the infamous Trace Hutton writhing on the sheets.

"Aver—*ah, fuck*—" Every time he tried to interrupt her, she sucked harder, licked faster, and moaned louder.

"Mmm . . . mmm . . . mmm . . . ," she hummed, drawing him slowly from her mouth with suction that pulled her cheeks against her teeth and rocked shivers through Trace's big, strong body until his cock slipped from her mouth. "I think I have a problem."

He lifted his head from the bed as if he could barely keep it up, his eyes dark and dazed, his chest heaving for air. "W-what?"

"I'm afraid I might have found my own addiction." She closed her eyes, ringed the sensitive ridge of his head with her tongue, sucked him into her mouth with a hum of pleasure, then drew him out again. "Can I have this all to myself? Whenever I want it? Whenever I need it?" She stroked her tongue over him again. "Whenever I please . . . *sir*?"

Trace grinned, dropped his head back, and laughed.

Avery smiled and took him again, sucking the laughter into groans before saying, "This is no laughing matter. A girl needs what a girl needs." She stroked his shaft, spiraling her hand along the wet length. "I should warn you, it might interfere with your ability to work." She stroked him again, slowly, leisurely, letting her fingers float over all the sensitive ridges. "And have friends." She stroked him again. "And sleep." And again. "And eat." She sighed. "And, oh, speaking of eating . . . why am I talking so much?"

Yes, she was in trouble. The strangest kind of trouble ever. Who knew a woman could like cock so much? Who knew pleasuring a man could be a thrill that made her dripping wet? Never in Avery's wildest fantasies had she believed she would be a woman who would covet a man's cock, or the owner of that cock, the way she did now.

She couldn't comprehend any of it in the moment. She'd have to think about it later. All she could do now was devour him. Suck him and stroke him and eat him until his eyes crossed and his body shuddered and he came in a violet burst.

But Trace was doing his damnedest not to allow that to happen. He dragged at her hair and pulled at her jaw.

When she ignored him, he sat up and stroked his hands down her back. Curving over her, he whispered hot in her ear, "Avery . . . baby, gotta stop. Sugar . . . God, that's just too good."

Which only drove her harder.

He groaned and stroked his hands over her ass. "I'm gonna come if you don't stop."

He lowered his face to her back and his teeth grazed her ribs. The electric current short-circuited Avery's rhythm. She drew him from her mouth and gasped at the sudden sensation. Before she could slide him back into the hot, wet, dark depths of her mouth where she'd decided he damn well belonged, his hand followed her spine over her ass and slipped between her legs from behind.

Her sex—swollen, wet, and aching—opened, and her body arched, reaching for his touch, which took her mouth too far from where it wanted to be. But, God, that pressure. She was helpless against her body's need to rub against his hand as it slid along ripe folds.

"Oh my *God* . . . ," stuttered out of her mouth.

Trace pushed both hands over her ass and between her legs. His fingers slid along her opening, spreading wetness, warmth, and sensation all through her lower body. Avery whimpered and lifted her hips, pushing into his hands. Then his fingers were inside her. Stretching and rubbing. Avery dropped her head to his thigh.

She was about to push him back to the bed when Trace gripped her waist and growled, "Come here."

But the order was more a thought than an expectation because he was the one wielding her body. With the swiftest, smoothest move,

Trace turned her, and Avery once again found Trace's cock in a mouth-watering position at her lips. And the instant his warm, wet mouth closed over her sex, she realized, the same was true for him.

With a naughty thrill fueling her, Avery went back to work on Trace, while Trace's mouth mirrored the pleasure. And Avery found it far more difficult to concentrate when he covered her pussy and relentlessly ate and ate and ate at her until she was right on the edge, right there . . . Then he broke suction, leaving her stranded and throbbing and she whimpered, "*Trace . . .*"

The fingers of one hand sank into her ass cheek until a bite of pain hinted. The other pressed between her legs and opened, his fingers spreading her folds. "There we go," he murmured. "Hold on, sugar. Ten intense seconds and you're going to scream. Put my cock in your mouth."

She glanced back. "What?"

"Trust me. Put my cock in your mouth and keep it there."

That was one of those request-demands that flipped an erotic switch she didn't even know she had. And Avery eagerly impaled her mouth with his thick, hot cock.

When he was firmly embedded deep in her mouth, his tongue pressed against her exposed clit and Avery cried out at the shock of pleasure. The sound rippled over Trace's cock, and he growled in approval and started licking the raw bud. Circle after circle after circle, he wound Avery tighter and tighter with rhythmic moans of pleasure until she, far sooner than ten seconds, spiked into an intense orgasm. Her hips bucked and her mouth spontaneously sucked while she moaned with pleasure.

The stars aligned.

Everything made perfect, beautiful, wild sense.

Until Trace pulled from her mouth.

The moment of confusion was lost somewhere in an aftershock, and then Trace was facing her again, kissing her. He covered her hand with his, pressed it against his cock and murmured, "Avery . . ."

His hips bucked, his cock surged, and the power of his climax, the wild roll and thrust of his pleasure beneath her hand while his guttural sounds of pleasure filled her ear, brought to mind the memory of a summer thunderstorm from her time in Virginia . . . as it might feel from inside a glass house.

And she rode out Trace's tremors the same way she used to watch the thunderclouds whisk the storm out to sea, with a smile on her lips, a renewed sense of being alive, and profound appreciation for the experience.

SIXTEEN

Avery was exhausted by the time she filled her cases at Finley's Market with fresh desserts. She might have gotten a top-of-the-world jump start on her afternoon, thanks to Trace's midday delight earlier, but now at 6:00 p.m., after hours of fielding gossip over the events at the café earlier, she felt annoyed and oddly blue. Avery kept her head down, hoping everyone could read the don't-even-think-about-bringing-it-up tension in her expression.

She knew chatter over the search would die down in a day or two. And she knew the truth about Trace. But the looks in people's eyes when they asked her about the incident—their doubt in Trace, their concern for Avery's well-being in his presence, and their twisted excitement over something "else" bad happening at the "The Bad Seed," as if the building would forever be the dive that drew trouble—was testing her patience and her good will.

"What did you bring us today?" Shannon's voice turned Avery's attention to one of the store's owners, who was also one of Avery's good friends from high school. Her bright smile put a little sparkle back in Avery's day.

"Nothing but the best sugary goodness ever, and some exclusive new recipes."

"Oooh," Shannon cooed, eyeing the case. "Tell."

Avery piled the last of the brownies just so, creating the most attractive display when viewed from the front. "This is my trifecta of brownies." She pressed her finger to the top shelf. "These are my milky way caramel fantasy chews—"

"Oh my God." Shannon rested one hand on her pregnant belly, her big dark eyes glazing over.

Avery grinned and moved her hand down a tray. "These are my pumpkin-kissed cheesecake bites."

"Oh dear."

"And these"—she pointed to the last shelf—"are my Bailey's Irish Cream truffle twists."

"Oh." The hand Shannon had resting on her belly jumped, and she started laughing. "He really liked the sound of those. Must take after his daddy. Oh!" Another jump. "Jeez, kid."

She grabbed Avery's hand, laid it in the same spot, and covered it with hers. As if his mother had orchestrated it, the baby kicked again. Avery sucked a breath and laughed, an airy, fluttery, slightly uneasy laugh, not quite sure how she felt about the whole baby thing.

"Wow," she said, pulling her hand away. "He's strong."

"My ribs and my back are none too happy about that."

But no one would know. Shannon was glowing from the inside out.

A pang of mixed emotions kept Avery's belly floating for an uncomfortable stretch, while Shannon chattered about the pregnancy, then about business at the store. Avery listened with one ear while her mind drifted to the sweet bundle of love growing inside Shannon and how desperately Avery had wanted a baby once upon a time. In the early years, when she'd believed she and David would be married forever and those long deployments had become the loneliest stretches of her life.

As soon as she'd realized their marriage needed real work, the idea of a baby drifted to the farthest reaches of her mind. After her childhood, bringing a baby into a turbulent world had been the very last thing she wanted to do.

But now she thought of Trace, of how patient and gentle he was with his father. Of how he'd sacrificed his own freedom, his very life, for the love of his family. How he continued to sacrifice, all without ever complaining. And Avery realized he was exactly the kind of man who deserved to be a father the most. He was exactly the kind of man she would want as a father to her child.

And . . . *whoa. Whoa, whoa,* whoa. A spinning burst of sparks lit off in her gut, like a pinwheel sparkler at a Fourth of July parade.

No, wrong direction, Avery.

Talk about turbulence. If today was any indication, Trace's life was far more turbulent than Avery had ever imagined.

But even as she tried to beat her mind back into alignment with her goals as a single businesswoman, her thoughts were as ethereal as ghosts and kept drifting toward different scenarios. Scenarios she had no businesses dreaming about.

Shannon waved a paper in front of her, and Avery was grateful for the distraction. "Your sales are through the roof," Shannon was saying. "I can't keep your products in stock. Anytime you want to increase your deliveries, or mass-produce or incorporate or go IPO or something, let me know."

Attached to the paper was a check. A nice check that eased the perpetual tension across Avery's shoulders. "Wow." She frowned, thinking back over the month. "Is this really what you owe me?"

"Don't you keep your own books?"

"Uh, well, yeah. Sort of. I mean, I do, but, God, I'm so busy. When I'm dealing with someone like you, who I trust, I have to admit, I let the daily numbers slide. I just don't have time."

Shannon pushed the paper with all the accounting details of Avery's sales into her hand. "Well, hire my bookkeeper with part of this." She tugged a length of tape from the register and wrote down a name and a number, then offered that to Avery, too. "She's fabulous and she's affordable. Don't leave your finances to chance or trust, no matter how much you like someone. You never know anyone as well as you think you do, especially not when money or emotions are involved."

"Thanks." She folded the paper and slid it into the back pocket of her jeans. "Guess I should know better, right?"

"Oh," Shannon said, frowning. "Honey, I didn't mean you and David. I was talking about business."

"It's okay. I think it applies across the board." Avery smiled. "I'll call your bookkeeper and sit down with Delaney to talk about ways to increase production. Guess I need to hire even more people than I thought. Keep your eyes open for me, will you?"

"Sure thing. I may have a couple of leads. I'll text you."

She hugged Shannon. "Thanks." Pulling back, Avery told Shannon's belly, "Behave, young man," making Shannon laugh.

Avery said good-bye to Rita and greeted several regular customers on her way out. She was thinking about where to reinvest the extra money burning a hole in her back pocket when she heard her name.

And cringed inside.

She stopped and turned to MaryAnn Holmes waving from her car.

"Ah, *shit*," she whispered. And as the other woman hurried toward her, the worst kind of dread pooled in Avery's stomach.

MaryAnn pulled her aside near the line of newspaper racks outside the store. Avery forced an easy smile as if she didn't know what this was about. As if she could evade the inevitable by pretending it wasn't going to happen.

"I'm glad I ran into you." MaryAnn spoke quietly, her expression too intense for small talk.

"I hope everything is fine with Willow."

"Yes, yes. Fine. But that's why I stopped you." She was already shaking her head, and tears of frustration and futility were already clogging her throat. "What happened at the café this morning—it's a deep concern."

"MaryAnn, it was all a mistake," Avery said, using her best voice of compassion. "A rumor that was nothing but a lie. The police came, they looked around, they found nothing, and they left. End of story."

Oh, but no. That was not the end of the story—not for MaryAnn. Her eyes flashed with anger. "Just because they didn't find anything didn't mean it was a mistake or a lie. And I don't want Willow anywhere near that. What if she'd been there and the police had found something? What if she'd somehow gotten caught up in the blame?"

"MaryAnn—"

"I'm sorry, Avery. I know how much you need her, and I know how much she was looking forward to working for you, but she's applying for colleges soon, and with all the cutbacks and how difficult it is to get in now, I can't take any risks. Willow won't be working for you."

No, no, no. Avery felt the ground shift beneath her feet. She closed a hand on the other woman's arm. "MaryAnn, you're blowing this way out of proportion. I don't need Willow to start for a couple of weeks. We can postpone training if that would make you feel more comfortable."

"What would make me feel comfortable is having her work somewhere where the other employees are not ex-convicts."

"Trace isn't going to be there when Willow—"

But MaryAnn turned and walked toward the store's entrance, leaving Avery standing there with her mouth hanging open and a knife in her heart.

Avery took a breath and waited for the sting of hurt to subside.

Then she took another to control the wave of fear that rose in the wake of pain.

When both emotions rushed back in a moment later and tears blurred her vision, Avery walked past her car and continued down Main Street until she reached Wildcard Brews.

She pushed through the front door and saw Delaney toward the back of the open space, talking to someone on a ladder beside a huge metal tank in the pilot brew room. She glanced toward Avery with concerned curiosity instead of her normal cheerful greeting. Her sister had called earlier to check on her after word of what happened at the café circulated around town.

Then Avery had assured Delaney she was fine.

Now . . .

"Do you have a minute?" Avery asked.

Without hesitation, Delaney started toward her. Avery must have looked as bad as she felt because her sister slid her arm around her and pulled her into the office. After she closed the door, Delaney dragged Avery into a hug.

The unconditional show of support and love gave Avery the safety net she needed to let go, and once the tears started, they kept falling and falling.

Delaney held her tight, stroked her hair, and whispered reassurances with the confidence of a goddamned bullfighter entering the ring, just like she had when their mother left.

"I know how hard this is, but you're strong, Avery. You're so strong. So much stronger than I am." Like she had all those nights Avery woke to nightmares. "Whether this is about Trace or the café or David, whatever it is, we'll work it out together." Like she had when the kids at school made fun of her. "I promise you everything's going to work out." Like she had when their father yelled or hit them. "You're not alone, Avery."

And just when she'd cried herself out, a soft knock sounded on the door.

Avery didn't look up. She covered her face and wiped at the mess with both hands.

"Do I need to kick someone's ass?" Ethan's low, steely voice, laced with just the right amount of this-is-becoming-a-regular-thing made Avery burst out laughing.

But her exhaustion sucked away the relief like a vacuum. "MaryAnn Holmes," she said, pulling in a shaky breath and cutting a look at Ethan. "Think you can take her?"

His handsome face went deadly serious. Eyes narrowed, mouth tight in a contemplative frown. His light eyes darted toward Delaney, who gave him a yeah-probably nod and shrug.

To which Ethan said, "She doesn't drink beer anyway. Consider it done."

And he left, closing the door.

Avery started laughing again, and only when Delaney gave him a thumbs-up through the glass did Ethan wander away to give the sisters privacy.

"God, he's a dream," Avery said.

"He is. And it took me a damn long time to find him." Delaney reached out and tucked Avery's hair behind her ear. "Want to tell me what happened with MaryAnn?"

That almost unbearable weight came down on Avery again, and she grabbed a box of Kleenex off the bookcase nearby to wipe her face and blow her nose. Then heaved a stuttering sigh and said, "She doesn't want Willow working at the café because of what happened this morning."

Delaney frowned, shaking her head. "Because . . . ?"

Avery explained and Delaney made a that's-ridiculous sound. "I'm sorry." She propped her elbow on her desk and propped her chin in her hand. "We'll have to put our heads together and come up with some alternatives. You might just have to train someone from scratch. Is that really all this breakdown was about?"

"I think it was just the straw. Everything's been building." She sat back in the chair and crossed her arms. "Why'd you hire Trace?" When Delaney frowned, Avery clarified, "You seemed to know he had good character even though he'd been to prison. How did you know you could trust him? Everyone is so ready to jump to the worst possible conclusion."

Delaney thought about it for a second. "I first met Trace back when I was dating Chip. He was the one who—"

"Got in the fight at the bar and killed Ian."

"Right." Her smoky-blue eyes grew even darker. "But he was also a very successful drug dealer. And there were several times when Trace bought from him while Chip and I were together."

Avery sat forward, frowning. "Then how could you—"

"One, because he was buying prescription drugs. You don't have to hang around drug dealers long to figure out that men Trace's age don't buy prescription drugs for themselves. They buy them to sell or they buy them for someone else."

"And two?"

"He didn't buy enough to sell."

"Is there a three?"

"His father was always waiting in the car."

Yes, Avery could see it. She nodded.

"You don't look surprised," Delaney said.

"I figured it out on my own. Why didn't you tell me this?"

Delaney lifted a shoulder. "Because it was really neither here nor there. He bought drugs illegally and went to prison for buying drugs illegally. He knew it was wrong, but he still did it. I'm not saying I don't feel for the guy—I mean, who would understand more than us, right?"

Avery nodded.

"But the biggest reason I didn't bring it up," Delaney said, looking a little sheepish, "is because from the first day you met him, I saw the spark between you two. And because I know you've got a heart the size of *Asia*. And because I knew you'd do what you're doing right now."

"And what's that?"

"Discounting the fact that he was convicted of a crime because he did it for what he thought was the right reason."

Avery propped her elbow on the desk and leaned her forehead into her hand, glad she was so tired. If she weren't this would have started a fight. "And that would be bad because . . ."

"It's a little hard to adequately put into words." Delaney took a deep breath and released it in a measured stream. She thought for a moment before speaking. "Regardless of the reason Trace did what he did, regardless of the circumstances under which he did it, the bottom line is he ended up in prison. He spent three years in a maximum-security prison. For three years, one thousand days, twenty-four hours a day, Trace lived, ate, drank, slept, and breathed with real criminals. Men who murdered, raped, stole, conned, cheated, lied, and otherwise broke heavy-duty laws to get in there. Chip ran with guys like that. Hell, I've dated guys like that. And when I told you that Trace has scars, I meant that there is no way Trace could have lived through that and come out the same harmless kid who went in."

Delaney heaved a breath, sat back, and leaned her temple against her fist. "I trust Trace with the business, with the building, with your opening date. But do I trust Trace with my baby sister?" She made an I'm-not-so-sure face. "Do I trust Trace with my baby sister who loves all creatures great and small, and who just got out of a shitty marriage and deserves the world?" She made another face, this one pained. "I would love to say yes, because I recognize the look in your eye when you're with him. But . . . I can't. I'm sorry, Avery. Your safety comes first for me."

Avery's head came up, and she gave her sister a disbelieving, "My safety?"

"You know what I mean. The safety of your heart. The safety of your future. The safety of the life you're trying to build here. This incident with MaryAnn is the very problem that will forever plague Trace, the same way my past will, in some ways, forever plague me." Delaney squeezed Avery's hand and blew her own struggles off with, "I've tarnished the Hart name enough for three generations. I'd like you to have a life that's bright and shiny."

Avery laughed softly, torn between appreciation for Delaney's love and frustration over . . . over what? Over the fact that Trace wasn't all he should be for Avery to risk her heart?

Her phone chimed, and Avery closed her eyes with a groan. "Oh my God, if this is bad news, I seriously think I might go postal."

Delaney offered her hand, palm up. "Let me look."

Avery handed the phone over to her sister and covered her face. "If it's bad, I don't want to know."

"Mmm, doesn't sound bad."

Avery took a cautious peek from beneath her lashes.

"Sounds like Trace has a surprise waiting back at the café."

"Really?" Avery's load instantly lightened. "Does it say what? Dare I hope it's a finished roof?"

Delaney handed the phone back with a smirk. "Telling what the surprise is generally ruins said surprise. And he's a man. I doubt his surprise has anything to do with a roof."

Avery took the phone and tried not to seem like her whole day had turned around with one text from Trace, but . . . "If it's not a roof, I hope it's a clone of me. Or maybe five. One for baking. One for marketing. One for business. One for recipe development."

"One for sex," Delaney added in a smart-ass I-know-you're-going-to-do-it-even-though-I-told-you-not-to tone.

Avery stood and matched Delaney's playful smirk with an extra dose of attitude. "Oh, hell no. No freaking clone is going to take the best sex I've ever had."

Delaney rolled her eyes. "So much for one night."

Laughing, Avery hugged her sister. "Thank you. And I do hear you. I just . . ." She pulled back and met Delaney's eyes.

Delaney shook her head and stroked a hand down Avery's hair. "You don't have to explain. I've got my own 'I just' right out there." She hooked her thumb toward the door.

As soon as Trace caught sight of Avery's Jeep on the road below, he shut down his floodlights, tossed his supplies into a secured box, slid his hammer into his tool belt, and hurried to secure the tarp over the small portion of the unfinished roof.

By the time he reached the ground, Avery was pushing her car door open, and Trace stood near the porch with the grin of an idiot and the anticipation of a five-year-old at Christmas. Only his anticipation was all for Avery.

"Hey," he called to her as she collected some bags from the backseat.

"Hey. How's the roof coming?"

She didn't sound right. He wasn't sure why, just sure that extra little spark of Avery was missing. But the days were growing shorter and shorter, and it was already dark, so he couldn't read her face as she started toward him.

"Good. Almost done. Need another hour at the most."

"That's great news." Instead of stopping a couple of feet away to talk, she walked right into his arms, pressed her face to his chest and sighed. "God I needed this."

Her distress shaved the edge off his excitement. He held her tight. "Rough day, baby?"

She nodded against his chest, and the fact that she didn't talk about it told him just how bad it had been. It also told him she wasn't ready to rehash it quite yet.

"I think I can put a smile on your face."

She laughed. "You know you can put a smile on my face."

He reached down and swatted her butt. "Get your mind out of the gutter, Cupcake. This is totally unrelated to sex. Though you're welcome to share your excitement over what I'm about to show you with me later."

"Oh, yeah? Who's with your dad?"

"Zane's got him tonight."

"Mmm." She lifted her face, pressed her lips to his neck, and kissed him there. "Then I might take you up on that." She stepped back and finally looked up at him. "What's the surprise?"

Trace took one look at her puffy, tired eyes and her drawn features and knew she'd been crying. All his excitement drained. "What happened?"

She shook her head and tried to brush it off, but Trace cupped her face and forced her to meet his gaze. "What. Happened?"

She sighed. "I lost Willow."

Ah shit. Willow was going to be Avery's backbone. "*Why?* You were giving her an awesome job and a real leg up."

Avery lowered her gaze to the bags in her hands, straightening them as she shook her head. "She's getting ready for college, has a lot going on. Her mom wants her to focus. Thought it was too much for her to take on right now." She returned her gaze to Trace, and he immediately knew there was more to that story. He could see it in her eyes. "But I talked to Delaney, and we've got a couple of other possible replacements we're going to contact tomorrow." She patted his chest. "It hit me hard initially, but once I put it in perspective, I'm fine. So, I'm really ready for good news. And your surprise couldn't have come at a better time. Let's see it."

Anger rumbled through Trace; he was sure the fiasco here earlier in the day had contributed to Willow backing out of the manager/assistant-baker position. But he didn't want to add his own emotions onto those he could see still weighing Avery down, so he took her hand, threaded their fingers, and walked her around to the far side of the building, where he'd parked the rental truck.

"Culinary Depot called," he told her.

She gasped and her grasp tightened in his. "Oh my God, really?"

"There's that spark I love." He grinned at her as they rounded the front of the café. "Really. And I took a break from the roof to go pick up your appliances because I knew the sight of these babies on your property would make you feel a whole lot better than a finished roof. Even though I'll be done with the roof tomorrow morning."

At the sight of the truck, she sandwiched his hand in hers and squealed.

Trace laughed, led her to the back of the truck, and pulled open the doors. He couldn't have been happier for Avery if she'd won the lottery. Because this café and these appliances were *her* lottery.

They were all wrapped and taped, but Trace had loaded them so there was space to walk down the middle, and now he lifted Avery into the truck and watched her inspect each piece with the joy she deserved in her life every day.

He could honestly say he'd never felt more satisfied with any job he'd ever done. And while he'd seen this kind of equipment dozens of times, Avery oohed and aahed over every little detail—the handles on the fridge, the knobs on the range, the racks inside the ovens, the finishes, even the goddamned wheels.

She stood there a long moment in silence, utterly still, her back to Trace. "It's all so . . ." She finally murmured, "So . . . real." Turning, she faced him, fingers threaded at her chest, a wobbling smile and nerves jumping in her eyes. "Oh my God."

She piled her hands over her heart and looked at the floor of the truck, her chest laboring as if struggling to breathe.

Alarm wiped Trace's smile away. In one leap, he was in the back of the truck, tilting Avery's face up to his, and he found her blue eyes swimming in tears. The pulse in her neck thumped fast. "Baby? What is it?"

"I . . . don't know. It's . . . so real. So . . . overwhelming." The tears spilled over. "There's twenty thousand dollars of equipment in here. What if . . . God, what if this place tanks? What if I can't make this work? What if I can't *do* this?" Panic cut into her expression. She pressed one hand to her forehead and one to her stomach, like she was going to be sick. "Holy shit," she whispered, looking around again. "I . . . Oh my God."

She covered her face with both hands, and when she swayed, Trace was glad he was standing right there to steady her.

"Hey, don't let your fears run away with you." He pulled her to him and wrapped her in his arms. "You can totally do this. You have your entire family behind you. I'm behind you. Even if the unforeseen happens, none of us are going to let you tank. But most importantly, *you* won't let yourself tank, Avery, and you know it."

Her warm sigh of relief drifted through the cotton of his T-shirt. But her muscles remained tense, and a tremor shivered through her body. Her arms were curled around his waist, fisted in the back of his shirt, holding him close. Her cheek rested against his chest.

"Shh," he murmured, stroking her back. "You're in the final stretch. This is where everything comes together. You've done all the heavy lifting—now let it carry you through. You just have to focus on the small details—stocking your fridge, finalizing your staff, and getting the word out about your grand opening. You need to direct this nervous energy into leveraging all the plans and people and marketing programs you already have in place, baby. It's all going to come together. Have faith in yourself." He kissed her head. "I have five hundred percent faith in you."

She turned her face into his chest and rested there a minute. Trace closed his eyes and laid his lips against her hair, kissing her head, breathing deep the soft floral scent of her shampoo. She awed him in so many ways he couldn't even describe half of them. And the guilt he felt over

JT and the trouble he'd brought her at the most stressful time of her opening ate at him now.

Avery finally heaved another sigh, then turned her face up to his. And God, she looked exhausted. Beautiful and real and tough and young and so damn exhausted. He wished he could do more for her.

"Are you up for a hot shower?" she asked. "I couldn't sleep right now even if I do need it. What I really want is the feel of your body against mine. That is about the only thing that's going to distract me from the stress right now."

He smiled and thumbed away the wet path on one cheek. "I am at your service."

SEVENTEEN

Even with Trace lying close beside Avery in her bed, one heavily muscled leg over hers, his tanned arm across her hips, and his dark head on her white pillow, she couldn't relax enough to fall asleep.

Her gaze blurred over the worksheets open on her laptop, and she pressed her eyes closed, rubbed at them, then refocused on the screen. She had to squint, partially because of her dim light drifting in from the bathroom, and partially because fatigue kept messing with her vision. When her anxiety started to spiral to a peak, Avery only needed to look over at him and watch his slow, deep, even breaths for a few moments before she magically settled.

She reached over, ran her fingers through his thick black hair, and murmured, "If only I could bottle you."

He stirred, snuggled closer, tightened the arm at her hips, and settled again. Warmth suffused Avery's heart, and those damned tears stung her eyes again. She'd gone years without crying. Years living more or less numb. She hadn't realized how numb until she'd gotten here and old friends and estranged family refilled her life with warmth and love, acceptance and happiness.

But Trace . . . whatever had formed between her and Trace was even deeper. Something altogether different. Every moment they spent together seemed to intensify whatever this was between them. Tonight they'd showered and kissed and touched but hadn't made love. Trace knew she was stressed and preoccupied; Avery knew he was sore from working on the roof. So they'd taken turns massaging away each other's tangles and knots, with a lot of thoughtful silence and a few short discussions on her next steps as she jotted notes and framed up the next two weeks of her chaotic life.

It was one of the most enjoyable, most comforting evenings she'd had in years.

Now he was lost to sleep, and she was once again drowning in angst.

"You can totally do this. You have your entire family behind you. I'm behind you. Even if the unforeseen happens, none of us are going to let you tank. But most importantly, you won't let yourself tank, Avery."

His faith in her made Avery smile. Regardless of whether or not the faith was warranted, he was right about having her family behind her. And it felt pretty good to hear that he was behind her, too.

Avery drew in a slow breath and released it on a sigh. Scooting lower in bed, she set her lists and outlines aside, snuggled even closer to Trace, and closed her eyes. There in the dark, with Trace's heartbeat against her side, Avery put together a list of action items in her head, "to-dos" for the next two weeks to support her grand opening.

As she sank deeper toward unconsciousness, something called Avery back to the surface. Woozy, she opened her eyes, focused on the ceiling, and took in her surroundings. Nothing had changed. Trace still slept soundly beside her. She hadn't even kicked the papers to the floor. But something . . .

A sound pulled her gaze left, to the window overlooking the side of the building. A shuffle? A scrape? She wasn't sure. Vague, uneasy sensations forced her mind to focus. She pushed herself up on her elbows and listened harder. An engine. A car engine. But her Jeep and Trace's truck were parked out front.

No, Trace's truck wasn't here.

The moving van.

Alarm burst in her belly and radiated outward. "Trace. Wake up." She pushed his arm off her along with the covers and rushed to the window. The truck was still dark, but it was moving, sliding slowly out of its parking spot, the gravel crunching under the tires. "Oh my God, *Trace*."

He was already at her side, and he slammed his hand against the window. "No! Motherfucking sonofabitch!"

He spun and grabbed his jeans from the floor. Jerking them on, he ran for the door.

"Trace?"

He ran down the stairs, yelling, "Where are your keys?"

"What? Why?" Avery stood at the top of the stairs, confused, scared. "What are you going to—"

"You fucker," he yelled toward the parking lot, then pivoted, and the glare he shot back up at her stabbed like an ice pick in her gut. *"Where are your keys?"*

"O-on the counter."

She hurried toward him in nothing but his T-shirt in time to watch the truck speed down the driveway, still no lights on. Panic skittered through her body, tying icy knots in its wake.

"Trace, what? I'll call the police." She turned toward the stairs and her cell, where she'd left it on the bed, but kept watching him over her shoulder. "Don't go, Trace. I'll call nine-one-one. Let the police handle it."

"Like they handled that bullshit this morning?" he yelled running for the door in bare feet and jeans. "*Fuck that.* Call Zane. Tell him which way I'm headed."

He flung the door open and ran to the Jeep.

"No. Trace—" Avery started after him, but froze, caught between grabbing him or her phone.

He made that decision for her when he backed into the driveway, spitting gravel at the café in an angry spray.

◆ ◆ ◆

Trace pounded his food on the gas pedal, slamming it to the floor. "Goddamned fucking *idiot*."

Seriously? Did he really think he was going to get away with stealing *kitchen appliances*? Did the fucker think *at all*?

He caught up with JT within three seconds of hitting a straightaway on the quiet country road that led out of town. But then they'd hit another cluster of curves, and Trace had to wait for another straight section before he could get in front of the truck to try to force JT to slow down.

In the meantime, Trace laid on the horn, hoping to spark even one gray cell in that pea-size brain of JT's that told him he was caught and all he could do now was pull over. But, no, JT did what JT did best—he played more games. He skidded around a turn and flung the truck into the oncoming lane to block Trace's view. Rubber smoked on the asphalt, and the truck fishtailed before it straightened and sped into another turn.

"Jesus . . ." Trace imagined all that equipment flying around, his stomach dropped, and he immediately backed off. "Relax. Just keep him close—let the cops catch up."

Or Zane. Hopefully Zane. Trace didn't trust the cops to do anything right by him. Especially not with Austin prowling around and Zane off duty. And he couldn't call and tell Zane where he was, because Trace had realized almost immediately that he'd run out of the café without his phone. *Fucking brilliant.* But hell, he'd barely gotten pants on.

After another few reckless curves, it was clear that either JT was drunk off his ass, purposely driving to damage the equipment, or both. And if this went on much longer, all Avery's appliances would be rendered useless. Trace had no idea how that would play out down the line with insurance. All he knew was that Avery didn't have the time or the money to recoup a loss like the one that JT threatened—all because of Trace.

He was following several feet back, when JT overcorrected for another curve. Trace's foot jumped to the brake pedal as the truck tipped onto two wheels. He sucked a breath. *"No-no-no-no-no . . ."*

Please God no.

When the truck bounced back on all four wheels, Trace started breathing again.

Fuck this. He wasn't waiting until Avery's dream was dust and she was bankrupt to end this bullshit.

At the next straightaway, he gunned the gas. One glance at JT in the driver's seat, and the smug grin on his face told Trace exactly what this was about—revenge.

Trace's mission solidified. He would *not* be waiting for anyone to end what should never have started. Trace was ending it right here. Right now.

When he had a couple hundred feet on the truck, he stayed in the center lane, slowing JT without allowing him to pass. He realized he would probably owe Avery—or in this case, Delaney and Avery—a car when this was over. But he'd rather owe one of them a car than cost Avery twenty grand in appliances and a solid start to her business.

And just as Trace had come to grips with the whole car thing, JT rammed the back of the Jeep with the truck. Trace lunged in the driver's seat like a crash test dummy. His teeth clacked together hard, pain shot through his jaw, and the bitter taste of blood filled his mouth. Metal crunched and groaned. The Jeep lurched, hiccupped, and stumbled. That one hit alone had totaled out the Jeep's worth.

"Mother*fucker* . . ."

He put all thought of consequences out of his mind. And did what had to be done. Trace gunned the engine, gained a couple hundred feet on the truck, and skidded to a stop sideways, blocking the road before JT had time to build Jeep-crushing speed.

Trace covered his head with both arms, shielding himself from the glass. Time slowed. The horn blared. The headlights reflected off mirrors, flashing against his closed lids. The brakes locked. Skidded. Squealed.

He was breathing hard when the slam of a door made him realize he hadn't been hit. Trace's mind clicked on. He pushed out of the Jeep, standing just in time to meet JT's fist with his jaw. Pain and shock mingled. Trace jerked back, hit the car, and automatically rolled to put his back to JT until he could get his head straight.

"You're fuckin' pussy-whipped," JT yelled, his words slurring.

"And you're drunk. Fuckin' idiot. I think you're *trying* to go back to prison."

Trace sidestepped the front fender before facing JT, and when the other man took another swing, Trace had room to move aside. JT stumbled a little, collected himself, and turned on Trace again with a look he'd seen too often in prison. A silent you're-going-down look.

"Did you think you were going to fence this shit?" Trace asked, trying to distract JT's slow mind so he could get an opening to take him to the ground. "As if no one would wonder where a fresh ex-con got brand-new commercial kitchen equipment?"

"See, that's your problem, right there, Hutton." JT jabbed a finger at him. "You think you're so fuckin' smart. Always thought you were better than the rest of us. But you're not. You're no fuckin' different."

JT lunged at Trace, hooked an arm around his neck, and punched him in the abdomen, right over his kidney. Pain exploded in Trace's side and spread through his gut. The burn, the hold, the punch, the darkness, the cold—it all took him right back to Folsom.

Trace mirrored JT's hold, locking his forearm around the other man's neck, and with a guttural growl of fury, Trace jammed his knee into JT's groin.

JT grunted; rasped, "Fucker"; and grappled for room to take another swing.

Before he got the chance, Trace grabbed the front of JT's shirt, yanked him upright, and drove his fist into his face. That sickening, flesh-on-flesh sound only dragged Trace deeper into the darkness of his past. He shoved JT up against the car and glanced toward Wildwood, hoping for headlights. For salvation.

Before he could focus, JT shoved Trace back with both hands, and he used his body weight to take Trace to the ground. The bare skin of his back hit the asphalt and burned like fire. Trace yelled first; then the pain stole his breath and gave JT the opportunity to get in a couple of good shots to his face. But once Trace found his equilibrium, he pulled out all the stops.

He rolled JT to his back and punched him until the bastard didn't have the strength to hit back. Then Trace held him down as lights approached and sirens sounded in the distance. A car screeched to a stop, and the door opened.

"Holy fuck, Trace."

Zane.

"Took you long enough." With his chest heaving for air, Trace sat back on his heels as Zane swung out his cuffs. With the headlights shining directly on them, Trace got his first good look at JT. His face was cut and bloody, lips split, eye already bruising. Sickness rolled through Trace's gut. Had he really inflicted that much damage? To avoid the uncomfortable answer to that question, he asked Zane, "What the fuck were you doing?"

"*Me?* What the fuck are *you* doing? Jesus Christ, I can't tell who's hurt worse. Do you need an ambulance?"

"Yeah," JT coughed, "he—"

"Shut up," both Trace and Zane said at the same time. Then Trace added, "You're getting nothing but a trip directly back to Folsom, fuckin' prick."

Zane spoke into a handheld radio, telling the deputy on duty he had the suspect in custody and was bringing him back to the café, then looked at his brother. "You need a trip to the ER."

"As soon as I get these"—he glared at JT, whom Zane had pulled to a sitting position—"*stolen appliances worth twenty grand* back to their rightful owner. That, you piece of shit, would be considered grand theft, which I'm pretty damn sure would amount to a felony—and your fuckin' *third strike*. Take a big, deep breath of air. It'll be the last you get outside prison."

Zane jerked JT to his feet. The man leaned toward Trace. "You'd better hope I don't get out, 'cause I'll be coming back for you, Hutton. And next time I won't be keeping my hands off that bitch that's got a ring through your nose."

Trace saw red. He lunged for JT and caught his neck just as Zane jerked the man back and out of Trace's grip.

"Shut your fucking mouth," Zane said in that cop tone Trace had heard far too often during his life. "Or I'm gonna give you back to him."

Avery was normally pretty good under pressure. She'd had many occasions as a military wife to support other members of military families in times of crisis. But she was, admittedly, not doing so well now.

As soon as the first deputy's car showed up at the café, Wildwood residents seemed to appear out of nowhere. Some wandering over to ask if she was okay, like Mark, who still hovered nearby despite Avery's suggestion he go home. Now there were three cruisers in front of the café, lights blinking in the 2:00 a.m. dark. The last to show up, just minutes before, was Austin. He'd climbed from the car and spent several minutes talking to the other two deputies before starting toward her.

And, God, her nerves were already shot. She didn't have the patience for him. All she could think about was the look on Trace's face when he'd left. His anger so sharp, so intense, she'd been pacing with all sorts of horrible thoughts and fears and insecurities filling her head.

Austin paused his slow swagger about eight feet away. "Zane found Trace and JT."

Avery's footsteps stopped and her stomach seized up. Something about the way he'd phrased that made Avery cold. "JT?"

"You didn't know it was JT who stole the van?"

"No, I didn't see the driver." And now Avery's fear intensified. A fear that cut so deep, she couldn't process it in the moment. So she slapped a Band-Aid on and asked the hardest question of her life. "Are they . . ." She had to force air into her lungs to speak. "Is Trace okay?"

Headlights turned onto the driveway. Avery's gaze jumped that direction but didn't find the Jeep Trace had taken or the truck JT had stolen. She found Ethan's truck turning in. And her heart fell.

"Austin," Avery said, drawing his gaze back. "Is Trace okay?"

Austin's gaze returned to the road, where Zane's black SUV slowed and followed Ethan's truck. "Well, here comes Zane. I guess we'll see."

Her focus jumped to a third set of headlights behind the SUV and found the rental truck coming in behind Zane. All Avery's air whooshed out in relief. A second driver meant Trace had to be okay.

She didn't get a chance to think about anything else before Ethan and Delaney parked and her sister rushed to her, wrapping Avery tight. "Are you okay?"

Suddenly she wasn't so sure. "I just want to make sure Trace is okay."

As the other cars made their way to the café, Avery explained what had happened. And by the time Zane stood from the driver's seat, Delaney and Ethan wore the same grim expression.

"He's in the back," Zane told the other deputies. "Put on gloves. He's bloody. You should probably call a medic."

"Shit," Avery said under her breath, and she pulled free from Delaney to rush to the driver's side of the van, ignoring the deputies as they moved toward Zane's car. She put her hands on the door and looked through the window. "Trace?"

He put the car into park, turned off the engine—everything in super slow motion—then looked at her through the glass. And a chill traveled the entire length of her spine. His eyes were dark and guarded. His face smudged and dirty.

She pulled open the door, already choking on his name. "Trace?" The light came on, and all the shadows turned red. His face, his chest, his arms—he had blood smears and drips and splatters everywhere. "Oh my God. What . . . ? How . . . ?"

"I'm okay," he said, his voice low, gaze cast down and away as he climbed from the truck with the pained movement of an eighty-year-old. "What the fuck is everyone doing here?"

Sirens grew closer, and as soon as Trace moved from the truck, she saw the blood remaining on the driver's seat and gasped. He turned and followed her gaze, which gave her a look at the mess of blood on his back. Sickness roiled low in her gut. One that was dark and confusing and deeply troubling. "Oh God, Trace."

The emergency vehicles turned up the driveway.

"Who the fuck called them?" Trace muttered, then yelled at his brother. "Goddammit, Zane, get everyone out of here. This isn't a fucking circus."

"No, you need them," Avery told him. "Delaney, send the ambulance over here first."

"No." His dark, almost feral bark shocked her quiet. He kept his eyes down. "The last thing you need is everyone watching me get patched up from a fight with the convict I hired and who tried to steal your equipment." His voice was low and harsh in a way that pierced her chest with a cold streak. "I've caused enough trouble for you for

one fucking lifetime. I'm fine. Everything is superficial. I'll go to the ER after I talk to the cops and check the equipment. Right now I'm going to put a shirt on and wash my face so I don't look like a fucking animal."

Avery just stood there, stunned silent as he walked past and quickly disappeared into the café. She pulled in a stuttering breath, her chest as tight as if she'd been physically hit. Her gaze focused on the seat again, and she swallowed hard. The thought of him hitting the ground with his bare skin . . . of how he'd gotten the bruises forming around his eye and cheekbone, the cuts on his lips, nose, chin, cheek.

Avery started to shake. Tears flooded her eyes. He'd just been in bed with her forty-five minutes ago. Safe and happy and so gentle . . . Her mind spiraled and tangled. Her thoughts jumped around. Things started to disconnect. Nothing made sense.

"Hey." Delaney's soft voice slipped into her thoughts. "You okay?"

Avery shook her head and gestured to the seat. "What?" Then to the café where he'd disappeared. "He . . ." Her brain chugged, chugged, chugged, but the gears wouldn't turn. She pushed both hands into her hair and choked out, "I don't know what's happening."

Ethan passed, squeezing Delaney's shoulder and murmuring, "I'm gonna check the equipment."

Avery crossed her arms tight and followed. She held her breath as Ethan fought with the doors. Finally saying, "They opened fine earlier."

"The equipment probably just shifted."

Avery's stomach dropped.

Fifty feet away, two cops flanked JT and pulled him from the back of Zane's SUV. The sight of him made Avery pull in a sharp breath. His face looked even worse than Trace's. One eye bloody and swollen shut, lips cut and puffy, cuts everywhere, blood everywhere. Trace may not have given JT that black eye and that cut lip in the picture she'd seen, but he most definitely had given him everything that was fresh tonight. And the amount of damage stunned her.

Trace had done that.

Her Trace had done *that*. With his own hands.

She shook her head, overwhelmed by the severity. By the sheer brutality.

Avery tightened her arms, suddenly so cold. Feeling so small. So weak. So fragile—emotionally and physically. The way she used to feel around her father.

The cops sat JT on a gurney, and the EMTs started working on him.

"You take that one." Trace's voice startled Avery, and she turned her head back so fast, she lost her balance and stumbled a little.

Delaney grabbed her arm to steady her and gave her a concerned stare. "Avery?"

"Just lost my balance," she muttered.

"Trace," Austin said, coming around the end of the truck. "We're going to need a statement."

"Yeah, just a minute."

He helped Ethan unblock the doors, and each man pulled one door open, exposing all her gorgeous equipment, equipment that she'd painstakingly chosen, paid her last dollar for, and needed installed immediately to open the café on time, thrown in the back of the truck like a mishmash of garage sale leftovers.

Avery covered her mouth, stifling a sob.

"Fuck." Trace bit out the word and put his hands on his hips. And while he was staring at the mess in the back of the truck, blood was seeping through his T-shirt.

"Not too bad . . . ," she heard Ethan say, but his voice faded in and out. "Everything looks intact . . ."

But she couldn't follow the conversation as blood created a dot-and-blotch pattern on Trace's back. Her head went light. A ring started low in her ears and built as her vision dimmed.

"Whoa, Avery?" Delaney's voice brought Avery back when she was halfway to the floor. With Delaney's help, Avery caught herself before she fainted and straightened, but Delaney looked scared.

Trace turned, his frown so dark, his face so bruised, so cut, she saw a whole different man there. "Avery?"

He closed the distance with his brow pulled tight. Her gaze caught on his hand rising to her face, his fingers in a gentle curl, the way they were when he cupped her face. But she caught the sight of his knuckles, raw and red and still bleeding.

Avery saw her father's knuckles from all his drunken brawls, the knuckles he'd raised to her and Delaney and Chloe so many times. And she flinched and shrank away.

Trace's hand froze; his gaze dropped to his hand and held. And something happened behind his eyes. Something she didn't recognize.

He dropped his hand, and the combination of resignation and pain on his face tore at Avery's heart. "I . . . I'm sorry. I didn't mean to—"

"No. It's okay." He nodded. And when his head finally lifted, he looked like an empty shell. "It's . . . right. It's the way it should be."

She shook her head. "What?"

He put his hands at his hips again and kept his focus on the ground. "I'll call a buddy of mine who lives nearby. He just had a job fall through. I'll have him come and finish up."

She stepped out of Delaney's hold with a new lick of fear and pain twining inside her. "*What?*"

"The only way you're going to save any face on this, the only way your business is going to survive for your opening, is if I walk away and you tell everyone you fired me." He met her gaze, but it was in a guarded, distant, businesslike way. "I'll call my friend, have him over here in the morning. He's good, and he's got a crew. I'll work out the payment with him. He'll have you up and running in two days. You'll make your opening."

An icy shaft speared her right down the middle. "You're *walking away* from me?"

"Avery," Delaney's voice interjected softly. "You need to think about your business right now. I think Trace has a smart idea."

"Fuck smart ideas," she said, but she said it to Trace, not to Delaney. "You promised you'd have this ready for my opening day."

Even as she said it, she realized how stupid she'd been to believe another damn promise. When would she learn?

He remained cool and distant. "It will be ready for your—"

"No, *you* promised." She closed the distance between them and jabbed his chest. "*You promised* me, Trace."

"If I stay and finish this job," he said deliberately, "you won't have a business to open."

Avery wanted to scream that she'd rather have him than the business. But she'd been here before. She'd tried to tell David she'd rather have a husband who was gone as much as he was gone than to end their marriage. And look where that had gotten her.

She couldn't force Trace to love her now any more than she'd been able to force David to fall back in love with her then. And she couldn't even force Trace to let *her* love *him*. She'd held on to David six years too long. She wasn't going to make that mistake again.

"I'm not going to keep you where you don't want to be." She pushed the words out, but she was breaking inside. "So if you don't want to be here, go. But I'll find my own way to finish the job. Tell your friend to find other work."

To keep herself from watching another man she loved walk out of her life—she was two for two, quite a record—Avery turned and walked away first.

EIGHTEEN

Trace wanted to die.

He lay sprawled on his bed, belly down, head turned so his good cheek pressed against the pillow. The right side of his face, where he'd taken most of JT's punches, was swollen, and his back had scabbed over. Mostly. He'd needed nine stitches to close various deeper cuts on his face and hand.

The day after a fight was always the worst. He'd learned that in the prison infirmary.

His dad appeared in the doorway. "What was I going to the kitchen for?"

"Ice." It was the third time his father had returned to ask. And he didn't even remember having to ask the time before.

He gave Trace that blank stare.

"Ice, for me, Dad."

"Oh, right." He nodded, but still stared, confused. "What happened to you?"

Trace sighed. "Can you just get the ice?"

"Sure, sure."

But after his dad left the room, the television clicked on, and a chair in the living room creaked.

Trace groaned and reached for the Advil on his nightstand. He popped three pills into his mouth and washed them down with water, wishing they would do *something* for the pain in his chest.

When he replaced the bottle on the nightstand, his gaze held on the clock: 2:15 p.m. He wondered how Avery was handling everything today. Wondered if Delaney had found someone to finish the café for her. He'd tried calling Avery twice already in hopes of talking her into letting his friend come help, but she wasn't answering.

Not that he blamed her.

And fuck, that just made all the memories flood back in—the panic on her face when she'd begged him not to go after the truck, the relief swamping her when he'd returned, the alarm when she'd seen his injuries . . . But the worst—the very worst—had been her fear. That spark of fear when he'd reached out to touch her . . .

A throbbing ache kicked up at the center of his chest. Yeah, that was the real killer. After everything they'd been through and shared, she was still afraid of him.

But again, he couldn't blame her. He'd been thinking about this for the last twelve hours while he hadn't been able to sleep. He had been beaten up and covered in blood. JT had looked just as bad. By going after JT like a vigilante and kicking the other man's ass just to get the appliances back, Trace had proven that while he may have paid his debt to society, he was still living on the edge of acceptable behavior.

And for the good girl who lived to please and nurture others with an ingrained need to make all things right, Trace had to look like a broken man with too many missing pieces to salvage the whole.

"Why aren't you at work?" His father was in Trace's room again and now shuffled to Trace's bed and lowered to the edge.

Trace had already told his dad a half-dozen times why he wasn't at work, but he told him again. "Because my job is over."

But in some ways, Trace felt like his life had ended along with that job. At least the spark of life that had kept him going over the last few months. A spark named Avery.

"Then why aren't you finding a new job? You've never been one to sit around."

Trace huffed a laugh, but he didn't smile. "Because I hurt everywhere."

George looked at Trace as if noticing the bruises and cuts for the first time. "Oh, yeah, you're a mess, aren't you? Probably couldn't get a job lookin' like that anyway."

"Good point." And just one more bubble burst.

The front door opened, and Gram's voice floated down the hall. "Hello, boys. I brought goodies."

George's face lit up. His posture straightened, and a smile turned his mouth. "Avery brought turnovers."

Trace groaned. His father could remember Avery and her apple turnovers, but he couldn't remember to bring ice from the kitchen.

Pearl stepped into the bedroom. George's smile fell, and he shot Trace a look. "I don't think that's Avery."

"Good eye, son." Pearl found that amusing. "And what are all the handsome men in my life doing back here?" She didn't wait for an answer. Pearl started toward Trace and ran her hand over his hair the way she had when he'd been sick as a kid. "Poor Trace. How are you feeling, honey?"

"As good as I look." And he couldn't take all this fuss. Gritting his teeth, he forced himself to sit up. "Since you're here, Gram, I'm going to run to the café."

If he could stand without passing out.

His grandmother didn't like that idea, but she was too busy answering George's questions about apple turnovers to keep after Trace, and he slipped out of the house. He rehearsed his apology for the tenth time since he'd returned home that morning on his drive. His palms were sweating when he turned onto the café's driveway.

His hopes died when he found the Jeep missing from where Ethan had parked it in front of the café last night. Ethan's truck sat in its place. That meant either Ethan and Delaney were here or they'd taken the Jeep into the shop and Avery was using Ethan's truck until she could afford her own car.

Considering the simple logistics of making sure everyone in the family had a car would now be a huge ordeal since Trace had gone and put one out of commission.

Footsteps on the gravel tripped his heart. He turned his head, hoping to see Avery.

"Hey." Delaney walked toward his truck instead. She didn't look angry, but she didn't look happy either. She leaned against Ethan's truck, her gaze narrowed against the sun. "You look worse than refried shit."

"Feel worse."

"You should." Her gaze slid over his arm and rested on his hand. "Bet those knuckles hurt." Her tone quieted. "My dad had knuckles like that."

Trace's mind flashed to the moment he'd reached out to Avery, to her eyes darting to his hand, to her flinch . . .

"I just talked to Ethan," Delaney said, cutting into Trace's thoughts. "He's at the insurance adjuster's office. They have the police report and talked to the truck rental company. There will be some hoops to jump through, but they're going to give us market value for the Jeep, less our deductible."

Trace's brain realigned, and he breathed a little better. One good turn of events. "What's the deductible? I'll get a cashier's check from the bank and drop it off later today."

"Well, since you actually had your head out of your ass when you rented the truck and took out insurance with the rental company, it's going to cover the deductible."

Wow, why couldn't he get that lucky in other areas of his life?

"Too bad all your decisions couldn't be so well thought out," Delaney said.

Bingo.

He nodded again, wondering what the best decision would be now—to check on Avery or just leave. The whole idea of walking away last night had been so he wouldn't be associated with her. Yet here he was . . .

He'd made such smart decisions up until Avery. Ever since then, he'd been impulsive and reckless.

And spontaneous and alive.

And happy.

"Didn't expect to see you here again." Delaney crossed her arms and gave him that contemplative look.

"Guess I probably shouldn't be." He glanced at the café, wishing he could turn back the clock and pick up the phone to call the cops instead of going after JT himself. "I just . . ."

"Love her."

Trace was nodding before he processed the words. "What?"

"Love her," Delaney repeated as if he were dense. "You just love her. I know."

His mouth formed words, but all that came out was "I . . . uh . . . that's . . . well . . ."

Delaney laughed, the sound filled with true amusement. "You're an even bigger idiot than Ethan was. He'll be glad to hear he's been taken off the top of that list." She pushed off the truck. "I've gotta get down to the brewpub." She rounded the front of the truck calling, "Don't torture yourself anymore—Avery's not here."

Everything inside Trace slid two inches lower.

When Delaney reached the driver's side, she paused and met Trace's gaze. "And don't bother coming back for a while. She's postponing the opening. She took a mental health trip to the coast."

"Ah, *fuck*." He dropped his head back against the seat. He felt like he'd swallowed a rock. "Everything I did last night was so she could open *on time*."

"No," she said with you-dumb-fuck attitude. "Everything you did last night was because you're *in love with her*. Jesus Christ," she muttered, "why do such smart men act like such morons when it comes to women?"

She asked the last more of herself as she climbed into the truck. The passenger's window was open, and she continued speaking to Trace as she pushed the key into the ignition and started the engine. "You had such potential, you know?"

Trace lifted a brow. "Potential?"

She turned and met his gaze. "Yeah, potential. You know, that thing that happens when you drag yourself from the trenches and keep going. You had yourself on a great track. You'd suffered and sacrificed and worked your ass off. You took this job for next to nothing for the mere possibility of gaining work from it."

Delaney looked through the windshield at the café and gestured to it. "That place is potential personified. You took it from an eyesore that everyone in town wanted to rip apart to a gorgeous place where they can gather together."

Trace sat there, speechless. He'd been so focused on getting the building done, he hadn't taken the time to appreciate how far it had come. How far he'd come.

How far he and Avery had come. Together.

"Or, well," Delaney said, "you *almost* got it there." She tipped her head, turning her gaze on Trace again. "The way *you almost* reached your own potential."

The knife in his gut twisted.

Delaney put the truck into gear and laid her arm over the seat to back out. "It's a shame, Trace." Her gaze was sad but sincere. "Because you made Avery really happy. Like cheek-cramping, four-year-old-on-a-playground happy."

Delaney backed out and continued down the drive, leaving Trace swimming in turmoil.

Avery stared out at the moonlight on the ocean from the cozy corner of the breakfast nook in her cottage and lifted the hot chocolate to her lips.

Warmth and rich chocolate coated her mouth and drenched her tongue, and Avery let her eyes slide closed so she could savor the beauty of it. The only thing that could make this better was a hit of Bailey's Irish Cream.

And Trace.

Her phone vibrated against the table, pulling Avery from that impossible fantasy with a painful jerk. She ignored the message, but her mind drifted to all the texts, voice mails, and e-mails she'd gotten from people not just all over Wildwood but from all over the *county* and beyond, fussing over the fact that she'd put her website and her space at Wildly Artisan on holiday status.

As for rumors that she was giving up on Wild Harts, those she quashed immediately, explaining she was taking time away to finalize details and recharge for the opening.

Which was true.

Sort of.

She'd done a lot of work in that direction, but she hadn't tackled the most important task—replacing Trace. That still felt too . . . too permanent? Too disloyal? She only knew she hadn't been able to deal with the thought of having someone else go in and finish what Trace started.

He chose to leave.

Her cell vibrated with another e-mail. Avery groaned and rubbed her eyes.

The outpouring of interest created a strange mix of gratitude and anxiety—gratitude for the interest and the business, anxiety that she wasn't fulfilling every order. But it was good to know that even after everything that had happened, there was still an overwhelming interest in her bakery and café. She wished she could share that with Trace.

With a focused, deep breath, Avery forced the anxiety to quiet, reminding herself like she had every five minutes during the last three days that her mission in life was not to make everyone else happy, but to make *herself* happy *first.*

If she were to truly make herself happy first, she'd already have hunted down Trace and hashed out what still felt like an ugly knot between them until she could fall into his arms and he would catch her.

"You can't make him stay," she reminded herself. "You can't make him love you."

And she shouldn't even want him to.

She'd been doing this round-and-round game for three days, and she was ready to trade heads with anyone who had more control over their thoughts than she did.

Her computer chimed with her scheduled Skype call from Delaney.

Avery breathed a sigh of relief, hoping her sister could break this cycle, and clicked into the software. Her sister appeared on the screen with a tired smile. "Hey there. Before we start, I do not want to know how amazing the beach is. I do not want to know how beautiful the weather is. And I do not want to know how relaxed you are. Deal?"

Avery frowned. "Trouble with the pub?"

"No, I just want a vacation. Want my boy all to myself for a few days."

Yeah, Avery could relate. She may not have a boy anymore, but that didn't mean she couldn't still covet the one who'd been hers for such a short time.

"So, you've had three days to relax, get your mind headed down the right path again," Delaney said. "How's it going?"

"Good." Avery looked at the charts and lists she had laid out around the table. "I've nailed down two cooks, a part-time baking assistant, four waitresses, four kitchen staff, and a commercial cleaning service. I just need to get them start dates. I also signed on with Shannon's bookkeeper. But I'm still looking for an assistant for me and a manager for the café. Lots of applications, but I haven't found those perfect fits yet."

"Holy shit." Delaney gave her a shocked-but-irritated look. "What happened to the decompressing part?"

"It's called boredom."

"It's going to be called burnout if you don't let yourself relax."

"How can I *not* relax on this *gorgeous* beach with this *perfect* weather—"

Delaney stuck her fingers in her ears and squeezed her eyes shut. "La-la-la-la-la . . ."

Avery grinned and took another sip of her chocolate.

When Delaney stopped acting like a two-year-old, she said, "That is *not* the kind of vacation I had in mind. How'd you do all that from a little cottage by the sea?"

She rested her elbow on the arm of the chair and her chin in her hand. "Same way I'm doing it now."

Delaney shook her head. "Well, when you get back you can turn in that tin can rental car. Kevin at Dent Pros pounded out the Jeep's hatch and repaired the latch. It's not exactly pretty, but it's functional. It should tide you over until you can spare some cash for something nicer."

Avery thought of Trace again. Wondered what other side effects he might be suffering from the trauma. Thought about asking, then pushed it aside. "That's great. I'm so glad the insurance is going to come through for you."

"I sent you the completed police report. I think you'll find it . . . enlightening."

Avery made a face. "I'm not quite ready to read that."

Delaney nodded. "Did you get my e-mail about your menus?"

"I did," she said, thankful for the change of subject, "and I've streamlined the website offerings to coordinate with Wildly Artisan, which will cut back on the number of products and create a rotating schedule of items so there's always something new available."

"Sweet."

Avery bit her lip against the urge to ask Delaney if she'd seen Trace. If he was okay. If he'd left town. If she knew where he'd gone . . .

Instead, she cleared her throat and tackled the hulking elephant clinging to her back like a chimpanzee. "I guess I should get someone to finish up the construction."

"I walked through with the building inspector yesterday," Delaney said. "He's ready to sign off as soon as that corner of the roof is finished and the appliances are in. I have to tell you, he's impressed as hell at the work Trace has done. Said he's never had inspections go as easily as they have with Trace at the helm."

Avery's heart swelled and grew heavy. Her ribs felt small and achy. "Yeah, well, you know your contractors. I guess it's time to toss me a few more referrals."

"I'll ask around, get numbers of people who might be available on short notice, and e-mail them tomorrow."

"Thanks," Avery said, suddenly tired and sad. "I miss you. How's Phoebe?"

"We both miss you, too. She's fine. Busy as usual."

A moment of silence stretched, and Avery stared out at the strip of ocean illuminated in cool white light. The depression that had been circling for days now settled in, making her feel melancholy and lost.

"Do you want to talk about Trace, Avery?"

His name sent a shock wave through her chest. She looked at the screen. "I'm just still really . . . I don't know, *confused*, I guess." So many thoughts and feelings crowded her; she felt too small for her body. She shook her head, overwhelmed. "No, I don't want to talk about him."

Avery disconnected with her sister, feeling anxious and unsettled. She pulled on a hoodie with plans to venture out onto the sand for a long walk when the phone rang.

She groaned and checked the display. Vince Brady's name came up.

Avery answered. "Hey there, Vince."

"Hi, Avery. Hey, I'm sorry to bother you while you're taking a few days off, but I just wanted to touch base with you to let you know that with the drought and all we're coming into the end of the season a little early.

I know you like all your produce fresh and we're doing our final harvest on pecans, almonds, and walnuts this week. Thought I ought to tell you."

"Oh . . ." That news spun Avery when she wasn't expecting it. She knew what day it was, knew how many days she had to each holiday. But somehow the end of harvest gave Avery a whole different perspective. It signaled a sharp sales peak over the holidays, then several long, quiet months before summer.

Suddenly, Avery's mind tripped into gear with this hit of urgency, and her mind churned over recipes, cash flow, and storage space.

"I need to do a little planning," she told him. "Can I call you back in a few?"

After a quick look over her finances, she saw what she feared: she was going to have to choose between landscaping for the café and grabbing the nuts fresh at a bulk price, which would save her money in the long run, but . . .

But if she didn't get over herself and find a contractor to finish the damn café, she risked getting such a late start on the holiday season that it wouldn't be worth opening the café until summer. If that happened, she would be both putting her life on hold again and falling backward financially.

Her stubborn streak flared. *No.* She'd come way too far for that. She picked up her phone and texted Delaney.

> Can you get the information on the guy Trace suggested? A contractor friend who had a job fall through? I'm coming home tomorrow.

Then she dialed Vince's line at Brady Farms and started toward the bedroom to pack.

NINETEEN

Avery's short drive home was filled with angst and second-guessing, but her renewed mission to retake control over her life won out.

She had a list as long as she was tall, filled with action items, and the very top was graced with Trace's name in all caps. Clearing the air with Trace was her very first "to-do." He'd acted out of complex and powerful emotions that night he'd pushed her away, and she was going to confront him to make sure that was what he still wanted. If it was, she would accept it, let go, and move on. But she couldn't live with a lingering sense of loose ends and bad feelings between them.

Driving back into town with all its quaint cottage bungalows, wide streets, and mature trees swamped Avery with the comfort of home. But when she got to the intersection of Chapel and Kingston and glanced toward the house on the corner, Trace's truck was gone from the driveway.

Avery's stomach dropped. An edge of panic snuck in. She parked in front of the house and approached the door where she rubbed sweaty palms against the denim at her hips. She knocked, crossed her arms, and waited, shifting from foot to foot. When no one answered, she rang the bell and waited, her stomach knotting even tighter.

Still no answer.

Her panic turned to dread. If he'd already up and left town, then she had her answer, didn't she?

With her stomach in a knot, Avery walked around to the back of the house and peered through the French door leading to the kitchen. She knocked again and tried the handle but found it locked. Avery cupped her hands around her face to peer through the glass where she could see the kitchen, dining area, and into the small living room. All the home's original furnishings were still in place but nothing more. The rooms were spotless, neat, and completely depersonalized, reminding Avery of a hotel room after it had been cleaned by housekeeping.

She closed her eyes and pressed her forehead against the glass.

Hurt and disappointment broke through her barriers and flooded her body, sagging her shoulders and pushing tears to her eyes. Avery turned, slid to the concrete stoop, and wrapped her arms around her knees, resting her head there.

She thought she'd run out of tears during the last few days, but she'd been wrong. They rolled from beneath her lashes, leaving dark-blue puddles on her jeans, but her eyes dried quickly, and her pain deepened from the acute slash across her heart to a more chronic ache in her chest.

He'd moved on.

Now she'd have to find a way to move on, too.

Again.

She fought to keep herself from thinking on the short drive through the quaint streets of Wildwood toward Main. Avery kept pushing thoughts out of her mind as they popped in, unable to fathom coming to grips with Trace's loss. With David, the end had been drawn out and unsettled for years. This was far more traumatic and hurt much more deeply. Trace had been there one day, loving her, making her world full and happy and right, then gone the next.

When she turned onto Wild Harts' driveway, her thoughts were in the past, remembering men she'd known in the military who'd died overseas. Filled with memories of her efforts to comfort their young wives and help with the couples' young children. And by the time she pulled the car to a stop near the front of the building, she felt so numb she wondered whether she had a pulse.

Then she focused out the window, saw the state of the café, and her heart thumped hard, reassuring her she was indeed still very much alive.

Her gaze scanned the front of the building, where rows of bright-green shrubs lined the landscaping boxes and clusters of pansies and petunias flanked the entrance. The stair banister was in, completing the stairs and finishing off the quaint, wide, covered porch with a real zing of style.

"Oh my God." Her heart surged again. She pushed the car door open and stood. Dragging her phone from her back pocket, she speed-dialed Delaney.

"Hey there," Delaney answered, upbeat and chipper. "Are you still coming home today?"

"I'm home. Did you do all this?"

"You're at the café?"

"Yes, how did this all happen?"

"Look around. If you still have questions, call me back."

Her sister disconnected and Avery frowned at her phone. "What the . . . ?"

She pocketed her cell, climbed the stairs, and tried the door. It was unlocked, and she stepped in. The café's familiarity immediately wrapped her in comfort and a renewed excitement. The break had been good for her. No doubt about that.

Avery crossed her arms and scanned the space. Her gaze paused on the range-oven combination that had been installed directly in front of her, behind the counter. The stainless steel gleamed against all the white cabinetry and tile, and the sight stole Avery's breath.

"Oh God . . ." She pressed a hand to her racing heart and moved farther into the space, looking everywhere.

All the crown molding had been installed and painted. The finishing touches on the floor and the cabinets were in. The stainless overhead pan rack had been installed above the butcher block and stocked with all her new pots. Not only were the tables and chairs set up throughout the main eating area, but the tables were stocked with condiments. There was even a new podium set up near the door with a laminated seating chart, neither of which Avery had planned.

"Oh my God . . ." She just couldn't think of anything else to say. She was overwhelmed.

Only when she started into the back and the main kitchen did Avery realize she hadn't seen the moving truck holding her appliances outside. And when she stepped inside, she knew why—every one of her appliances was installed. Her refrigerators, her ovens, her massive stovetop, her industrial blender, her sinks. Supplies that must have come during the last few days had been unpacked and organized on shiny chrome shelves. All her handheld appliances were lined up and stored on another, her dishware on another, her packaging supplies on yet another.

There wasn't one thing out of place.

Turning a circle, taking everything in with a giddy bubble in her chest, she texted Delaney, `Did you and Phoebe do this?`

She started up the stairs, eager to see how the event space was shaping up. At the top of the stairs she stepped into a room that stole her breath again. Not only was the flooring in, but it was buffed to a glossy shine. The fireplace's stacked-stone face continued all the way to the vaulted ceiling. The huge windows had been trimmed out with molding, the recessed lighting had been installed and finished off, and natural light flooded the space.

Her phone buzzed, and Avery blinked away tears to read Delaney's message: Nope.

Staring at the answer stirred other thoughts, and those thoughts stirred anger. If Delaney and Phoebe hadn't done this, then the only person left was Trace. Which meant he was trying to ease his conscience by hiring his friend to finish the café even when Avery had told him not to.

A scrape sounded in the apartment, drawing her gaze to the closed door. Complete with molding and handle hardware. A soft shuffle sounded, followed by silence again.

She clenched her teeth, now caught in an impossible situation—facing this stranger who'd made this place absolutely dreamy and telling him to get out.

Yes, it was wonderful to have the café finished, but not out of guilt, and not so Trace could clear his conscience, as if that were all it would take. And now he'd gone and put this other contractor in the middle.

Avery took a deep breath and moved to the apartment's door, pushing it open slowly to look into the rooms before she stepped in. Her little living room was neat, every book in place on the side table, every magazine stacked on the coffee table.

Movement sounded in her tiny kitchen toward the back of the space, and Avery wandered farther, taking in the light-amber hue of sunlight spilling over the shining floors.

She was forming a congenial get-lost message for her guest when she stepped into the opening for the kitchen, where a man wiped down the new handle on a closet door, his back toward her.

A man with wide shoulders, small specks of blood on the back of his white tee, and raven-black hair.

"*Trace?*" Her voice came out filled with *what-the-hell?*

He swiveled, eyes wide. Or *one* eye wide. The other lagged behind, still a little swollen, still extremely discolored with bruises. "Hey. I didn't think you'd be back for a couple more days."

God, he looked *awful.* She grimaced and covered her mouth with tented hands. Shadows and bruises, cut and swollen lips, black eye . . . and after reading the police report, she knew he'd gotten all his injuries in self-defense. That hadn't surprised her, but it did make her feel even guiltier for the way she'd flinched when he'd tried to touch her.

"Oh my God. Tell me you feel better than you look."

His lip twitched into a split-second smile, but it was gone before Avery could appreciate it. "I'm okay." He shrugged. "Sore. Ugly. But . . . okay."

"I stopped by your house on the way here. Looks like you're all packed up and moved out."

He glanced away and nodded. "Yeah."

She wanted to ask him where his father was, but venturing too deep into the personal areas still felt dicey. "I didn't see your truck out front."

"It's on the other side, by the kitchen. I had to haul in the shelves and put them together."

She narrowed her eyes, completely lost. "I don't understand. You told me you couldn't finish."

He looked down at the bar cloth he'd been using to wipe the table. "Well, I did some thinking. And you were right. I did make you a promise. But I can't say I did it all myself, as much as I wanted to. I had to call in some help—that contractor friend I told you about. He did the heavy lifting. I took care of the small stuff. A couple of his guys came to help with the landscaping."

"Trace, I can't afford—"

"I paid them," he said. "From my money."

Disappointment carved a hole in her belly. "So that's what this is. Follow-through."

"Partly, yeah," he admitted with a kind of annoyance that told Avery he believed that was more important than she did.

She crossed her arms. "And the other part?"

His sighed, set the folded towel on the table, and looked directly at her, bruises and all. "I thought getting away from you was the only way I could do right by you. But when Delaney told me you postponed the opening, I realized that instead of helping you, all I did was add yet another problem to your mountain of challenges."

This was sounding all very . . . mature. All very . . . clean and businesslike. And even though Avery wasn't interested in acting mature or businesslike, she did her best. "Well, perfect. I guess you've passed the professionalism test."

She clasped her hands around her arms. A hot bath, a nap, and a private crying jag was on her immediate agenda, but not in that order. Especially not when tears were already burning her eyes.

"I'm tired." She couldn't make herself pretend anymore. It took too much energy. "I'll make sure you get the rest of the money I owe—"

"I'm not here for the money." His stern voice drew her gaze again. "I'm here to finish. I'm here to fulfill my promise. I'm here to show you that I'm not giving up. I'm not walking away from you or from us." He pressed his hand against the breakfast bar, face set in a deliberate way she'd seen before, one that told her he was dead serious about following through. But his voice remained patient and compassionate. "I know the way I handled the situation with JT was wrong. And I don't expect you to just believe me when I say it won't happen again. I plan on sticking around and proving it to you."

She frowned, confused. "Trace, I don't—"

"Dad and I moved in with Zane to save money. We got notified that Dad qualifies for Medicare, so we're going to start searching for a memory-care home nearby. I've picked up three new small jobs over the last few days, here in town. A bathroom remodel for Shiloh, a friend of Delaney's; a custom-cabinet job for a lawyer down the other end of Main Street; and a new roof for Gabe Snyder. Ethan's letting me use part of his warehouse space to set up shop. I smoothed things over with Mark, and he's considering my bid on the kitchen remodel. It looks like he's going to take it. And Caleb's letting me bid on the market's expansion project. I should be out of Zane's apartment and on my own in three months, tops."

Avery's mouth had dropped open at some point. Before she could find anything to say, Trace went on.

"I'm here for you, Avery, and I'm here to stay. I don't care how long it takes for me to prove that the other night was an event I never plan on repeating, or to wipe the smudges from my name around town, or for you to trust me again. I'm going to make it all happen because I love you, and I know, right here, right now, *this* is where I belong."

Having him repeat her own words back to her made her huff a laugh, and tears spilled over her lashes. She wiped them away with shaking hands, and when she looked up again, Trace was right there.

He slipped one arm around her waist and cupped her face with the other, rubbing her tears away with his thumb. His troubled gaze held on her cheek as he stroked it. "And I'm going to make it my mission to stop these tears."

Avery closed the distance between them, pressing her body against his and curling his soft cotton tee into her fingers to keep from touching him somewhere that would hurt. "I have no doubts, Trace." She pushed up onto her toes and kissed him gently, avoiding the cuts on the left side of his lips. "Not one." She kissed him again. "And I've loved you since that day we met and you told me I had a killer smile."

Trace grinned . . . as much as someone could with cuts on his lips. He wrapped his arms around her waist, pulling her body back against his. With his face pressed to her neck, rocking her back and forth, he murmured, "God, I missed you. The last three days felt like three months. Don't ever go away again . . . unless you take me with you."

"That's a deal." She crossed her arms behind his neck and pulled back to smile into those gorgeous blue eyes of his. "So what do you think? Is this place ready to open?"

He grinned. "Hell yes."

She kissed him, gently, away from his injuries. "Will you be at my side when it opens?"

He gave her a look. "I don't think my face will be healed by your opening day."

"My opening day has been canceled. I'm sure you'll be fine by the time—"

"I wouldn't count on it, Cookie. Your sister has her own agenda, and she's never taken direction very well."

Avery pulled in a sharp breath. "She didn't . . ."

Trace laughed. "You're right, she didn't. She didn't tell anyone you were postponing. She decided it was easier to cancel at the last minute than it would be to get people excited about the opening again. So that gives you about five days to bake and train before the opening."

Avery laughed, overwhelmed with gratefulness for her family. For Trace. She leaned into him and asked again, "Will you be at my side when it opens?"

His grin returned, and he pressed his forehead to hers. "I'll be with you as long as you want me."

Her heart filled, and all the unease that had been jittering inside her for years, calmed.

She combed her fingers through his hair. "Then I hope you're prepared to stay around for one hell of a long time."

He kissed her and held her tight, whispering at her ear, "Hell yes."

TWENTY

"And it's time to pick another winner." Phoebe's voice came over the microphone, filling the café and filtering over the exterior speakers to the diners seated on the patio, where heaters kept the fall chill away for the grand opening of Wild Harts.

The customers cheered, but that didn't stop George from playing the piano. Nor did it stop Henry Baxter from singing along with George to "Blueberry Hill" by Fats Domino—much to the customers' amusement.

With a coffeepot in one hand and a champagne bottle in the other, Avery scanned the space, searching for flutes or mugs to refill. She was stunned by the sheer number of people stuffed into the café. The restaurant had been filled to capacity since they opened the doors at 6:00 a.m.; six hours later, both the indoor and patio space remained packed with an hour-long wait list.

A giddy flutter passed through her belly, leaving a deep sense of awe and gratitude.

"This prize," Phoebe said, "is three free breakfasts for two here at Wild Harts."

She called off the ticket number, and a moment of silence ensued. Then Amber, a young woman who worked at Finley's Market—and Mark Davis's date for this event—jumped up. "Me! That's me!" Everyone clapped, and Avery laughed.

"Behind you." One of the waitresses passed Avery coming out of the kitchen, her arms laden with plates. "Hot food."

A moment later, another waitress came at her from the opposite direction. The cooks were cranking out great food; the waitresses and bussers were kicking ass and turning tables. Phoebe and Pearl acted as the emcee team for activities, announcements, and door prizes. Delaney, Ethan, and Zane roamed the café and the patio, chatting, refilling drinks, making sure everyone was happy.

Avery wandered to a table where Betty, wife of Avery's piano tuner, Henry, sat with five other members of the Geri-Hat-Tricks bridge club.

"Refills, ladies?" Avery asked.

"Oh, yes, please." Betty was the first to lift her champagne glass, but orange juice layered the bottom.

"Would you like me to refresh your mimosa?" Avery asked.

She gave a shrug. "Why water down the good stuff with orange juice?"

"Good point."

After emptying another bottle, Avery thanked the women for coming and started toward the breakfast bar, where cases of champagne waited beneath the counter.

Uncorking the bottle, Avery took in all the familiar faces. At least half the artists who rented space from Phoebe at Wildly Artisan were here now or had already been in. Belle Davis had pulled through on her promise to bring her entire office staff to the opening, including Dr. Morrison and his wife. Sheriff and Mrs. Holland had been on the patio chatting for hours, along with several deputies. The Mulligans, all Delaney's and Avery's friends from school, the owners of Finley's Market . . .

The whole town was here.

Except of course Austin, for which she was grateful. It was better for everyone. She understood the hurt lingering over his brother's death. But she didn't understand his attempts to place blame on innocent people or to bully others over to his way of thinking.

Harlan joined the older group at the piano, and George transitioned from "Blueberry Hill" into "Ain't That a Shame." In a corner near the piano, Willow had set up a children's area, where kids now sat at a small table and drew or played with toys on a colorful carpet.

Movement on the stairs to the second floor, the event space as well as Avery's apartment, drew her gaze. Trace came down the steps and into the main restaurant with the couple from out of town he'd taken off Avery's hands half an hour ago, offering to give them a tour. He was animated, gesturing as he spoke, pointing out different aspects of the remodel, and the simple sight of him flushed her heart with joy.

Dressed in black slacks and a deep-blue button-down shirt with the sleeves rolled up on his forearms, Trace looked mouthwatering. He turned his head, caught her gaze, and grinned. A little over a week since the fiasco with JT, his face still bore remnants of their fight. But instead of being considered a leper as he'd expected, he'd been hailed by most as a hero for saving Avery's business.

Trace walked the couple to the door and shook hands before they left. Avery longed to get him alone to show him just how much she appreciated all his support. Then sleep twelve hours. She was exhausted.

Avery wandered back into the seating area where Willow came up beside her. "Mother alert, two o'clock."

She glanced toward the front door where MaryAnn Holmes stood, looking around. She let out a breath of resignation. The day after the incident with JT, Willow had come by the café to check on Avery. She'd also come to tell Avery that she wanted her job as manager back, and that she'd given her mother an ultimatum: get over her resistance to Willow taking the job, or Willow was moving out. But Avery had reservations about how willing MaryAnn would be to honor their agreement.

"Don't worry," Willow said. "I was extremely clear with her. If she says one wrong thing, you tell me. Becky's got a bed ready for me at her house."

Avery smiled. "I'm sure it will be fine. How is everything else going?"

"Fan-freaking-tastic," Willow told her. Then she added, "We're out of pastries."

Avery's smile dropped. "We can't be. There were mountains—"

"Gone. Every last one."

"But we baked twenty hours a day for days—"

"Not even a crumb left," Willow said matter-of-factly, "and we have dozens of orders for more."

Avery's breath whooshed out in shock.

Trace came up to them and slid his big, warm hand up the back of her dress, slipped it under her hair, and caressed the nape of her neck. And, Lord, that felt good.

"Add one to my name," he told Willow, then shot a sly grin at Avery. "I just got another kitchen remodel bid."

Willow broke into a smile. "You're gaining on her."

The amount of work she and Trace had been offered since they'd opened the doors that morning had become a running competition, with Willow keeping tallies on potential jobs stemming from the day. She'd been booking parties, catering gigs, and wedding cake design appointments for Avery all morning. Trace had a bevy of construction jobs lined up, everything from laying concrete to complete home renovations.

"Are you sure you don't want to lift the cap on your Thanksgiving pie orders?" Willow asked playfully. "I have a very long list of people hoping you'll cave under the pressure."

Trace laughed, the sound deep and rich. "Good thing we added that extra oven."

"Holy shit." Avery pressed a hand to her hot cheek and looked to Willow. "God, I hope you're ready to start baking."

"I like the sound of that." MaryAnn approached, her demeanor substantially friendlier today. "She is amazing in the kitchen."

"And I can't wait to get her in there." Avery offered her hand to MaryAnn. "We're okay?"

MaryAnn's gaze darted to Willow, then back to Avery. "We're good."

Relief eased Avery's shoulders, and a smile spread across her face. "Would you like me to find you a seat—"

"I'll just grab a chair with my book club."

"Great. I'll send a server right over." Avery stopped one of the waitresses and directed her to MaryAnn.

The portable phone rang in Willow's hand, and she moved away from the group to answer.

Suddenly, between the swamped restaurant and the buzz of activity, Avery and Trace were alone, in that intimate cocoon they seemed to be able to find anywhere.

Looking into her eyes, he slipped his arms around her waist. His lips tilted in a slow, soft smile. "Hi."

She leaned into him, mirrored his smile. "Hi."

"How are you holding up?"

"I'm ready to fall into bed with you."

"Mmm, ditto, baby."

She glanced toward the piano, where George attempted a rusty version of "Great Balls of Fire." "I can't believe how that's come back to him."

"I can't believe how that's brought him back to us," Trace said. He pressed his forehead to hers. "I don't think I've thanked you yet."

"I don't think you have to."

He kissed her softly, and Avery felt overwhelmed with gratitude and happiness. "I still feel like I'm in a dream. All anxious that I'm going to wake up and I'm still going to be fighting to reach this dream."

He lifted his head. "You've done all the fighting. Now you're reaping your reward."

"I dreamed about this day for a long time, you know? Until a few months ago, I thought that's all it would ever be, a dream. And even after I started down the road to making it a reality, I must have second-guessed myself a thousand times."

He lifted a hand to stroke her cheek.

"In my heart of hearts I knew I'd get here. But this opening has exceeded my every last wild dream. And you know why?"

He grinned. "Because you're beating me in job prospects?"

Avery laughed and lifted her hand to cup his jaw. "Because you're with me. This wouldn't mean half as much to me without you here."

The humor in his expression faded, replaced by deep and serious affection. He combed one hand through her hair. "I wouldn't want to be anywhere else."

"How do you feel about today?" he asked. "About the events and wedding cakes and four hundred sixty-two pies you'll be making?"

Avery laughed. "Amazing beyond words." The men at the piano collectively introduced a new song from bygone eras, "Earth Angel" by the Penguins. Harlan, Henry, Pearl, and Phoebe had joined George in singing the sweet ballad.

"Good." He bent his head until his lips softly touched hers. "Because I love you beyond words."

The emotions those words evoked were so beautiful they hurt. She took his face in her hands and held his gaze. "I love you, too. So much."

Trace wrapped her in his arms, swept her back in a dramatic dip, and kissed her in front of a café full of customers . . . and essentially all of Wildwood.

A burst of whistles and applause erupted around them. Avery broke the kiss with laughter. The feeling of being completely loved swam through her for the first time in years.

When Trace pulled her upright, the old-timers decided to jazz things up again with "Old Time Rock and Roll." Customers started clapping to the rhythm and signing along. Trace twirled Avery beneath his arm, then pulled her in to dance with him. Across the restaurant, Ethan grabbed Delaney and joined them on the makeshift dance floor.

George handled the piano fairly well, but when the group's worn vocal chords stretched to shout the lyrics, notes went haywire and laughter sprinkled through the café.

Surrounded by her family, her lifelong friends, and the man she loved, Avery felt all the loose ends in her life weave together into a perfect tapestry. Smiling up at Trace, she knew she'd been right since the very beginning. It might have taken her a while to get here, but there was no doubt she was right where she belonged.

ABOUT THE AUTHOR

Skye Jordan is the *New York Times* bestselling author of the Renegades series and other contemporary romances, including the first novel in the Wildwood series, *Forbidden Fling*. Born in the San Francisco Bay Area, she holds a bachelor's degree from California Polytechnic State University–San Luis Obispo and spent two decades working as a sonographer at UCSF Medical Center. Today, when she's not writing, she volunteers at a clinic in rural Mexico. She is the proud mother of two college-age daughters and lives in the historic town of Alexandria, Virginia, with her husband of twenty-five years.